Kingdom of Sleep

Books by E. K. Johnston

A Thousand Nights
Kingdom of Sleep

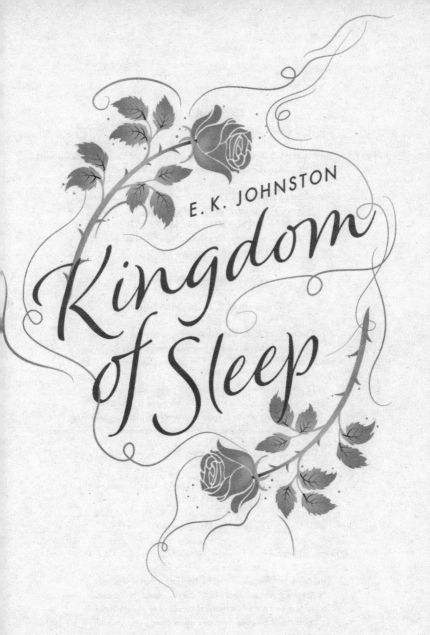

E. K. JOHNSTON

Kingdom of Sleep

MACMILLAN

First published in the US 2016 by Hyperion, an imprint of Disney Book Group
First published in the UK 2016 by Macmillan Children's Books

This edition published 2017 by Macmillan Children's Books
an imprint of Pan Macmillan
20 New Wharf Road, London N1 9RR
Associated companies throughout the world
www.panmacmillan.com

ISBN 978-1-4472-9039-1

135798642

A CIP catalogue record for this book is available from
the British Library.

Designed by Marci Senders

Printed and bound by CPI Group (UK) Ltd, Croydon CR0 4YY

To Rachel, who dealt the worst game of
Settlers of Catan in the history of humankind.

We know exactly how we came to these cold, hard mountains, and we remember everything that we have lost since we arrived here.

We were a proud kindred, once, taking what we wanted from the petty humans, and nesting on our ever-growing power. We were made strong in that desert heat, tempered by sand and blood and bones. We stretched out our hands and our will, and used that which we seized however we wished. We made bodies that could not be killed, and we began our slow domination of the world we inhabited. Then one of us rose too high, took too much, and was brought down.

The world is made safe by a woman.

She took the evil that she knew and bound it up with bright iron

1

she had dreamed into existence. She found a place for evil to roost, far away from the people she loved. She made for evil a home where it would be weakened and starved, where the earth itself would be a poison to it. She did the very best she could.

And, for a while, that was enough. The mountains were not kind to us, as she knew when she sent us here to suffer. For generations of human life, we were too weak to leave them. We would not die, but we could no longer send out our spirits with the fiery vengeance we had carried before our defeat. We were beaten. Lowered. Angered. We hungered and we thirsted, and we lamented what we had lost in the hot desert sand. And we remembered every modicum of it.

The creatures she made to be our keepers hemmed us in, keeping us weak and struggling. Their iron horns and fiery breath caught us on the slopes without mercy, and their flames brought out new strength in the earth's power over us. Their songs and laughter were torture to our ears. Even their little feet and little stingers made our unending lives a misery, turning the ground again and again to magic beyond our control.

But we endured.

Humans came to the mountains, to cross them at safe passes, seeking a pathway to the sea. The land on the other side was better, fertile enough for growing food and soft enough for cattle. First, villages sprouted up to mock us, prospering where we could not go; then, towns and trade routes; and finally, a kingdom in its own right. We knew that if we were to rise again, we would have to do it before they gained full mastery of the land they had claimed.

Our first attempts to leave the mountains were met with disaster. Time, perhaps, or hubris had dulled our sense of ourselves, and we were hopelessly overmatched. We were not yet strong enough to face a horde of human fighters, much less the creatures who jailed us. There was iron everywhere now, it seemed, plucked from our very prison and smelted into bright weapons, and even jewelry, that we could not abide. Our wounding was beyond the mortal measure of pain. We retreated. We regrouped. And, oh, we abhorred it.

From my hated sanctuary, I looked down upon that kingdom, and I knew that another way must be found. We could not take, as we once did. We could not force and pillage as we liked. I would not wheedle, and I would not beg; but I would ask, barter, and trick. I would find weakness, and I would push it until it cracked. They would give me what I wanted and think that they had bested me. I had only to outlive them, after all, as my kind did not die. And so I learned.

There are corners in the world that are too dark to see, and there are edges that are sharper than they appear, ready to snag the unwary. There are those who do not fear the things they should, and there are those who would bargain with the devil herself for the sake of their greed.

The world is made safe by a woman, yes, but it is a very big world.

ONE

THE LITTLE ROSE was only five years old when her parents ruined my mother and brought ruination to my own life. I can tell the story like I was there, though I wasn't. Even if I had been, I had only six years to my life then, and my memory would likely fail me on the finer details. So it is better that I heard the story from others, others I trusted. That means I know the truth.

My mother told it to me, and the others who fled with her repeated it, and I learned it at their knees. By then, I was old enough to card the wool and spin the thread—I was my mother's son, so my spinning was to be expected. When you spin, there isn't much to do besides talk and listen, but at the time I needed to learn more before I could do my share of the talking. As a result, I was a very good listener. The words I heard were woven into my heart, and I wrapped myself up in the details I gleaned from them as I would a blanket: once my mother had been a proud woman, and a wealthy one, and then a spoiled little princess had ended it all.

The Little Rose was born in Kharuf to the king and queen of that land. It had been seven generations since the King Maker had split his country along the mountain seam, bequeathing half to each of his sons to avoid a civil war. In Qamih, prosperity was easy. The soil was fertile and the weather was fine for much of the year. The Maker Kings still ruled there, throne passing from father to son when they died. There was an unnatural blessing upon that land, for even when it should have gone ill for them, it did not. We in Kharuf might have a drought—heather withering on the slopes, while the sheep starved—but their fields were always well watered. We might have too much rain, and lose villages to mudslides, but their crops never faltered.

Even with such a neighbor to compare with, Kharuf was not always unpleasant. I do not recall much of my early years there, but my mother assured me that we were always well kept and cared for by the king. Ruling a smaller kingdom as he did, it was said that King Qasim knew all of his subjects by name. This was of course an exaggeration, but Qasim and his wife, Rasima, did well by their people, and

5

their people loved them for it. The Maker Kings might live in a castle three times the size of theirs, and never fear that the game in their forests would run out, but in Kharuf we had a king who was not afraid to shear his own sheep, and a queen who could tend a flock as well as she could weave a tapestry.

The birth of the Little Rose, called Zahrah by her parents, did not change that, not at first. The Little Rose was a pretty child, my mother told me. She had the same dark skin as her parents, brown eyes, and a mouth that smiled before she had teeth. Her hair was the color of wheat in high summer, which was unusual but not unheard of. It was said that long ago, one of the Little Rose's ancestresses had married a man who had pale skin and hair the color of rice cooked with saffron. Pale skin was not ever seen in the line again, unless someone fell ill and the color was unnatural, but every now and then, light hair reappeared. It was less a mark of kingship, though, than it was a reminder of where our people had once come from. No, in the Little Rose's case, her kingship was assured by her parents' careful stewardship of Kharuf—at least, it was until the day that the Little Rose turned five.

No one ever argued that the birthday party was less than magnificent, even afterward, when talk of the day was confined to hushed whispers of faded hope. At the time, the partygoers were thoroughly charmed. All I remember is that I was in bed with sheep pox and couldn't attend, but my mother told me that the queen herself had made sure to send me a plate of sweetbreads, and a handkerchief she had embroidered with her own needle in an attempt to make up for it.

In the main gallery, where the castle people gathered to celebrate, it was a much merrier time. The subtle glow of the candles highlighted the gold thread and deep purple silks of the tapestries. The royal harpist played so perfectly in tune that the crystal goblets at every place setting sang with her as she plucked each note. And the food, the food was perfection beyond the sweetbreads I had been given, each succulent morsel resting in finely decorated vessels.

This was why Kharuf loved its king and queen so much. The Maker Kings sat at high tables and did not speak to any but the most important lords and merchants. They had fine glass and inlaid spoons to eat with, but the lower tables had only rough fare. They lorded their creations over each and every one: their roads and their harbors, the bright steel of their soldiers' helmets. In Kharuf, what the king ate was eaten by all, and the cutlery in the queen's hand was the same as that in the hand of the lowest scullion.

Qasim and Rasima had, as tradition dictated, invited each of the magical creatures that guarded humanity to the feast. Where a common shepherd might put out purple cloth and a few iron nails if they wished to attract the attention of our protectors, the king and queen had commissioned wrought-iron figures of each creature, paying the smiths quite handsomely, it must be said. They had placed each gift in a purple silk bag that the Little Rose had, with help from my mother, stitched herself.

Perhaps it was the care that they had put into the invitations, or perhaps the creatures themselves sensed that they might be needed at the party, but each of them came. This was not tradition. We might pay lip service to them, or see a fiery feather or bright flash flitting through the heather at night, but no one had laid eyes upon any of the guardians in decades. I was devastated for weeks afterward to have missed them, for I did not think I would ever see their like again. My mother described them to me, though, as lovingly as she could, even while her life was falling to shreds all around her.

The piskey and the sprite had been the most entertaining. Both of them fliers, but small enough not to cause alarm on the scale of the others, they had danced with one another in the air above the tables, the harpist providing accompaniment for their antics. The sprite swooped and dove, to the delight of the children, while the piskey shed fine gold dust behind her as she flew in stately circles.

The dragon arrived with an apology, of all things, as she was only a child herself, and was worried she would appear uncultured in so fine a court. Her mother, she explained, would be unable to fit inside the castle without breaking the roof, and so the younger, smaller dragons had cast lots to see who would get to attend. Rasima did an admirable job of keeping her face straight and welcomed the dragon with all the pomp and ceremony she would have given an elder statesman, before calling the steward to settle the great beast somewhere close to the main hearth.

My mother could never quite recall where the gnome had sat. Sometimes when she told me about her, the gnome stayed at the king's knees, and whispered to him about which flocks should graze in which meadows. Sometimes, the gnome disappeared to the kitchen garden and sank her hands into the soil there. Sometimes my mother forgot the gnome entirely, which I would have thought unfair, except gnomes were shy, and far happier to repay any gift they received quietly and immediately before going on their way again.

The phoenix perched on the back of the unicorn, and the two did not eat, nor speak to anyone once they had greeted the king and queen. They took their place, unbidden, beside the princess, and the Little Rose stared at them, quite forgetting that she had gifts she was meant to be opening and food she was meant to eat. They had gifts of their own for her, of course—gifts that would ensure she grew to be a good and wise ruler—but they were not the sort of gifts a child could open, or even readily understand. Instead, they were gifts to her body and to her mind: discernment and resilience and grace and the like, each tailored with a ruling queen in mind.

And so the birthday celebration was a remarkable success, a wonder for all those in attendance, even for the small boy who was sick in bed and would only ever hear about it secondhand. If the feast had ended as well as it began, the stories would have been much shorter. My mother would not have been forced out of her home, I would not have lost all I cared about, and the kingdom of Kharuf would have continued its quiet march through history.

As it was, a demon came, and the march was not so quiet after that.

TWO

I ROLLED HARD ON THE DIRT, and would have come up spitting grass had we not trod it all to mud some hours ago. I had to use my fingers to scrape my teeth clean.

"Come on, Yashaa," said Saoud. "You can do better than that."

It was true, and we all knew it. Saoud hadn't laid me out on the ground like that since I was twelve, and I'd been only just tall enough to carry a bow staff without tripping on it. With six more years of experience to my credit since then, I hit the ground only when I wished to, as part of a feint or as a way to lure my opponent past his center of balance.

"Get up." Saoud waved his staff in front of my face.

"Unless you yield, of course."

I had no intention of yielding. Usually when Saoud and I sparred, we were evenly matched, but he had finished another growth spurt in the past few weeks and was still finding out where his arms and legs had ended up, and I was trying not to take advantage of it. Moreover, I had argued with my mother again, trading words until she could no longer speak for coughing, and that made me angry. I didn't want to hurt Saoud like I had hurt her.

"I do not yield," I said, bracing my weight on the staff to get to my knees, and then my feet.

"No mercy, Yashaa!" That was Arwa, cheering from the fence post. Her voice was still high with youth at eleven years of age, but hearing it always made me feel better. Tariq sat beside her, four years older and far more unsure of his seat upon the rails.

"Oh, please have mercy," Saoud taunted, grinning so I would know he didn't mean it. "Spare me, Yashaa, from your powerful blows and quick—"

That was as far as I let him get. I could have hit his staff aside and taken him at his knees, but that would not have been sporting. Instead, I tapped lightly on his left hand where it gripped the wood; well, as lightly as you can tap with a bow staff, which is to say: not very. He bellowed, of course, but he did drop back into guard, which gave him half a chance. It was still over very quickly.

12

"I'm glad we're on the same side," Saoud said, as I pulled him to his feet. "When it counts, I mean."

It always counted, but I wasn't going to tell him that. He knew it as well as I did, and if I said the words it would only remind him that his father, once our teacher, had left him here with us and gone off to do who knows what. And that my mother had probably been the one to drive him away. Instead we bowed, and I passed my bow staff to Arwa, who used it to balance herself on the fence rail; first standing, then walking, and finally spinning on one bare foot, the staff whirling in the other direction above her head. Tariq gripped the rail harder, as though his balance was transferable to her.

"That makes me so uncomfortable," Saoud said, and I smiled.

Arwa had come with us from Kharuf, strapped to her mother's back. Almost a year old, she should have learned to walk while we journeyed, but because of the steep slopes we climbed and the wagons on the roads we traveled, her mother had been afraid to set her down very often. She was held by everyone in the convoy at one point or another during our two years of travel, and by the time her feet finally touched the ground, we were all a little worried that she wouldn't ever take to walking as she should. Technically, I suppose she didn't. Now, she had no fear of heights, and could climb almost anything. Her balance was so perfect that Saoud's father used to joke that she must have been crafted by a sword-master. I looked forward to facing her at her best in the sparring circle someday, once she had mastered the basic forms. It would certainly be an interesting match.

Tariq was less gifted, less sure of his physical strength. He excelled at strategy, though. Saoud's father would tell us that Tariq might only strike one blow, but it would be the only one he needed. Tariq could hold his own, at least for a while, but his chief talents lay in other areas.

"Yashaa!" came a voice from our circle of tents. "Your mother wants you."

Saoud grimaced, but I knew he wished he still had a parent to yell at him. Arwa threw me my staff, and laughed as I nearly dropped it. Saoud looked away as she jumped down from the fence, but he needn't have bothered. She didn't show off.

"I'll come with you," she said. "Your mother has my spindle."

I nodded my head, and we headed back toward the tents. Tariq watched, ever keen-eyed, even if it was something he had seen a hundred times, while Saoud began one of the solitary drills that his father had taught us. I had only known Saoud a few years. He and his father were from Qamih, and had no ties to Kharuf at all, except through us. We tried not to treat him as an outsider, Tariq and Arwa and I, mostly because we knew how much that hurt, but he didn't understand the spinning, or why we still clung to it, though it had been some years since spinning had done us any good.

There were four main tents and two smaller ones in our encampment, plus an open-air kitchen. It was a far cry from the castle that my mother talked of when she was feeling nostalgic, but it served us well. We camped near a crossroads, and merchants knew where to find us. We did not have very much to offer, but we were cheap, and the work we did was good.

After the demon laid its curse upon the Little Rose, most of the spinners had gone on the Silk Road, into the desert. Across the burning sands was the kingdom from which our ancestors had come, and they could do their work there, which they could no longer do in Kharuf. We knew the desert kingdom still existed because their traders crossed the desert with camel caravans, but few people from Kharuf ever made the trek. My mother hadn't gone because she loved Queen Rasima, and because she was afraid that I was too young to survive a desert crossing. She waited for two years, until I was eight, while everything in Kharuf fell apart around her. Then she took the last few spinners still at court and went, not through the desert after all, but across the mountain pass to Qamih.

They had hoped that in this kingdom of tradesmen and merchants, they would find a place where they could do their work and be paid for it. But Qamih was different from the home they had left, and on this side of the Iron Mountains, a harsh guild system prevented unlicensed crafters from selling their wares in public markets. The guilds were also behind the trade agreements that Qasim had been forced to sign with the Maker King, which beggared Kharuf at every turn while the coffers in the Maker King's capital overflowed. It was impossible for a spinner from Kharuf, even one as highly respected as my mother, to be given the credit she was due. New spinners, especially talented ones, were unwelcome competition.

We couldn't stay in the cities or towns, and so we wandered for two years, Arwa on her mother's back and me carrying my mother's loom, until Saoud's father, who had found us on the road and hired on as a guardsman even though we could barely afford him, took us to the crossroads, to camp with the other non-guild traders there. He understood spinning even less than Saoud did, and wanted to train all of the children in combat. My mother disapproved but never directly forbade it, even when it became clear that I was more enthusiastic about fighting than I was about spinning. For Arwa and Tariq, spinning was a game that, once they had mastered it, became as important as breathing. For me, who could remember the castle and the king's face and the way the Little Rose laughed from her place at the table, it was a hateful reminder of what we had lost.

We could hear my mother coughing before we reached her tent. Arwa stopped in her tracks, and looked up at me.

"Can you get my spindle?" she said. "Maybe bring it to dinner?"

"I will," I told her. "Go and see if they need help cooking."

Arwa's mother had died of the sickness that plagued my mother. It wasn't contagious—at least, not in the traditional sense, or we would have been driven out of the crossroad camp—but it was hard to watch, and harder still when you knew the outcome. Magic is not common in the world, but from what I have seen of it, it is mostly cruel; and, at least when it comes to the magic that hurts the ones I love, tied back to the Little Rose. Tariq's father had died of it first, a drowning gurgle that grew more and more quiet, until all breath was gone; then Arwa's mother; and now my mother was ill. I didn't know what we would do if she died. The other merchants were reluctant enough to keep us as it was.

I took a deep breath, and lifted the tent flap. There was light inside, because of the lamps, but the air was heavy with the herbs my mother burned in the brazier to help clear her lungs. I didn't like the smell very much. Mother was sitting up, and spinning. I had asked her once why she could never keep her hands still. She hadn't answered, but instead had smiled, and told me to coil the yarn so it didn't knot on the floor. I was glad to see her spinning now. Some days, her hands did not have the strength for it.

17

"Yashaa," my mother said to me, "thank you for coming. Do you feel better now that you have hit Saoud for a while?"

"Yes, Mother," I said, my voice clipped. I had hoped, for a moment, that she was going to apologize for being so obtuse earlier. We had quarreled over Saoud's father, again, and it had brought us no closer to understanding each other than it ever did. "It is not from hitting him, though. It is from moving with purpose."

"There is purpose to all movement," she said to me. "Even in the simple coil and rhythm of spinning."

"What did you wish to tell me?" I hoped I was changing the subject. I didn't want to fight with her again.

"I have had word from Saoud's father," she said. "I wanted to tell you what he discovered."

"Is he coming back?" I asked, unashamedly eager. He had turned a little strange when Tariq's father died, as though seeing our curse play out in front of him made him regret throwing in his lot, and Saoud's, with us in the first place. He traveled much more after that, but he always came back—or he always had before.

"No," said my mother. "He is too busy to come back. But he has sent me important news, and you need to hear it."

"Then tell me," I said, sitting at her feet as I might have done once to hear stories of the Little Rose.

"Kharuf is dying," she said. "The people are starving and there is no money. Even the king and queen struggle.

The Little Rose cannot spin, and so no one can."

I wanted to say something about how Kharuf had been dying for years, and that Qasim and Rasima's struggle meant nothing to me, but my mother raised a hand, and I held my peace.

"There was a blight in the wool last season," she continued. "They could not sell very much, which meant they had no money to buy cloth."

Once they had spun their own thread and woven their own cloth, I thought. But I knew better than to say it out loud. It would be wasted breath, and my mother had no breath to waste.

"Qasim has made a deal with the Maker King," my mother said. "The Little Rose is seventeen now. When she is eighteen, she will wed Prince Maram, and by that marriage, Qamih and Kharuf will be united again, and the Maker King will get whatever name his people choose to give him."

"What has this to do with me?" I asked. "We have left Kharuf, and we have never been welcome in Qamih."

"If the kingdoms are united, there will be a treaty for the spinners. There must be," my mother said. "You shall go to the Maker King's court, by the sea. You must find out who is negotiating the treaty, and make sure you are included in it. Take Tariq and Arwa with you."

"No," I said.

19

I couldn't leave. We were barely surviving here with the work spread between all available hands. If we left, if I took Tariq and Arwa and we *left*, then there would be no one but strangers who barely tolerated us to watch over my mother. I shook my head.

"What about Saoud?" I asked, my words slow as my thoughts raced.

"He will stay at the crossroads," my mother said. She had never loved Saoud, so I didn't understand why she would keep him behind, especially since his father was gone. Maybe she wanted to be sure of his father's loyalty, though neither he nor Saoud had ever given us cause to doubt them, as far as I could tell. "He will be old enough to hire on as a guard, soon."

"What about you?" I asked then. "I could stay too, and be a better guard than Saoud. We could all stay here."

"No, Yashaa." She started to cough. I waited. It seemed now that when she coughed, she coughed for hours. Finally her throat cleared. "You will go. Take the others. If you do well, you will be able to make a real home."

"I have no home," I told her, anger flooding into my voice. I didn't look at her face when I said it, because I knew I would hurt her. "The Little Rose saw to that."

"Yashaa," she said. "It is a terrible net, that magic. The Little Rose suffers as much as any."

I did not care about the suffering of the Little Rose,

beyond an ugly gladness that she did. I only wanted the conversation to end.

"Arwa needs to pack her spindle, if you are driving her out," I said, my voice as cold as I could make it.

"I will put it in the basket with the other spinning tools," she said. Her breathing faltered.

I made myself meet her gaze. Her eyes were full of tears, as though she was sad to see us go, as though she hadn't so casually dismissed the boy I held in my heart like a brother. Anger filled my chest, crushing my lungs the way the Little Rose's curse crushed my mother's.

I did not understand. I didn't understand how a woman so weak could have such an iron will. I didn't understand why she had so much power over Saoud's father, over the crossroads camp. Over me. I did not understand my mother at all. But I loved her, and so I went to gather my things.

THREE

WE WERE A STRANGE PARTY on the road, Tariq and Arwa and I. My mother had struggled to stay standing as we left her at the opening of her tent. It was the farthest she had walked in some time. I tried not to think about the chance that she might die before we made our way back. Saoud did not see us off, having been sent out hunting in the early hours while we were taking our leave of my mother. I was furious, and I could see that Tariq and Arwa were likewise upset. At least he had been with us while we packed, and while we strung together what little plans we could. I tried not to think about losing him, either.

We didn't take a wagon with us. Even if we had an ox

to pull it, we didn't have the means to feed the creature that would do the work. There was grazing aplenty on the plains of Qamih, but there were great forests there too, and clay flats that stretched as far as the eye could see. So we went on foot, carried what we could, and prayed for good weather on the road. Tariq did most of the praying. Arwa was happy enough to say the words, and earnest enough to believe that someone heard them, but my faith in such things had long since waned. Tariq, though, believed with the conviction of one who had seen the world, and chosen faith to spite it.

In the foothills of the Iron Mountains, we had an easy time. The way was mostly downhill, and there was plenty of game for Tariq to catch in his quick-made snares. Saoud's father had shown us all the trick of making them before he'd taught us staff fighting. "You must be able to feed yourselves before you can defend yourselves," he'd said. At the time, I remember thinking it was ridiculous—what good was it to eat in the wild if you were prey to anyone who might stumble across your path?—but now I was glad that Tariq, at the least, remembered his lessons.

It was early in the year for pinecones, the best kindling, but with Arwa in our company it wasn't too much of a concern. She could climb the trees more easily than the cones might fall, and seemed to take delight in pelting us with them as Tariq and I assembled camp every night. She was taking her eviction from the crossroads harder than we were, so we didn't berate her for it too much. Coming as it had so soon after the death of her mother, Arwa felt the loss of her makeshift family, particularly the company of Saoud, most keenly.

I missed him too. When we walked, I made Tariq lead us, with Arwa in the middle and me behind her to cover their backs. There were large animals, with teeth and claws to match, in the mountain forests, and there was not a lot even the most powerful king could do to keep the roadways safe. If Saoud had been with us, he could have covered the rear, and left me free to lead. Tariq was not wood-blind by any means, and the road was clear enough, but he tended to get distracted.

Accordingly, when I woke up the next morning and found Saoud patiently feeding the last of Arwa's pinecones to the dwindling fire, I only laughed and pointed out that he could have started the porridge if he was going to be awake anyway. He walked to the food pack, shooing away two bees that were hovering over top of it.

"You're not going to send me back?" he said.

"You say that as though I could."

"Your mother said it was spinner's business." He would not meet my eye, pretending to measure out the grain for breakfast, when I knew he had done it so many times he could tell by weight alone.

"My mother says that about everything when she wants

to cut you and your father out," I said. It hurt me when she spoke like that. I could imagine how Saoud felt. "Are you coming with us for our sakes, or because you want to see your father again?"

"Can't it be both?"

"Of course," I told him. "Only, we might miss him in the capital. Or on the road. Or maybe my mother lied, and he has other business altogether."

"Then I will go with you, wherever you end up." He meant it to have the solemnity of an oath, but the effect was somewhat marred when Arwa emerged from her tent halfway through his declaration, crowed with joy, and threw herself into his arms.

"Took you long enough," she said, once she had rescued our breakfast from an untimely fate and hung the pot above the fire so that we might eat sometime before noon.

"Yashaa's mother is difficult to escape once she gets her mind set on something," Saoud informed her. We all knew it for the truth. Even ill, her determination had been enough to get the three of us evicted from the only company that Tariq and Arwa could remember. I imagined she had set Saoud to any number of mundane tasks to prevent him from running off. For a moment, there was a pain in my chest—my heart, not my lungs—as I remembered how my mother and I had parted, but I ignored it. Saoud was here. Everything was much improved now.

25

Tariq crawled out of the tent we shared, blinked twice, and then accepted our new circumstances without comment before heading off to the river to wash. By the time he came back, the porridge was ready, and the tents were struck and rolled. Saoud carried no tent of his own, because he would have had to steal it, and that was something he would not do. We would have to sort it out once we stopped for the night, but not now, because it did not take us very long to break our fast and be on our way. I ate quickly, and the others followed my lead. I was eager to be moving, even if I wasn't overfond of our destination. Arwa and Tariq were both intimidated by the fact that today we would leave the forest. They had both left before, of course, but they did not remember it as I did, and they didn't know what they might find there.

"Look!" said Arwa, who had taken the pot to the river to rinse it. "It was on a rock, right by the river's edge. I must have just missed it."

There was a soft glow coming from her cupped hands. The pot hung from the crook of her elbow, bowls stacked neatly inside. Tariq peered over her shoulder to look, and his eyes widened at what he saw.

"Yashaa, have you ever?" he asked, breathless, as I reached them and looked down into Arwa's hands myself.

There wasn't a lot of it, but it was unmistakable: fine golden powder, with a soft glow and the slightest smell of honey. I had only seen it once before, when I snuck into the Great Hall at the castle in Kharuf after the Little Rose's fateful birthday party. The maids, most of them weeping, were cleaning the floor, but I had still been upset over having missed everything, and wanted to see even the remnants for myself. One of the girls had called me over, perhaps understanding that I did not yet know how much the world had changed, and showed me what she had collected in her dustpan.

"It's from the piskey," she had said to me, her voice kind, and her face streaked with tear tracks. "It's for luck."

"It's for luck," I echoed, as Arwa poured the dust into my hands. "It means they watched us, heard us, and approve of what we're doing."

"What, going to the capital to beg?" Saoud said, suddenly bitter. His knuckles were white on the staff he carried. "I know what your mother would have you do. I heard the merchant master tell her that not even pity for children would sway a Maker King, no matter who was negotiating the treaty. We could send Arwa before them in rags, and they wouldn't feel the slightest bit of concern for her."

Arwa blanched at the idea, fingers unconsciously twisting in the frayed hem of her headscarf. The cloth was good, but she had worn it for a long time, and it showed. When she ran or climbed, Saoud's father had said the broken wisps of her veil trailed behind her like piskey dust, but now that we saw both veil and dust together, we knew that he had spoken the words only as a kindness to her.

"You will never have to do that," I promised her.

"What will we do, then?" she asked. I watched as she made her fingers relax their hold. There was still dust on them, gold against the brown of her skin. It was beautiful.

I looked at Saoud, at Tariq. What could we do? We could walk for days and days, only to throw ourselves at the questionable mercy of the Maker King. My mother, hoping against hope and unable to travel herself, thought that I could secure a future for us. But it would be a future that she wanted. A future for me to spin out the rest of my days in Qamih, and hope for whatever meager prosperity I could wrench from people who were not my own. Always I would be the poor relation, the hanger-on who had no other place to go. I would do that, and gladly, for my mother, if it caused her breathing to ease, but I knew that it would not. Despite the sourness of our parting, I loved her. She was my family too, even if I didn't agree with her dreams for me and for my future. I would survive, as she had done until her strange illness took hold of her. But I looked at Tariq, at Arwa with her gold-dusted hands and threadbare veil, and I knew that I could not be satisfied with that little for them.

"Whatever we do," I said, "we will do it together, do you understand? If you don't like my mother's plan, if you have another suggestion or an idea, you must tell me what it is."

They nodded. There was a fire I hadn't seen before in Saoud's eyes. I felt as though the bones along my spine were tempered iron, making me strong. The gold dust glowed against my skin, and reminded me of something that I had missed for too long. There were no answers here. But there might be some to be found, if we looked in another place for them.

"We will not go to the capital," I said. "We will not beg for scraps at the table of the Maker King of Qamih. It's time for us to go home."

It felt very strange to say the word.

Tariq stilled. More than any of us, he wanted to see the heathered fields that were his birthplace once again. His was the longing of a memory half real, half constructed. My memories were firmer, and Arwa had none at all, save an idealized version of the Little Rose that I could never bring myself to tarnish. Tariq believed in Kharuf the way he believed in everything else: he had heard the story many times, and when he reasoned his way through its inconsistencies, he found surety, not doubt.

"We will go back through the woods, and cross the mountains," I said. "We will go back to Kharuf, to our birthright there."

"What about the curse?" Tariq said.

I let the gold dust fall to the ground, where it mixed with the dirt and disappeared, save for the occasional glint when

29

it caught the sunlight. I brushed my hands on my kafiyyah. It was my turn for white knuckles on the staff I carried, the staff I would use to fight and support my steps on mountain paths. I held on with all I could, the way I held on to the stories my mother had told me about her life before her ruination. The way I held on to the truth.

"If we go to Kharuf, we will fall victim to the curse ourselves, as our parents did," Tariq said. He didn't sound afraid, and Arwa didn't look it. "It will come into our lungs and choke us. The Little Rose does not spin, and so neither can we."

I had never believed it to be that simple. I don't think Tariq did, either; he only spoke plainly to bring an end to the conversation. I thought about the golden dust again, and let myself consider the full scope of the world. It was hard for me to do. I liked the straightforwardness of staff fighting, the ease of movements my hands had done a hundred times before. Whether I liked it or not, that also meant spinning, and spinning meant the curse. I knew in my heart that Tariq was right. The magic spun around the Little Rose all those years ago must have grown in potency, the threads of it twisted more tightly by the pull of each season's turn. We could not just blunder into its webbing.

"We haven't spun in Kharuf as they did," I said. "And we haven't spun here as much as they did. Maybe we won't be as sick. There must be a way."

Tariq considered it, but I knew it would take him a while to decide. He would sift through all that he knew.

"It will take us some time to reach the pass." Saoud knew the look on Tariq's face, too. He pulled out the map his father had given him, and traced the line that would be our route so that we could all see it. "Let alone to cross the border. We can think on the way."

"It would make us less vulnerable to bandits, if we keep moving," I said. I tried to sound neutral, so that Saoud would voice his opinion too.

"I don't like it," he said. "But it's better than trusting the Maker King's alternative."

Arwa brushed the last of the gold dust off of her hands and was only a simple spinner-girl again. Tariq doused the fire and buried the smoldering remains. Saoud took his staff too, and looked at me. I squared my shoulders, pretending confidence I did not entirely feel, and started walking back in the direction of the rising ground.

The four of us would go together.

FOUR

WITH SAOUD'S INCLUSION, we woke early every morning to spar before we took up our journey again. Though I was the better fighter, Saoud had his father's gift of teaching, and could square off against Arwa and Tariq so that they learned. If I tried it, I would probably break their fingers. It was not that I lacked control, Saoud's father said, only mindfulness of how my opponent moved. I was a bruiser, Saoud an artist, and we each of us had our place.

Right now, my place was stirring the pot by the campfire while Saoud and Arwa did their best to knock the other off their feet. Tariq had caught three rabbits the night before—game had been good to us in the mountains—and we had put the remains of the last one into the porridge to thicken it. It was plain road fare, and nothing special, but compared to the dried meat and fruit we'd have for lunch while we walked, and whatever Tariq might conjure up for us to roast that night, this meal was a promise that, at least at the outset, the day would not go too far ill.

With a victorious cry, Arwa leveraged her staff behind Saoud's knees and dumped him into the dust. She was getting better. Soon he was going to have to stop giving her openings.

"I know, I know," she said, laughing, as Saoud rolled to his feet. "If I shout then I cannot claim a surprise attack."

"What else?" asked Saoud.

"I dropped my elbow, I looked down at your knees before I swung for them, and I didn't retreat quickly enough to avoid you kicking me, if you'd wanted to," she recited. "Do I get to have breakfast now?"

"It's almost ready," I told her.

"I am going to the river, then," she announced, and disappeared into the greenery that flanked our camp.

Saoud looked like he might have protested. The farther we went up the mountainside, the more dangerous the road became. The main road was well kept, of course, so that the wool convoys could come through, but we were avoiding that way lest any word get back to my mother. Our path was steeper, the river's current faster, and the possibility for danger more present. Arwa was no spoiled flower, like the Little Rose in her pretty castle, but she was in our charge, and Saoud and I were still trying to figure out the line between protecting her and giving her the privacy she required.

"I'm still in earshot!" she shouted, and Saoud rolled his eyes.

"Get the bowls," I told him. "And get the water bucket ready for heating so we can clean up as soon as we're done."

Tariq, whose sparring lesson had been done before Arwa's, had already struck the tents, and soon enough we were on our way again. With the path more difficult to see, I was even gladder of Saoud's decision to join us. I could discern the way ahead, and he could guard the back. For all our planning, though, it was Arwa who first saw the signs of danger.

We walked steadily uphill all day, and though the morning had started off fair-weathered enough, the sun was shrouded in light grey clouds by the afternoon, and rain was gathering in the leafy canopy above our heads. Arwa had stopped walking to wring out her veil when she gave a low cry, and waved frantically to Saoud.

"It's a bear print," he said. "Nothing else in these mountains is that size, save the dragons, and they have three toes."

"There's no water in it." Arwa's voice was so muted,

she barely said the words aloud.

The forest around us grew, all of a sudden, impossibly large and dense and dangerous. We listened, ears straining against the gentle patter of water on leaves and boughs above us, hoping to hear some sound of the beast that tracked us, but there was nothing but the rain.

Saoud moved slowly. He'd been using his staff as a walking stick, as had we all on the ascent, but now he reached behind him to tie it to his pack. I did the same. Arwa and Tariq had to lay theirs on the ground, and I made a note to fix their packs at the earliest opportunity. Tariq had two knives in his belt, the legacy of his father, but Arwa had only her eating knife. I had a set of matched blades, and Saoud had the long knife that his father had given him when he reached his sixteenth summer. Not very good inventory for going up against a bear.

"Arwa." Saoud said it in his father's voice, and I knew that Arwa would listen to him, even if she didn't like the words he said. "Climb a tree."

It wouldn't defend her against a bear forever, but it was the best thing I could think of too, so I only nodded when he said it. Arwa bit her lip, clearly upset at the idea of leaving us behind, but cast about for the best option and then disappeared above our heads without a single word of protest.

"Tariq, stay out of its reach. Bear skulls are hard, but

they've got eyes and a maw like any creature. Do you think you can hit either?"

Tariq looked at the knives in his hand. He had some practice at throwing them, but never at anything more mobile than a bale of hay. Still, he met Saoud's gaze and swallowed hard.

"Try to keep it still, if you can." He didn't say it like he had very much hope in the matter.

"Yashaa, keep to Tariq's side," Saoud said. "I will circle behind it."

"Is that the best idea?" I asked.

"It has kidneys, same as a man does." Again, I couldn't think of a better idea.

At last, there was a noise from the woods around us. Not a broken stick or a stumble, for bears have too much woodcraft for that, but rather a rustle in the leaves that was not from the rain. We turned toward it just as the bear came out of the underbrush and saw us.

It wasn't a large one, which was good news for us. Without a bow, we would have been hard-pressed to put down a full-sized male. This one was black, and when it stood to roar at us as it entered the glade, it was no taller than Saoud's father. But it was very wide; its arms stretched out far enough to grasp all three of us at once—to crush us without ever having to bloody its teeth or claws. It dropped back on its paws to come toward us, and I saw its face for the first time. I had never seen a live bear before, but I knew that something about it was wrong. Its eyes ... its eyes were wrong.

"Yashaa!" shouted Saoud, and I refocused on my task.

"Move, then!" I replied, but he already was.

Crouched low, and legs spread wide, he circled the bear as it paced toward us. Beside me, Tariq was shaking so hard I thought he might drop his knives. He had seen the beast's eyes too, and I knew that he remembered, as I did, stories of a faraway garden littered with statues that were impossible to look at without feeling a twist in your soul; statues carved because a demon had wished it done. It was bad enough to face a bear, but a bear with a demon inside of it was even more terrifying.

The bear roared again, and this time I thought I heard another's voice on top of the beast's. Another bear might have passed us by—surely there was better prey in these woods—but the demon in this bear hungered for our blood in particular and would have it, if it could.

Saoud was all the way around now, waiting for us to get the bear's full attention, but it was holding back. I knew the demon was working against us, using its own intelligence to keep the bear from its full ferocity, even as it planned to bring that same force down on us as soon as it could. We needed something to bring the bear out, to make the demon lose control.

And, from above, Arwa saw it too, and saved us. She had nothing to hand but whatever pinecones she could grasp from the branch on which she stood, and that is what she used. Her aim was true, pelting the bear around the ears and muzzle until, pushed to animal rage, it charged the ground where Tariq and I were standing.

To his credit, Tariq didn't hesitate at all. The first knife left his hand before the bear had taken two steps, and it hit the creature's shoulder. It was already roaring, so I couldn't tell if it felt any pain at all, but Tariq's second knife took one of those terrible eyes—and that, we could see, the bear felt. It reared, pain and confusion in its voice; the demon pressed it forward, when all it wanted was to retreat. Then Saoud was behind it. He was as strong as anyone I knew, and it still took both hands on the hilt of his knife to pierce the bear's hide. He went low and left of the spine, hoping to strike something important there, and he must have hit a vital target, because the bear—no, the demon—screamed as the iron pierced it.

Before the creature could turn on him, I stepped between those flailing front legs and drove my knife into the bear's other eye. My blade was longer than Tariq's, long enough to reach the beast's brain, and that was its end. It caught me with a paw as it fell, and I staggered back as blood filled my eyes; but it did not rise, or even move, when it hit the ground.

I sat there, in the bloodied glade, while Arwa used one

of her spare veils to bind my head and Tariq retrieved and cleaned our knives. When I could see again, I looked for Saoud, who cradled his knife in his lap. We had taken down a bear with a demon on its back, and it hadn't been the end of us to do it. The mountains seemed just a little bit smaller against the expanse of the sky.

FIVE

WE DID NOT CONTINUE on that day, so that we all might have some time to recover. We moved only just far enough from the bear to avoid any opportunistic scavengers that might take interest in so large a corpse. Saoud took some of the better meat, but we had no means to preserve the bulk of it, so he was forced to leave it on the forest floor. This rather galled all four of us: we had each known enough hunger to be reluctant to leave food behind to spoil.

The wound I sustained bled fiercely, forcing Tariq to scavenge for moss when Arwa's spare veil became too soaked to be useful, but it seemed at first to be mostly superficial. The morning after, though, I had a terrible headache and any light at all only heightened the pain. When I tried to walk to the river to wash the blood out of my hair, I stumbled and could not keep my feet. Saoud took my arm and led me to the fire, where he was roasting bear meat for our morning meal.

"My father has told me of injuries like this," he said, returning his attention to the spits. "They bleed a lot, and even though the mark they leave is small, they can rattle the inside of your head. We should not have let you sleep last night."

"I don't know if you could have stopped me," I told him. "I slept longer than you did, and I'm still tired."

"If you sleep, you may fall into a slumber from which you cannot be woken," Saoud said. "I would rather poke you with a stick every ten minutes all night than risk that. I don't want to have to carry you over the mountain pass."

"Your concern is touching," I said.

"Yashaa, I'm serious," he said. "There's nothing we can do to make you better except force you to rest."

"You just said I couldn't!" I protested. Rest was out of the question. We had too far to go.

"You can't sleep," he said. Arwa came to sit beside him, and Tariq took a bucket to the river because it was clear I was not going to make it on my own. "One of us will make sure you stay awake today, and tonight we will wake you every quarter mark. We'll be able to travel again the day after that."

41

"Saoud," I began, but his face was his father's: deadly serious and not to be gainsayed.

"Even that might not be enough," he said. "That was not simply a bear, and you know it as much as I do. It fought with another's strength, and it struck you directly on the head. It's miracle enough that you are only mildly wounded."

"Three days of travel lost, and that's mild?" I wanted to sound angrier than I was, but the truth was that I was bone-weary and couldn't muster the energy.

"For a bear and a demon, I think so," Saoud said.

At the word "demon," we all stilled. We had been brought up on stories of the wonderful creatures who had loved Kharuf-that-was, who had given gifts to its blasted princess, but sometimes we forgot what they had been made to do. We had come out of the desert, and so had they. Where we had brought sheep to pen up or herd on the heathered slopes, they had brought beings much darker, and the mountains were the prison they had used for the pen.

Arwa's knife was in her hand, cutting the cooked meat into portions, and I saw that it was bronze, as most eating knives were. Saoud followed my gaze, and I knew he understood.

"Here," he said, passing over his small iron dagger to her. "Keep this on your belt, even when you sleep."

She nodded, and the knife disappeared under her long tunic. Saoud's father had told her that unless she grew up to be a giant like him, her best defense was to convince others she was not a threat, and so she always concealed the weapons she carried under her clothes. That short a blade was a poor protection, but the iron in it would keep her from the worst.

"At least we'll be able to use more of the bear," Tariq said.

That was a comfort. Fresh meat was always a treat for us, regardless of how we came by it. I couldn't help Saoud and Tariq dress the bear—too much walking, too much bending over, and Saoud said I wasn't to carry anything heavier than a bowl of porridge—but I could wrap the cooked meat in the leaves that Arwa collected, so at least I wasn't completely useless in my infirmity.

By evening, the worst of my headache was gone, though I still could not stare at the fire for long, and I was exhausted. Worse, I was bored out of my mind. The others had taken advantage of the day to mend tears in clothing and bags and fix what they could of our gear. When I tried to focus on something, though, my eyes swam and my head pounded anew. I would have even been grateful to spin, but I could barely hold my hands still for Tariq while he wrapped the last of his thread around them.

He sighed when the job was done, taking the skein and putting it carefully in his bag. Both he and Arwa had brought carded wool for spinning on the trip. Each night, at the fire, they had brought out their spindles and worked them, spinning thread for no particular reason other than that they could, and that they found it to be a comfort. Arwa had run out of wool the night before the bear attacked us, and this was the end of Tariq's supply.

"I know spinning is not your favorite," he said to me, "but it's all I have left from my father."

"I know," I said. Maybe when my mother—no, I wouldn't even give that consideration. Instead, I ran a practiced hand over the thread in Tariq's bag. "It's well-made," I told him. "Even and strong. He would be proud of you."

"It's not like we can spin in Kharuf anyway," he said. That had been his decision after much consideration. He closed the bag and stowed it with the rest of his gear.

That was the other story from the mountains. The Little Rose could not spin, and thus no one in Kharuf could spin. Qasim had made a proclamation of it, and that law had driven most of the spinners from his land. Those who stayed—like my mother, who stayed for love of the queen— knew only suffering. I would not let Tariq and Arwa suffer if I could do anything to prevent it.

"That is why we must break the curse," I said.

There was stunned silence. I could almost hear Tariq's mind as he considered all aspects of what I had said, and selected which bit to take apart first.

"Is that your plan?" Saoud said. "Or are you just speaking whatever words come into your battered head?"

"It's not the injury talking," I told him. "It's the only

solution that works for us long enough to be truly useful."

There were several more moments of silence while Tariq thought. The longer he was quiet, the more a desperate sort of hope began to rise in Arwa's eyes. I had to look away from her.

"We don't know how it will work at all," Tariq finally pointed out. "We don't know what it will do to the Little Rose, to break her curse."

"I don't really care what happens to the Little Rose," I said, more harshly than I had intended.

"Yashaa." Arwa sounded upset, but I pushed forward. This would not be easy, and it was best to air all of the problems as soon as we could.

"Is it fair that so many suffer for the sake of one girl, princess or not?" I said to her. "Is it fair that she lives in a castle while you live on the side of the road, and your mother paid for her craft with her life?"

"Of course not," said Saoud, speaking carefully. "But I didn't like killing the bear, and it was possessed by a demon that wanted our blood."

"I don't want to kill her," I said, realizing belatedly that my words had been vague enough to suggest it. "But we have to do something. Do you think Kharuf would be better under the Maker Kings?"

"Why do you care about Kharuf at all?" Saoud asked. Usually he and his father kept clear of our debates about spinning and our homeland, but committed as he was to us, I couldn't fault him for joining in now.

"I don't," I told him. We both knew I spoke too quickly, but I pushed onward, gesturing to where Tariq and Arwa sat. "I care about them. I want them to have the life they were meant to—to be respected for their craft, and honored for the history of their work."

"Then why don't we just keep going after we cross the mountains?" he pressed. "Why don't we take the Silk Road and cross the desert? Let the Little Rose grow old and die and take her curse with her to her tomb. You've been made unwelcome in two kingdoms, Yashaa, but you know there is a third that will have you, and have you gladly. You have only to get there."

We were strong enough to make the desert crossing now; I did not doubt that. And perhaps one of the spinners who had gone there would recognize me, or at least my mother's name, and make us welcome. But it was all too uncertain.

I felt like my brain was on fire. Demon bears and piskey dust, spindle whorls and desert roads—it was too much. I wanted my mother to be healthy and to stop looking at me like I had betrayed her by preferring the staff to the spindle. I wanted Tariq to be left alone with enough carded wool to spin himself back to the happy child I remembered. I wanted Arwa to have charge of a room full of weavers, as her mother had done in the castle of Kharuf-that-was. I wanted the

Little Rose to pay for what she had brought down upon the people that I loved. I wanted to unleash twelve years of hunger and uncertainty on her, and make sure that she felt, in her marrow, the pain that she and her parents had caused.

Overcome, I pitched sideways and Saoud caught me back from the fire. I fought him off, weakly and with no real effect, except that he let me go when I regained some measure of steadiness.

"Perhaps we shouldn't make any decisions until you feel better," Arwa suggested, her voice as delicate as her footsteps when she walked the fence rail.

"I am fine," I told her. My head was pounding again, and I looked away from the fire.

"Promise me you will at least consider taking the desert way," Saoud said.

"Would you come with us?" Arwa asked. "We might not be able to get word to your father."

"I will go with you, whatever path you take," Saoud said. "My father will find us, or he will not; but when he left, he told me that I had learned well from him, and that he trusted me to find my own way."

We were quiet for a long moment. I had never asked Tariq or Arwa what the last thing their parents had said to them was. Their illness had left them disoriented at the end, and it was possible that whatever words they'd managed to speak on their deathbeds were not useful. If I had spoken with my mother for the last time, I was not proud of how we had parted. For all my bravado, I didn't have Saoud's certainty. His father had blessed him. My mother had coughed, and I had abandoned her.

"We will return to this conversation when we can better see the paths that lie before us," I declared. "The Silk Road is a good idea, but there are many things we must consider before we take it."

"Even if we are only passing through Kharuf, we need to focus on the curse. It will affect us, though we don't know exactly how much," Tariq said. "The stories we do know are messy, and contradict one another all the time."

"My mother has told me the truth, I know it," I protested, even though I knew that the stories she had told me had changed over the years, and she must have left things out, thinking I was too young to hear them.

"Your mother told you the truth as she saw it," Tariq said, precise as the pointed end of the spindle he loved so much.

"He's right," said Arwa. She passed me a cup of water, and I took a small sip.

"I know that too," I said. "I just . . ."

Tariq took my hand and squeezed it. I knew he understood.

"Magic is complicated, and we must know all of the details before we can act," he said.

"How do you suggest we do that?" Saoud asked, but I knew there were only two answers.

"The impossible way," I said, marshaling my thoughts, "would be to find the piskey or the demon who was in the Great Hall when it happened."

We all shuddered at the idea of facing another demon. The bear had been enough. As for the piskey, they were the tiniest of the creatures that guarded the mountains, and could remain concealed forever, if they wished to. Certainly, they had made no move to help Kharuf thus far.

"What's the possible way?" Saoud asked. I met his gaze.

"The possible way," I said, heart racing against the bones and muscle in my chest, "is to go to Kharuf, to the castle, and ask the Little Rose."

ii.

My kind do not spend their days at craft or art. Our deepest desire is not for the making of a thing, nor for the thing itself. Rather, we thrive on the skills of those who make. We steal that time and that power, and we turn it to our own souls, and that is how we grow. Once, I had struck deals with shepherds and merchants, and knew only paucity of spirit in return. But I could wait for them to die and then strike new deals with their children, and their children's children, and, thus, I gained some measure of true power.

I went down from the mountains, not to conquer, but to trade. I found a king who had two sons and feared that, when he was dead, they would turn on each other with his kingdom as their prize. It

was a quiet fear, for the boys loved one another very much, but I
nurtured it, whispering tales where I could about kingdoms that had
fallen thus, and before long, the old king could barely sleep without
nightmares of blood and fire.

And then I told him what to make.

He set my mountains as the border and crafted two kingdoms,
one for each of his sons. To the elder would go the clay flats and forests and fields and the harbor in the west, and to the younger would
go the heathered slopes and deep dells of the east. It was not an even
split, but it put his needless fears to rest, and turning him into the
King Maker gave me more power than I had hoped for. Power enough
to deal with his house for generations. I gave the Maker Kings of
Qamih their name, and for seven generations, they made roads, and
safe harbors for ships; city walls and a great army; and their subjects
gave them names to match their work. All of it fed into me without
their realization. I used that power to control my own kin, to keep
them from taking foolish risks in the lowlands, and to shore up their
strength against the bitter iron that wounded us so deeply.

Kharuf, where they herded sheep and little else, was nothing to
me, except that I needed it to be, and I needed it to wither toward
inevitable doom. And slowly, slowly, it did, presenting an ever more
tempting target for the latest of the Maker Kings, who had no title
of his own yet, and who hungered for conquest.

Finally, I saw my chance. A girl was born to Kharuf three years
after a boy was born in Qamih; ideal for an arranged marriage, if
their parents could be convinced. The timing was perfection, beyond

what I might have engineered. Kharuf already hovered on the brink of desolation—one or two hard winters, or a summer with too much rain, would be enough to send it over into desperation—but I would leave nothing to the mercy of possibility. When the proposal was made, it would be accepted.

There had been one like me before amongst our kind. He had taken a king and ruled that king's lands, but in the end he had been undone, and his undoing had ruined our kind for time nearly beyond measure. I would take no king, not directly. Instead, I would have the girl, the Little Rose. I knew she would be raised from infancy to rule: given the best education, taught to do everything from spinning thread to planning battle strategy. Her mind would be a fortress, each stone of it laid with the will to lead, and once I took it, I would make it impregnable. She would be queen, but once married, she would not be the focus of power—at least, not until I decided it was time for her to be.

I waited five more years, almost nothing compared to my wait thus far, and then I went to the castle in Kharuf where the Little Rose spent her days. It was her birthday, and the Great Hall was full to bursting with her subjects. This suited me, as I fed as much on fear as I did on craft. I spent the afternoon in the kitchens, unseen, and watched as the cooks prepared a feast that almost didn't require my help to be stunning. As I lurked, I felt the approach of the beings who might undo my plan before I could begin it.

It was tradition to leave offerings for the creatures that kept my kind hemmed into our mountain prison. It was not tradition for them to actually attend. Perhaps they sensed me. Perhaps they were, at last, aware of my actions over the previous decades. Perhaps it was poor luck on my part. In any case, I had not come this far to be thwarted now. I cast aside my dignity, and waited, crouching in the kitchen embers, while the feast went on above. I waited while each of my hated jailors gave a gift to the Little Rose, and as they gave their power to her, I held back a flood of laughter. They gave her gifts to make her a better queen. Without meaning to, they would only strengthen my designs.

At last, I could stand to stay in hiding no longer. I left the kitchens and went to the Great Hall in a storm of darkness and flame. I looked upon the Little Rose and I gave her a gift of my own: a promise that, someday, we would achieve great things together, and her own people would suffer greatly if she tried to work against me. In the face of my fury, only the piskey spoke, adding the wisp-thin thread of her magic to the strong-spun cord that was my own. Her gift to the princess was so laughable that I let her bestow it, as though sleep could protect her kingdom from my designs.

I left them there, in panic and devastation, to reason out the depth of the doom I had presented to them. The effects would not be felt in full right away, but time would show them how far their fall was destined to be. The Little Rose would live; I had seen to it. She would grow up as blessed and talented as my jailors had decided to let her be. And then—then, she would be mine for the taking.

That would give me Kharuf, but I did not wish only for that sheep-infested mire. I wanted Qamih as well, and I had plans for *that, too. Each year of my enforced exile in those hated mountains, each moment spent pandering to one Maker King after another, all of it would come to fruition in the endless meadows of Kharuf. My kind make no art, it is true; but if we did, then the curse I gave to the Little Rose, to her parents and her kingdom and her people, would be our greatest work.*

SIX

THE WAY THROUGH the Road Maker's Pass was easy, thanks to years of long trade between Qamih and Kharuf, but we did not take that road. Even after our encounter with the demon bear, Saoud and I deemed it unwise to travel in view of others. Bears, we had learned, we could handle. We were less sure of ourselves if confronted with a group of armed men. Banditry had not always been a problem on the trade route that linked the two kingdoms, but as the ruination in Kharuf increased, so too did the number of desperate souls upon the road. It was, Saoud's father told us, the simplest of mathematics.

"Why doesn't the Maker King fix it, like he did in

Qamih?" Tariq had asked, prying his knives out of the target while Saoud's father lectured. My mother liked our weapons training little enough, and cared even less for when Saoud's father taught us politics, but that had not stopped us from learning either. "We could all call him the Peace Maker after he does it."

"The Maker King will have peace, I think," said Saoud's father. "But he will do it in another way."

We never asked what that way might be, not even Tariq, and questions came to him the way that breathing did to the rest of us. Saoud's father would freely tell us many ugly things, so we did not press him when he did not wish to be pressed.

Now, I realized our path would have been easier if we had. Tariq was right about the version of the story that I knew from my mother: it was in many pieces, and we had put them together differently over the years. My mother told me about the creatures and their gifts to our princess as I lay sick in bed, and if there was an oddness to her face as she said the words, I thought it was because she was sad I had missed the event. Six-year-olds can be selfish, and I never thought that maybe, maybe, there was more to the tale she was telling.

I had not realized the extent of the darkness until weeks later, when my sheep pox had healed, and I had gone back to the spinning room to sit at my mother's feet. It should

have been the same as any other day in the spinning room—
wool came in, carded and bundled for us, and thread went
out, each skein destined to be a part of a better work—but
something was different. My mother wouldn't let me spin.

They whispered, the spinners, where once they had chat-
ted freely. Spinning was a craft of the eyes and hands, and
left the mind free for talk. At my mother's knee, I learned
as much about how Kharuf ran as I learned about her craft.
But that day they were quiet, as though they did not wish
for me to hear. I heard them anyway, of course, because it
was a small room, but the words I remembered were strung
together along an uneven yarn, such that I might have spun
in my first months of working.

"The Silk Road is the only way," I heard, and "Mariam
is already sick. It has only been two weeks!" and "They
cannot expect us to stay here. They cannot expect us to
live like this."

My mother said nothing, just spun on and on, as though
the evenness of her thread and the steadiness of her work
would be enough. She spun as the room around her emptied,
of spinners and of that which they would spin. The wealth
and wool of the kingdom went to Qamih, and returned in
the form of cloth we should have been able to make ourselves. The food we ate became plainer fare. Other artisans
followed the spinners out of the castle, back home to their
own meager villages to scrounge for work, or across the

sand in search of something better in the land their ancestors had called home. Arwa's mother coughed, and pressed
a hand against her belly; but she would not leave my mother,
and my mother would not leave Kharuf.

In the end, it took a royal decree. It was nearly a full year
after the fateful party, when most of the spinners had gone,
and those who stayed spent more time idle than they did at
their craft. King Qasim stood on the dais in his threadbare
purple robe, his face gaunt, and without his crown upon
his head. Queen Rasima stood behind him, the Little Rose
in her arms, even though she was six now, and too big to
be carried. We stood in the Great Hall and listened as the
decree was read out by the king himself, so important that
he would not leave it to a herald.

"By order of King Qasim and Queen Rasima, rulers
of Kharuf," the declaration began, "the craft of spinning,
whether by wheel or by spindle or by means held secret to
the crafters themselves, is forbidden. Wool may be shorn
from the sheep and bleached and baled. It may be carded
and coiled, but it may not be spun into thread within the
borders of this kingdom."

There were so few spinners left in the court, a shadow
of the former glory we had once held here, and all of them
had stayed for love of their king and queen. Around me, I
saw drooped shoulders as crafters saw the ending of their
work. Arwa, not quite a year old now, made cooing noises,

but the rest of us were silent as we considered our future. Even Tariq knew to be still. Some of the adults would find another trade, perhaps, or limit themselves to the care of the sheep and the trading of raw wool. Most would leave, my mother among them, rather than give up the craft they had set their lives to the mastery of. In the Great Hall that day, hers was the only back unbent, the only face that was not overcome with despair. I remember her standing there, so determined in the face of the king's decree, and I felt my own body straighten to match hers.

On the dais, the Little Rose turned her face into her mother's shoulder. She was only six, but she was still a princess, and I hated her then, because she couldn't even look at us one last time.

And so we had left and wandered for two years, and then we settled for being poor spinners at the crossroads, when once we had made cloth for a queen. All that time, my mother told me, Tariq, and, eventually, Arwa, about the way the Little Rose had smiled at the phoenix above her chair at the birthday, and how the piskey had delighted her with aerial acrobatics. Her stories always ended well before the demon, and the curse, and maybe that was why Tariq and Arwa loved them so much, but I heard enough from others to understand it. The king and queen had been made to choose between their kingdom and their daughter, and they had chosen their daughter, to the ruin of all else. At the time, I had thought it was anger that gave my mother her determination, because that's where I always looked to find mine. Now that I was older, I was not so sure.

"I never understood why it was spinning," Arwa said, as we sat around the campfire. We were high enough in the mountains that trees were few, which made the fire difficult to maintain, but soon we would be across the top of the range. In the meantime, we huddled together and ate smoked bear meat with whatever plants Arwa had gathered as we walked during the day.

"What does it matter?" asked Saoud.

"I only mean that there are other crafts to pick from," Arwa said. "Why not blacksmithing? Or weaving? Why not farming?"

"It had to be something small," I said, my tongue so thick with bitter feelings that I could taste them. "Something that no one considers, something that goes unnoticed."

"How can spinning be unnoticed?" Arwa asked. "It is the base of everything."

"We know that," I said. "We have been taught it. But do you think the Little Rose looks at her dresses when she puts them on in the morning, and wonders how they are made?"

"That's not fair, Yashaa. Your mother taught the Little Rose to spin herself, and she was the most important spinner in the castle." She paused for a moment. "When she helped teach me, she said that spinning was the beginning of everything. Maybe that's why the demon picked it. Because that's where Kharuf begins."

Tariq and I exchanged a look, and Tariq shrugged.

"It's like fine silk, magic," Tariq said. "Most people cannot see the threads until they are unspooled."

"Why would a demon want Kharuf to be unspooled?" Saoud said. "Why make the curse at all?"

"I don't think demons need reasons," I said. "I think they just enjoy destruction."

Tariq looked like he had his own answer to that question, but didn't want to start an argument. I was not very reasonable when it came to discussion of the curse, and my head still ached, which made me irritable. I resolved to be less obstructive, but before I could say anything encouraging, Saoud interjected.

"My father says it is not wise to engage an enemy you cannot predict," he said.

"That is why we are going to find the Little Rose," I reminded him. "I fought the bear with you, Saoud. I do not wish to fight another demon, in any form, until I know more."

Saoud looked at me for a long moment, and then nodded. Tariq moved closer to Arwa, and wrapped his blanket around her. I would be so glad when we were back in the lowlands, where summer remembered that it was meant to be warm.

"Tell me again what you remember of the castle," Saoud said.

It wasn't very much. I remembered the Great Hall and the spinning room, and our own living quarters, but I could not tell him the shape of the gates, nor how many soldiers guarded them. Tariq remembered the Little Rose's playroom and nursery with some detail, but we had no way of knowing if those rooms would still be hers, or if she would have moved to different ones once she was older.

"We are going to have to find a village near the castle and ask questions," Saoud said. "I don't like that idea very much, but I don't like wandering into the castle and making an attempt on the princess with no directions at all."

"You're right," I said. "But how do you intend to get them to tell us?"

He was silent then, and so was I, as we cast about for a solution.

"I'll ask them," Arwa said.

We all looked at her, surprised.

"You'll just ask?" Saoud said. He wasn't mocking her, not quite, but he never could help smiling when he looked at her, so it looked rather like he was.

"People tell me things," she said practically. "You have seen them do it."

This was true. More than once over the years, we had

concocted some sort of plan to eavesdrop on the merchants who visited our parents when we had been forbidden to listen to their talk. The plans had always failed, but it had taken Arwa only moments to sit next to someone's wife, stir a pot over a cookfire, and ask the questions we wanted to have answered. She was small, and so they often thought she was younger than her true years. Even if they did not speak to her directly, they spoke around her without heed to her presence, and her memory for such overheard conversations was excellent.

"Very well," said Saoud. "But Tariq must go with you, even if he hides himself. I don't think any of us, even Yashaa or I, should be alone once we come down from the mountains."

"Or in the mountains," Tariq said, tearing a strip of bear meat with his teeth with particular ferocity.

"Yashaa, how is your head?" Arwa asked me.

I grimaced, for I had hoped that they had all forgotten.

"It's fine," I told them, which was not quite the truth. Saoud frowned. "It's better, in any case. The headaches are almost gone, and I can look at the fire without fainting. We have walked for days, and I haven't faltered. Sometimes I feel a bit light-headed, but my sight has cleared and my mind no longer feels fuzzy, like it did in the first few days."

"You will tell us if something changes?" Arwa pressed.

"I know you are well enough, but, Yashaa, we are all we have."

"I will," I told her, "and I know."

And silently I promised her that someday, I would make sure that she had more.

SEVEN

WE WEREN'T SURE IF the border between Kharuf and Qamih was at the highest point of the mountain pass, or somewhere else along the way. The mountains were not inhabited, for the most part, so it mattered little which kingdom laid claim to them. Anyone might climb partway up and trap for meat or furs, and anyone might scratch the surface of the mountain rock to look for iron ore, though most of what had been easily exposed was long since depleted. We knew that Qamih lay behind us, but we weren't certain where Kharuf would begin. At least, we weren't until we crossed into it.

There was a little creek, one we had followed down the

mountainside because it was clear, and if we kept to it, then we didn't have to carry our own water as we walked. It turned sharply south where we needed to continue east, and so we crossed. As soon as our feet touched the dry dirt on the other side, we knew that we were home.

Tariq, who spun the most of us, coughed so hard that his paroxysms took him to his knees, and there was blood on Arwa's handkerchief when he handed it back to her. For her part, Arwa caught her breath easily enough and kept her feet, though she swayed enough that Saoud put his arm around her shoulders to hold her up. My head, which had ceased to ache as the air thickened on our way down the mountain, pounded anew, though I too was able to stand.

"Give me your spindles," Saoud said. "Now."

Tariq didn't try to talk, but rummaged in his pack as his strength returned to him. Arwa retrieved both of hers— one from her mother, and one from the father she had never met—and I got mine.

"Are you going to break them?" Arwa asked, and she handed Saoud the tools of her craft. She didn't sound sad or scared, just resigned to whatever would be decided.

"No," Saoud said. "I will keep them for you."

He had sat around the fire in the evenings with us all these days in the mountains, and all the years before. He had seen how unconscious it was; how, as soon as we were settled, a spindle appeared in our hands and wool for us to spin. Even I did it, and my feelings about spinning were complicated. He knew that, though we might not mean to, our hands tended to find craft to work, and he knew that if he left us our spindles, we would spin whether we meant to or not.

"The king's decree was for our own protection, as much as it was for the Little Rose," said Tariq, as his spindle disappeared into Saoud's pack.

"Maybe," I said. "But he still drove our parents away to save one girl. I am not ready to forgive that so easily. Are you?"

"No," said Tariq, but his heart was not in it. He was still looking at Saoud's pack. "The magic must have grown stronger in the years since the curse was laid. Our parents weren't affected so quickly, even right after the birthday party."

"Can you walk?" Saoud asked, hoisting the pack onto his back again. "Are you ready to go on?"

In truth, my body was, but my mind had seen clearly for the first time the illness that was killing my mother. She had always kept it from us, even when Tariq's father and then Arwa's mother were dying in the spare tent. She never let us see the full power of her illness, never let us feel the fear of it in our lungs. I felt it now, though, in my own breathing, and when I looked at how Tariq's shoulders still heaved.

"I am," I said.

"So am I," said Tariq, pale and determined, and beside him, Arwa nodded.

Our pace was slow, though the ground was even and the air was plentiful again. Saoud took the front, and did not push us. I guarded the back, poorly, I'll admit, as I was halfway lost in my own thoughts.

I had always carried a spindle. Even though I hated it and loved it in turn, it had always been in my pocket, in my belt, in my pack. When we had no food upon the road, I'd had my spindle. When I was angry with my mother, angry with the Little Rose, I'd had it. I set it down only for sparring, when the manic energy of the staff or the knives took me over, and made me into a tool for crafting of a different purpose. The spindle didn't weigh very much, even with the weighted whorl, but I knew it was with me when I had it, and now that it wasn't, I felt its absence.

This was the burden my mother had borne that whole last year in Kharuf, when she stayed for love of the queen. To keep the spindle and feel her lungs fail her, or to give it up and always be searching for it? I had been without mine for not even an hour, and I was nearly mad from wanting it back. How had she lasted? How had she felt the pull and stretch of her craft and ignored it until she was safely in

Qamih, and could work again?

I nearly tripped when I realized it: she hadn't. She had spun for the king and queen, and for the Little Rose, even though she had felt it killing her. She had not been able to stop. Not even after it was made illegal. She had spun and spun, and unspooled, until finally she had crossed the mountains with the illness already set into her lungs, drowning her with every breath. She had done her duty—no, she had done more than that—and she had carried the price of it across the mountains, where it was still killing her. I wished I had been kinder.

Our days went well enough. We walked and walked, and there was plenty to keep us occupied. The evenings, however, were not so easy. Saoud sharpened knives until the sound of iron grating on the whetstone made Arwa beg him to stop, to give her some peace and quiet. But the quiet was even worse. I could hear Tariq's fingers move against the fabric of his trousers, spinning wool that wasn't there with a spindle he didn't have. I could hear Arwa's breathing, and wondered if it wheezed more today than it had yesterday. I could hear my own heart beat, hard against my ribs, for lack of anything else to do.

We sparred, each of us taking a turn against the others.

I even squared off with Arwa, and though I tried to go easy on her, she fought with such ferocity that I was forced to maintain my guard, and strike at her harder than I might have liked. We fought each other with the staff, and with our fists, and with knives, which was something Saoud's father had never allowed, because there was no way to make it safe.

"There is no *safe*," Saoud said, panting, when I reminded him of this. "There is no safe, and the three of you are wild here. Knives, I think, are the least of our worries."

We were lucky that he kept his head.

It was Saoud who planned how far we would walk each day, now, and where we would camp and what we would eat. Left to ourselves, Tariq and Arwa and I would not have managed it. We skirted what few villages we passed, and not even Saoud went into them to seek news or food. He would not leave us alone, and neither would he take us with him into a town. Instead, he shepherded us up and down the heathered slopes with the care and attention of the best herd master, and took care of us when we could not take care of ourselves.

One night, I woke to Saoud carrying Arwa out of our tent. She struggled against his hold, her veil and robe loose in the night breeze, and her arms flailed against him in use-less blows.

"What are you doing?" I hissed at him.

"She was trying to get into my pack," Saoud said, and I heard the words he would not say: she was trying to get her spindle.

"Please," she begged. "Just for a little while. Just for a little while."

"No, little goat," he said to her, and I heard his father's gentlest voice when he spoke. "You mustn't. You must sleep without it."

He put her in her tent, and then came back for his pack. I had never given it much consideration before. It was merely a part of Saoud, Saoud's pack on Saoud's back. He saw how I looked at his pack now, though, and sighed.

"Yashaa," he said. "We need a better way than this."

He was tired. We were killing him, and the spindles were killing us. I didn't know what to do. I couldn't stop staring at the pack. I watched while he picked it up, wrapped it tightly in his arms, and went to sit by the fire alone.

It was a long time before I could go back to sleep.

"Saoud," I said, when we rose gritty-eyed in the morning. Tariq and Arwa had gone to the river for water, and would not overhear us. "Saoud, tonight I should spin."

"No!" he said.

"Listen to me," I said. "This is what we know: spinning makes us sick. Not spinning makes us mad. I will suffer the least if you let me spin, and then you and I can make a plan when my head is clear."

He did not like it. I did not much like it either, but I knew that it was the only way. It would be only the finest thread, the smallest line between sanity and sickness, and I would hold it for as long as I could, but I needed a place to start.

"Very well," he said. "But I will hold the wool."

He would stop me before I spun too much, I knew. He would help me find the middle ground.

When Tariq and Arwa returned with the water, we cooked dinner and sparred until it was too dark to see. They crawled into their tents and slept, and Saoud and I pretended to do the same while we waited for them to quiet. Then Saoud went to his pack and pulled out my spindle and a handful of wool he had taken from Tariq.

As soon as he put the shaft in my hands, I felt better than I had in days. The weight of the whorl pulled my hands down, the way my mother had taught me when I was a child, and when Saoud gave me the wool, I knew that this was what I was meant to do. There was a tickle in my throat, even before I dropped the spindle the first time, but I ignored it.

I spun quickly and well, and long before I wanted to stop, the wool ran out. Saoud would give me no more. The thread was not my best work, but it was work, and I was glad of it, even though I coughed when it was done. Saoud gave me water, and I coiled the thread around the spindle shaft, finishing the job as I had been taught.

"Are you better now?" Saoud asked.

"Yes," I said. My throat betrayed me with a cough, and Saoud's eyes narrowed. "At least, my mind is better," I said.

"You look much calmer," Saoud said. "You have scared me these past days."

"I'm sorry," I said. "And I will be sorry later, too. I can already feel it coming undone."

"Then we'd better talk now," Saoud said, "while we still can."

EIGHT

IN THE END, THE BEST IDEA we had was to give Arwa her spindle. As she spun the meager wool that Saoud allowed her, her eyes lost the red-manic glint; her smile became the one I was used to, not the feral look of a strange girl who scared me as much as I am sure I scared her. The hardest part was watching Tariq, whose face grew longer and longer as he watched her spin, hunger writ on every part of his skin, and his fingers still moving absently against his thigh.

"I'm sorry, Tariq," I told him. I didn't try to still his hands, though I wanted to. "You know I don't hold you back to hurt you."

"I do," he said. "I do. It's only . . ."

I knew what he meant. I had only felt the call to spin since we had arrived in Kharuf and fallen under the curse. Tariq lived with it of his own accord, this calling to our craft, and loved it, all his days. Now he could not have it, and he felt mad for wanting.

Arwa came out of the tent. She had scrubbed her face, and was wrapping a newly washed veil around her head. She was dressed neatly, with none of the dust of the road on her knees, in the best clothes she had remaining. She looked like a poor merchant's daughter, one who could pay for what she needed, but could not pay very much. The truth—that she was not even that well-stationed—pulled even harder at my heart.

"Are you sure you are all right?" I asked her, probably for the tenth time.

"Yes, Yashaa," she said to me, and coughed lightly into her veil. "My head is clearer now, and I remember how the market works."

"We will be close by if you need us," Saoud told her.

I would be the closest, since my head was still clear enough. I would watch her as she went among the stalls. Saoud would be with Tariq, tucked out of the way but ready to come if we needed them.

The town we were close to had a fair-sized market. There were more than two dozen stalls, and we knew that more artisans and traders would set up in unofficial corners of the market to do their business.

"They talk to Arwa because she is small enough that they think it does not matter what they say to her," Saoud's father had told us. Arwa had overheard two merchants discussing how the Maker King's soldiers might be bribed to rout us out of the crossroads, despite the fact that it was our right to stay there. Arwa had been right next to them when they'd said it, her dress and appearance making it obvious who she was, and they had not cared. When she told Saoud's father, he had been able to remedy the situation, and the two merchants had found themselves unwelcome at the market thereafter.

"Do they think I am stupid?" Arwa asked.

"No," said Saoud's father. He used his gentle voice, so that the words would not hurt her when he said them. "They think you do not matter."

"Then they will pay for their own folly," Arwa said. It became a game to her. She would listen and report, and we learned to use the gossip she brought us to our advantage.

Now it was no game, and Arwa knew it, but she also knew that she was very good at it. She had dressed to match the part, and she walked into the strange town's market as though it was her second home, while I hung behind her by several measures and watched her work.

Her veil was another advantage in these situations. With half her face covered, men and women could not assume she was a stranger, because it was possible she was someone they should know. As long as no one asked her to fetch her parents, she could pretend to be local, and no one would suspect otherwise. I followed her as she made her way up one line of stalls and then back along the other, never lingering for very long at any one shop, but carefully figuring out which of the people she would go back to, and press for information.

Deciding she was safe enough, I retreated to the long tables that had been set out for taking lunch. It was early yet, and so no one else was seated there. I couldn't see the whole market from where I sat, but I could see enough of it. The selection was quite poor. There was no cloth for sale at all, only finished tunics and trousers, robes, and veils. These were more expensive than plain cloth, which might be made into whatever the buyer wished. I was not sure how anyone in this town could afford such luxury, but that stall was the most crowded, for all the shoppers at it had an uncomfortable desperation in their bearing.

I looked away, both to see what else the market had to offer, and because the finished clothes made me sad in a way I could not explain. There was a woodcarver across the way, and I watched him work with his apprentice while they waited for customers. Though their stall was full of utilitarian items like stools and sturdy cupboards, the carver and his apprentice made little frivolities while they sat. I watched the master produce a bird whose wings actually moved from a block of wood no larger than both my fists held together. The apprentice's work was not so fine, but the sheep she carved looked so real you might have shorn it.

Other stalls sold nails or potatoes or dried heather. The breadmaker's stall was nearly empty already. The butcher was busy, as was the candlemaker. I saw Arwa admiring a set of finely tapered candles at his stall for a moment. She smiled at him, and I knew she would compliment the work to see if he would bite. He must not have been too forthcoming, because she quickly moved on. I knew that busy stalls were less helpful ones for Arwa, because if a merchant had customers, they were not likely to waste time talking to her for longer than it took to figure out that she had nothing to offer for their wares.

After an hour had passed, Arwa appeared at the table with two figs in her hand. I didn't bother wondering how she'd got them. She passed one to me, and tucked the other one away. I knew she would give it to Tariq later, because he had missed the market entirely; unlike Saoud, he would be sad about it.

"I think the candlemaker's wife is the best chance," she said. "But they have been too busy all morning, so I haven't been able to get close to them again."

"We aren't in a hurry," I reminded her. "If it takes you the whole day and you learn something we can use, then it will have been time well spent."

"I know," she said. "It's only that I can feel the pull of the spindle again, and I want to be well away from here before—" She paused. "You know."

I did know. What I said instead was: "It is better to forget it while you're in the market."

"Of course," she said, shaking her head to regain the sense of it. She hadn't coughed in a while, at least. Neither had I. "This is very strange."

"It is," I told her. "I am sorry I can't be more help."

"I am glad to be any help at all," she said. "You and Saoud would have had a much easier time of this journey without me."

Arwa had been a part of us for so long that sometimes I forgot how much younger she was. I thought, instead, that she was only very small. But it was six years that separated us, not just height, and we hadn't spared her very much thought when we'd dragged her through the mountain pass. The last time she had done it, she had been a babe on her mother's back, one year old and never alive before her people were cursed.

"Remember who it was that climbed the tree and distracted the demon bear for us," I said to her.

She smiled. I passed her the half of the fig I had not yet eaten, and she took a bite.

"Come on," she said. "Let's go and see if the candlemaker's wife can spare us some time."

The crowd around the candlemaker's stall had thinned. Only two old women stood there, looking at the cheapest and stubbiest candles that were available for sale. They would not burn particularly clean but they would burn long, and a clever person might save the wax and make a new candle with some of their own string.

"But where will you get it?" said one woman to the other. "There hasn't been yarn in the market for months, let alone heavy string for candles."

The second woman scowled, but put down three small coins for the candles anyway.

"There's bound to be a fraying veil," she said to her companion.

This was Kharuf now, I saw. They sold the wool to Qamih, and it didn't come back as yarn or cloth. It came back as whole clothes: expensive, and good only for wearing. Spinning, I thought, showed its face in every corner of craft. I wondered where the candlemaker got his wicks and how carefully he guarded them.

"Can I help you, little one?" The candlemaker's wife had finally noticed Arwa.

"I've never seen candles so fine!" Arwa said, her voice a delight to the ears. "You could light one in a castle and not feel it was out of place there, I think."

The candlemaker's wife smiled, an expression half remembrance and half longing.

"Aye, little one," she said. "My father-in-law used to do just that. His candles were even finer than these ones, but there's no call for such wares as that anymore."

"You made candles for the castle?" Arwa asked.

"When first I was married nearly eight years ago, yes," said the woman.

"Did you get to go inside the walls?" Arwa's voice was breathless with childish excitement. "Did you see the gates? Did you get to wander the corridors looking for places that needed light?"

"No, little one," said the woman. "We only went into the courtyard and met with the steward. But, ah, I tell you, even the courtyard was a marvelous place. It was so wide, and the stones were swept clean of any dirt that might get run in off the road. They cared about what the castle looked like in those days. The iron gate shone, and the guards around it stood straight up at attention the whole time."

Iron and guards. That might be too much for us.

"And there was no lack of light, either," she said. "Except for one tower, which I always thought was odd. The other three towers were always lit up, so you could find the castle in the night. But one of them never had so much as a spark."

If it had a window that faced outwards, that could be our way in.

"Such a time you must have had!" said Arwa. She did not turn to look at me, but made a fist by her side to show

81

she knew I had what I wanted.

"Aye, little one," said the candlemaker's wife. "Now run along, before my husband realizes you're not going to buy anything."

Arwa giggled and fled.

NINE

WE MET UP BACK WHERE Saoud had hidden our camp, just as the sun was setting. We pitched the tents before we did anything else, as that was difficult to do in the dark, and laid a fire to cook supper. At last, we were settled for the night, and while we waited for the lentils to cool, Arwa told Saoud what she had heard.

"The market is very poor," she said. "Only the clothier has any money at all, and they all resent him for it. The clothes he sells are not particularly well-made, and often they must be pulled apart to fit the buyer, but the only way to get cloth is to walk to Qamih, so they must all buy from him."

"It's like they want us to starve," Tariq said.

"The king and queen are just as hungry," Arwa told him. "And nearly as poor."

"Not the king and queen," Tariq said. "*Them*."

"I don't understand," said Arwa, but Tariq wouldn't look at her, or talk any more.

It used to be straightforward, when we camped at the crossroads, but ever since we had come into Kharuf, and Tariq had all but coughed up a lung on the bank of the stream, I wasn't sure who we were anymore or where we belonged. The way Tariq said *them* chilled my blood, though, and I did not like to think about it.

"How close are we to the castle?" Saoud asked.

"Half a day's walk," Arwa said. "We could be there by lunch tomorrow, which gives us plenty of time to scout for the tower."

"What?" said Saoud, because Arwa had jumped ahead. She filled him in on what the candlemaker's wife had told her, which reminded her of the fig. She peeled it for Tariq while she spoke, and passed it to him. He ate it in two bites and still said nothing to her.

"Yashaa, this is a terrible plan," Saoud said when Arwa had finished talking.

"I know," I told him. "Can you think of anything better? We can't exactly enter the castle in disguise. We are clearly too young to be merchants, and they will recognize their own guards."

"Climbing a tower, though," Saoud said. "It's like something out of an old story. Do you think you can do it?"

"I can do it!" said Arwa in her very best market voice. It didn't fool us for a moment.

"No!" said Saoud and I together.

"No, Arwa." This time Saoud's voice was calmer, and he looked at her directly. "You are the best climber, it is true, but the climb is only half the work of this plan. What if the tower is full of guards? Or what if it is a prison? You can reach the top, we know it, but you may not be able to deal with what waits for you there. Yashaa will be an ugly climber, but he will be better prepared if he has to fight his way through the window."

Arwa sighed. I knew that while she understood what Saoud was saying, she felt in her heart that he said the words because she was too young to be useful.

"Someday you will be tall enough," I said to her. "And then you can take part in all the terrible plans that require climbing."

She laughed, and Saoud relaxed, and except for Tariq, who was still lost in the maze of his thoughts, we were all happy for a moment.

"They are going to be unhappy," Tariq said. "I know it. I know it."

"The king and queen, or their guards?" asked Saoud.

"No, no, no!" said Tariq. He threw his bowl on the

ground, and lentils went everywhere. "Them, them! How can you forget them?"

Saoud and I exchanged a look, and before I could help myself, I glanced at Saoud's pack. He sighed, unhappy, but went to where he had set it and opened the knots. Carefully, he pulled out Tariq's spindle and two handfuls of wool, and then returned to his place by the fire.

"Here, Tariq," he said, passing them over. "I will stop you if you cough so badly again."

I don't think Tariq heard him. He fell upon the wool and grabbed the spindle like they were the tools of his salvation. He had no leader thread, but that didn't stop him. He quickly twisted some wool to use instead. It wasn't the best method and would mean the start of his thread was bulky, but that hardly mattered. Once he had that, he set the rest of the wool close to hand, rose up on his knees, and dropped the spindle.

We watched it whirl, faster and faster as Tariq spun. His thread stretched thin in places, and was thick and uneven in others, but he didn't care. All he wanted, all he needed, was to feel the pull of the spindle's drop and the growth of thread beneath his fingers. Soon enough, the raw wool was gone, and Tariq grabbed at nothing for a moment before he realized that he reached out in vain. Saoud caught the spindle before it could reverse and undo Tariq's work, and looked down at the thread Tariq had made.

"I have made better," Tariq said. "But it was good to make anything."

Arwa nodded and helped him wind the thread up. I wondered if that made her feel better, or if only spinning would suffice. When they were done, Saoud took the spindle and packed it away again. Then he refilled Tariq's bowl with the lentils that remained in the pot and passed him a spoon.

"What do you mean when you say 'them,'" I asked, "if not the king and queen?"

Tariq swallowed. He was calm again, balanced like a perfect whorl as the world spun on around him.

"I have been thinking about the demon bear," he said. "We know from the oldest stories that demons can overtake a thing and make it theirs. Once they used people, but then they were weakened. I don't think our victory over the bear was as complete as it might have appeared."

"You mean we didn't kill it?" Saoud said. "Tariq, we *ate* most of it."

"We killed the bear," Tariq said. "But we didn't kill the demon. We just drove it out and away."

"Will it come after us?" Arwa asked.

"I don't think they can easily leave the mountains," Tariq said. "I don't think most of them are strong enough to. But I'm not talking about the demon that was in the bear. I'm talking about the demon that came to the Little Rose's birthday party, all those years ago."

Of the four of us, only Tariq had been in the room that night, and since he had been only four years old himself, he remembered nothing. They all looked to me instead.

"I didn't see it," I reminded them. "And I had the sheep pox, so I was fevered and dreaming anyway. I am not sure anything I remember would be useful."

"Tell us the story, how your mother told it," said Arwa, "and we will see what it means when we add it to what we have learned."

"You've all heard it before," I said. "You've all heard her tell it."

"We know, Yashaa," Tariq said. "I want you to tell it. Remind us of what we know, and we'll compare it with what we know now. It helps to do these things out loud."

So I told them the story as I knew it. How the Great Hall had looked, and how the creatures had come to give gifts to the Little Rose. I told them how five gifts were given, and then the demon came and gave the curse, and how only the piskey remained to countermand that great magic. She could not do much, but she could help the Little Rose, and the king and queen were grateful for it.

"Why couldn't she help us, too?" Arwa asked.

"Magic is about balance more than anything, and always has been since the Storyteller Queen made it in the desert," Tariq said. "Whatever the piskey did, she did as much as she could. Remember, the others had already done their magic and made a tangled net of the threads. We're lucky the piskey was able to do anything at all."

"Some luck," I said. "She still helped only the Little Rose."

"We need to know the exact words," Tariq said. "Not just the piskey's words, but the demon's words as well. Not rumors and not tales of them, but the words themselves."

"My mother would never tell me," I said. "I am not sure she knew."

"My father wouldn't tell me either," said Tariq, "but there has got to be someone in the castle who knows. The Little Rose must, because it's her curse."

"So Yashaa will climb into the dark tower and try to find a way to get us in," Saoud said. "And if you can't, you must find out on your own."

I nodded and then thought of something else.

"After the castle, we should go back to the mountains," I said. "I know it's not entirely safe there, but at least we will have our minds, and we will be able to spin."

"I agree," said Saoud. "There will be a cave or something, and we can stay there until we have decided what to do next."

"In the meantime, we bury the spindles here," I said. Tariq and Arwa both looked at me in shock. "I don't like it either, but remember: spinning is illegal in Kharuf. If we are caught tomorrow, and they go through Saoud's pack and find them, he will be in desperate trouble."

We didn't speak any further but finished our dinner in silence, and then we went to our bedrolls.

In the morning, Tariq took the small shovel we used to dig the fire pit, while Arwa looked for a tree that she would be sure to recognize again. There weren't as many trees on the heathered slopes, but she found one to her liking soon enough, and Tariq carefully peeled back the green layer of plants before setting it aside to dig the hole below. When he had gone down far enough, we placed all four spindles, with their whorls beside them, into a shirt Tariq had mostly outgrown and wrapped them tightly. Saoud had to place them in the hole, as none of us could bring ourselves to do it. Then he packed the earth down on top of them carefully before replacing the greenery on top.

We rolled up the tents and stowed our gear in our packs. Saoud didn't conceal the fire pit as he had done when we were in the mountains. There was less need to hide our tracks here, and a good chance that we would be returning to camp here again tomorrow, if all went as we hoped it would go. Still, there was a weight in my steps I couldn't explain, and a reluctance in every step I took away from the last piece of my mother I owned.

"Are you sure you will find it again?" I asked Arwa. For once, I sounded like I was the younger.

"Yes," she said. "We will find our old camp easily enough, because of the fire pit. No one else would look any further, but I will know to find this tree."

I looked back at the tree, only just visible from this distance, and frowned. It didn't seem particularly special to me, but Arwa was good at this.

"It will only be a day, Yashaa," she said. She did not remind me that I hated my spindle most of the time, and I was glad of it, for otherwise I might have wept to leave it behind in the dirt.

TEN

WE REACHED THE CASTLE well before noon and settled in to wait. We had no way of knowing which of the towers was the one the candlemaker's wife had told us about, except that it was one of the towers that guarded the castle's corners, where the view from the wall was obscured. Saoud's father had told us that the palace in Qamih was protected by a double wall that bent back on itself at the corners, so that there would be no blind spots. There was plenty of stone in Qamih, after all, and they could quarry it readily enough. In Kharuf, they had to be more economical when they built the castle, so it was a simple square, with the main keep in the middle, and the outbuildings all around it. It was, I suspected, far less grand than the palace in Qamih. And yet when I saw it, my heart lurched: this had been my home.

I had played in that courtyard, chasing balls or chickens; or Tariq, when it was my task to mind him. I had gone to the kitchens to look for extra bread between mealtimes, and the cooks had pretended I was stealthy enough to take it without their notice, slipping me sweets and more besides. One of those rooms had been the spinning room, where I had learned my craft at my mother's knee, and one of those rooms had been mine—where I'd slept, and where I had stayed when I was sick with the sheep pox.

"I don't remember it," said Tariq beside me, great sadness in his voice. "I thought I would see it, and remember. But I don't. I know I lived there, and spent three years in the nursery with the Little Rose, but I don't remember anything."

"It's all right, Tariq," I told him. "I don't remember very much, either. It's more that I know this was my home, our home, and that we were happier here than we have been anywhere else. Does that make sense?"

"Yes," said Tariq. "That's how I feel too."

"I feel like it's a story," said Arwa. "A story I've heard so many times that I think it's real after all. A good story. An important one. A story that I love."

"Me too," said Saoud.

We sat, and we watched the castle, and we waited for it to get dark.

"I see a light!" said Tariq.

The sun had just disappeared behind the mountains, and the sky above us was dark blue and blackening as we watched. Tariq was right: there were lights in the castle. Dozens of them in the main keep, though we could only see the topmost level over the wall. The Great Hall shone dimly, as though only a few lights were put there. The king and queen must have been taking their dinner somewhere else tonight. A few torches lined the walls.

The towers flanked the gate, and I had hoped they would not be the dark ones. It would be hard enough to climb the tower, and I didn't fancy doing it close to the gate, where the guards were likely to be concentrated. Saoud pulled my arm, and the four of us began our long walk around the castle, careful and quiet, to check the other towers.

The castle in Kharuf was not overly fortified. There was no moat, merely a ditch, and the land around the castle had not been flattened or cleared. There was a village over the rise to the east, so we went westerly, and stayed as low in the heather as we could. We passed what had once been the outbuildings, where the hunters and falconers had stayed. Now they lived inside the walls of the castle—not out of fear for their safety, but because there was space for them and their animals. With the spinners gone, the weavers and seamstresses and tailors had left too, and their rooms were taken over by those who remained behind in the service of the king. There were no patrols, nor any sign of them, though we did watch the torches moving along the top of the wall, and knew that the soldiers there took their duties seriously.

At last we came around to the north side of the castle. This side was darker. I looked up at the towers. One had a lit window, but the other was dark. The candlemaker's wife was right. That was our way in.

I took off my tunic, which was pale linen. Even with the dirt of the road on it, it would shine like a beacon against the dark stone walls. Saoud handed me his spare, dyed forest green. Wearing it, I would be well enough hidden, unless light fell on me directly, in which case I would be discovered anyway. My trousers were dark, so I kept them, but I left my shoes. Climbing would be easier in bare feet.

"Remember," said Arwa, "there are other paths than up. You can go sideways and get just as far as you can if you only look in one direction."

"I will remember," I told her.

"Go slowly," said Tariq. "If the mortar crumbles, they might hear you."

"I will," I said.

"Are you all right?" Saoud asked. "Is your head clear?"

"It is," I told him. "Having something to do helps, even if it is not exactly what I want to be doing."

He put his hands on my shoulders, and pressed his forehead close to mine.

"Be careful, my brother," he said. "And come back to us."

I tried to answer, but the words stuck in my throat. Instead I nodded, and slipped away from them, into the night.

I reached the ditch with no trouble, and paused to rub dirt on my face. It was brown enough on its own, in all likelihood, but I wanted to take no chances, and the dirt would make it more like the color of the night. I was about to brush my hands on my trousers when I remembered that Arwa sometimes climbed with dirt on her hands on purpose, to help her find grips. I flattened my hands on the earth again, and then rubbed them together so that the grit was all over my fingers and palms. Then I scrambled up the other side of the ditch, to the wall.

The stones were worn smooth by years of long exposure to wind and rain, but there were places between the blocks where I could find purchase for my hands and feet. I offered up a prayer to my ancestors, the ones who had come across the desert and brought magic with them, and began to climb.

I would have gone slowly whether Tariq told me to or

not. It was difficult to find good places to put my fingers, and they had to bear most of my weight because it was even harder to find good spots for my toes. My arms ached before I was even halfway up. I thought longingly of the rope I carried on my back. At least I would have that for the way down.

Course by course, I made my way up the side of the tower. When I reached the level of the top of the wall, I had to move sideways to make sure I was on the outermost corner. There were guards on the walkway on either side, though they didn't pass through the tower. I wondered, not for the first time, what could be inside. Saoud thought it was probably storage, but Tariq was less sure. I agreed with Tariq. There was nothing that needed to be stored up so high. The room ought to have been a guard's office or lookout, and yet with no light, it could be neither of those things.

Above me, high in the sky, the moon was rising. It was not quite full yet, but it was full enough. If it rose too high before I climbed back down, it would light the wall well enough for me to be spotted. That, more than anything, limited the amount of time I could spend in the castle looking for our answers.

At last, at long last, my fingers gripped the window ledge. This was the hardest part, not the least because I could feel the closeness of my goal and wanted it badly. The ledge was made of wood, so soft after all that stone, and I ignored the screaming protests of my arms as I pulled myself over it, so that I perched on the ledge, one leg in the tower room and one still outside.

It was not storage. It was not an office either, even an abandoned one. What it was, was very, very strange.

The room was wide, the size of the entire tower, with no divisions. I could not see a door, only two very high windows on the courtyard side, and an odd compartment where the door ought to have been. There was a cot with a straw tick mattress near the window. There were two pillows and a heavy quilt. There was a chamber pot and a low table with nothing on it. There was no hearth or brazier, and I wondered how the room was kept warm when the snows came.

The not-quite-full moon was shining through the courtyard windows, and I saw that the floor was thick with dust. Patterns were drawn into it. Lines a finger-width and wider, as the design called for. Flowers and men and horses, and swirls beyond counting.

And footprints.

I was so surprised I nearly fell out the window, but instead caught myself on the ledge and waited there. There was no door. No person could have fit out through the odd compartment I saw. Whoever had made those footprints was in the room with me. Slowly, I pulled my other leg through the window, and stood on my feet, as steadily as I could manage given the dark unknown I was peering into.

Over the hammering of my heart, I heard her. She laughed, when she realized I was afraid. Maybe no one had ever been afraid of her before. And then she stepped into the moonlight, and I saw her.

She was my age, or perhaps younger. It was hard to tell. I thought that maybe if she had lived in the tower for a long time, it would be like how we'd worried about Arwa when her mother had had to carry her on the road. If she never walked properly, if she never got to see the sun, then she would be small and frail.

Except Arwa had never been frail. And I didn't think this girl was, either. If she had been plague-ridden, they would have taken her out of the castle, or she would have died. The candlemaker's wife said that they had not come here in years, and yet this girl was still here. She could not be sick. She must be locked up in this tower for another reason.

She wore a simple dress and slippers. It was good cloth, for all it was a plain design, and the fit was very good. Her hair was mostly covered by a scarf, but a few tufts of it stuck out as though they yearned for freedom from their prison, and I knew that her head had been shorn. It was her hair that gave her away. The color of summer wheat, of rice cooked with saffron, carried across the desert by an ancestor old out of time.

"Hello, boy," said the Little Rose. I had never heard a human being sound more resigned. "Have you come to rescue me?"

iii.

The petty humans do not remember the moment of their making. They cannot recall that first spark of life, nor the painful pathway to their first breath of air. They do not carry the memories of their first word or their first step or their first food. They do not remember the beginning, but if they were a spinner in Kharuf, I gave them the gift of every feeling of their end.

This was how it went: first a tickle in the back of the throat, and then a cough. These things were easily ignored, shrugged off as summer colds or the whisper of pollen on the back of the throat. They drank tea with honey and put fresh flowers in the spinning room to clear the air. They threw the windows wide open and sent the rugs out to be cleaned. There was dust in the courtyard, they said to one *another; it was dust from the sheep brought in for counting.*

It was not the dust.

After the first tickle, the cough became more persistent. They struggled to breathe, and slept propped up on pillows or sitting in chairs. The faintest amount of smoke, from the hearth or from a torch or even from a candle, was too much for them, and they wheezed for air. They took walks along the top of the castle wall. They went out into the meadows, and sat under the shade of the broad-leafed trees that grew there. They tried compresses to draw out infections; they tried teas to clear the lungs. They tried every remedy they could imagine, except the one they knew would do the trick.

The spinners took council with each other and argued long into the night. No agreement could be reached, and so they left each master of the craft to make their own decisions. Most took their tools, families, and apprentices and set out on the roads, leaving Kharuf to seek their fortunes in other lands. Some few stayed behind and tried their hands at other crafts, but were not made content by them. No matter how busy their hands were or how occupied their minds, their bodies yearned for the downward drop of the spindle, the weight of the whorl, and the steady pull of growing thread, until they could do nothing but reach for the spindle once more.

No fewer than a dozen stayed and kept to their craft's traditions. They spun for the king and queen because they loved them, and they grew more and more ill as time progressed. When they finally died, it took days. They could not eat or take water, only breathe, slower and slower. The nurses who minded them measured every rise and fall of the chest, breaths spacing out so far that just when the caretakers were prepared to check the time and give the final blessing, the spinner would heave again. It drove the nurses nearly mad to hear it, rusty, slow breathing, echoing down the stone walls of the corridor where the spinners were brought to die.

The mind, by my design, was the last thing to go. When they drowned in their own lungs, they knew it, though there was no one for them to tell, even if they'd had the air and strength to do it. I gained nothing from this additional suffering, except that it entertained me to watch it unspool before me.

In the end, Qasim did the only thing he could think of. His last few spinners loved him so dearly that they would not forsake their craft for his sake, nor for his wife's, nor for the sake of the Little Rose. So he made a new law, and forbade all manner of spinning in his kingdom. There was a great bonfire in the courtyard when he had the spindles and wheels burned. And the last remaining spinners were driven out from his house.

Kharuf was a country made for sheep and little else. The sheep were still caught and sheared, but the wool could no longer be turned into thread, even in secret, so it was sold to Qamih. At first, the Maker King only sold back thread and yarn at a higher price than he'd paid for the wool. But his greed grew ever more, and in time, he only sold cloth. At last, he ordered his merchants to sell only finished clothes to the people of Kharuf, and they were so dearly bought that the people could barely afford to eat.

Their only hope was for the day that their princess would marry the Maker King's son, and the two kingdoms would be united once more. Then the Maker King would ensure they did not starve, and that wool and thread and yarn and cloth were fairly traded on either side of the mountain. It was a vain and small hope, but it was what they waited for on the heathered slopes of Kharuf.

It was not what I waited for. I waited for two kingdoms, one falling and one strong, to come together. I waited for a baby girl to grow to womanhood. I waited for an undeveloped mind to learn what a future queen is taught. I waited while her parents tried to protect her and their own desperate subjects from the tightly spun threads of magic that made up my curse. I waited, and I did not care how many spinners breathed themselves to death while I did.

And all the while, the Little Rose grew up in a dark room at the top of a stone tower, and the king and queen guarded the secret of her confinement more closely than they guarded the castle itself. For they knew what I knew — what I had declared to them on the day of her fifth birthday. The age I gave was a number pulled from the air to give weight to destiny. The truth was that I would have the girl whenever I wanted. I knew that her parents would do all manner of desperate things in an attempt to thwart me, and that in turn would serve my purpose. The spinners were cursed, the land of Kharuf was cursed, and the Little Rose could break it in a heartbeat — if only, if only they would let her have a spindle.

ELEVEN

"MOST OF THE PEOPLE who come here come to kill me." The Little Rose had a calm voice, a beautiful one, but I got the idea that she didn't get to use it very often. "Though before, they always came through the gate and pretended to be friendly before they turned to murder. They would want to see me, I suppose, to see what they were after. They would speak to my parents, and then when they saw me, they would fly at me with a knife. Killing me won't work, you know. I mean, it will work in that I will be dead. But it won't break the curse."

That she could speak of assassination so calmly chilled my blood. Not so long ago, I had considered harming her, too, and now the thought was wrapped in shame. I pushed it away.

"But you, boy, have not come here for murder," she continued. "Murderers bring masks and sharp knives or poison. Or they shoot an arrow from the roof of the rookery. That one nearly worked, only it was windy that day, and a great gust of air turned the arrow from its course. The arrow was the last one. My mother and father took steps after that, and now I am here. You are not like that. You brought me a rope."

I was still pressed back against the window ledge, unable to move or even to answer her. She spoke like she didn't care if I answered her or not. She moved about the tower room, fetching an extra dress from a small cupboard I hadn't noticed and a tiny necklace from the drawer underneath it. These she placed on the bed, and then began to strip the casings off of the pillows.

"I've considered the window before, of course," she said. "But it's dreadfully high, and none of the blankets they give me are ever any good for shredding."

She was, I realized as I watched her jam the dress, the necklace, and the quilt into the pillow casing, packing. She wanted me to take her with me. She expected it.

"I'm very sorry that I am so ill-supplied," she said. "They don't let me keep even my cup between meals, and I don't know if I have ever owned a pair of proper shoes. I expect

I will be quite a burden to you, but I promise to keep my complaints to a minimum. As you can see, I will not be leaving behind anything of value or use."

It was true. Even before she had taken the quilt off the bed, the room had been ill-appointed at best. My mind unfroze all at once, and I was nearly overcome with questions.

"Why are you up here?" I asked, as it seemed the best place to start.

"For my protection, of course," she said. "First, you see, there were several assassination attempts. Then I turned seven, and I started to wander away from my mother's side. I could get into anything then, and oh, I did."

"But it's a prison," I said, rather obviously. "And you are a princess."

"A cursed princess, boy," she corrected—rather primly, it must be said. "That makes all the difference."

"How do you know I'll take you with me?" I asked.

"You know who I am, it seems," she said, "but you have forgotten about the gifts. Most people do, you know, so you mustn't feel bad about it. Most people are rather focused on the curse, and I think that is understandable, so I will let it slide. But if we are to travel together, you must remember the gifts as well."

"Discernment of truth," I said. "Knowledge of worth." They were the gifts from the unicorn and dragon. She'd had my measure as soon as she laid eyes upon me.

"The very same," she said. The pillow casing was full now, and she was standing close enough that I could have reached out and touched her.

"Well, boy?" she said. I blinked at her. "The rope."

"My name is Yashaa," I said, not wishing to answer to "boy" for the rest of the evening. "There are three others in my party that wait for me in the hills. We have no real plan for our own escape, let alone yours."

"Why did you come here, then?" she asked. "If you had no real plan."

"We—" I paused, and then decided that this escapade was likely to get stranger before it was over, and she might as well know everything. "We wanted to know the truth of the curse. To see if there was anything we could do."

"You're in luck, Yashaa," she said. "I was there, after all. And though I do not remember the details with much clarity, I have had them explained to me many, many times. Take me with you, and I will tell you everything you want to know."

"You will have to leave your slippers," I said. "They will not grip the stone, and they will be of no use on the ground."

She toed them off obediently, and set them neatly next to her bed.

"The rope may hurt your hands," I told her. "I can carry you, or I can carry your bag."

She looked at her meager belongings. Then she looked at the other pillow casing. She got it quickly, and wrapped it around her hands. There was a lot of extra fabric, and her hands were now attached to each other, but the idea was sound.

"All right," I said, tying the rope around the leg of the table. "There's no way to untie the knot from the bottom, so they'll know how you escaped as soon as they see it."

"They'll know anyway," she pointed out. "The window is the only way in or out, until they break the wall down for my wedding day."

"Right," I said, flinching from her terrible pragmatism. I tested the knot. "Let me go first. And hand me the bag."

She did, and I tucked it up the back of my tunic. I looked ridiculous, but there was nothing for it. At least the bag was light. I pulled one more time on the knot, and then climbed over the window ledge. The moonlight was close to this side of the tower, now. We would have to go quickly.

I let myself down slowly, despite my rapidly beating heart, but it was only a matter of moments before my feet touched the ground. I looked up, and saw the Little Rose sitting on the ledge. She had kilted up her skirt so it would not billow in the breeze or get caught on a protuberance of stone. It was not as practical as Arwa's wide trousers, but it would have to do.

Her descent was much slower than mine had been. I

barely breathed as I watched the line of moonlight get closer and closer to where she climbed. Then she dropped and was standing beside me, unwrapping her hands. She smiled, a true smile this time, not the bitter thing I had seen in the tower.

"It's nice outside," she said, like she had never been outside the walls before. I knew that she and Tariq had been taken out together, for riding lessons and the like, but I shuddered to think of how long it been since the last time she had been free of stone walls and narrow windows. "Shall we go?"

"Follow me," I told her.

She did. Down the ditch, through the dirt, and up the other side. We didn't speak as we walked, keeping low and quiet, as I had done on my way in. My mind continued to unfreeze, and I realized that, for all my bravado, I had kidnapped the Little Rose. That she had come willingly— in fact, she had all but insisted—would not serve as an adequate defense if we were caught. And I couldn't just send her on her way. She had no shoes. Saoud was going to kill me.

Before we got to the others, I pulled her into a little hollow, and put my face next to hers.

"The others," I said, my voice low. "They are my friends. I take care of them."

"You don't want me to put them in danger," she said. "I'm

sorry, Yashaa. If I could get away without you, I would. But I need you."

"I know," I said. Her cold practicality was no different than my mother's when she had sent us away and separated me from Saoud. "We will manage somehow. That is Arwa— she's nearing twelve, and is the youngest of us. Tariq is fifteen, and Saoud is of an age with me."

"They will know me?" she asked.

"They will," I said. Even if her hair did not betray her, they would know her. "Princess, we were your friends once. Tariq and I were, at any rate. Arwa wasn't born until after you were cursed. We lived here, and then we left."

"You're spinners," she said. It was a surprise. The unicorn's gift hadn't told her that. She didn't sound frightened, though, merely determined.

"We are," I said. "Saoud is not, but he is my friend and my brother, and he will stay with us."

"All right," she said. "I will try my best, Yashaa. And I am sorry."

She could have been apologizing for any number of things, but I chose to believe she meant the kidnapping.

"Come on," I said, and pulled her to her feet.

We kept going through the dark. The way was easy enough, but there were thistles on the ground. I could only barely see them in time to step around them. The Little Rose didn't know what she was looking for. She must have stepped on at least three of them but made no outcry and voiced no complaint. If she kept this up, I thought, we might actually make it back to the mountains. She would need shoes, though. There was no getting around that.

At last we drew close to the place where Saoud, Tariq, and Arwa were hidden.

"Yashaa," whispered the Little Rose. I stopped. "There is one thing I have to tell you."

"What?" I asked.

"No matter how I ask, not if I beg and not if I order you, you must never, ever give me a spindle," she said. Her eyes shone in the light of the moon.

I nodded, thinking that the sky was bright enough that she would see, and understand.

"Yashaa, promise me," she said. "Promise me that you will never let me spin."

"I promise," I said. Her voice was almost regal, where it wasn't edged with frenetic worry, and I responded automatically; a spinner to the request of a princess. She would explain it when she was ready. Despite her gift-given trust of me, there was something she feared.

"All right," she said, her voice calm again. "I am ready to meet the others now."

We took the last hundred steps, up the low hill and down into the little dale where the others were hidden. They were sitting right where I had left them, ready to run at a moment's notice. My shoes were in Arwa's lap. She heard us first and looked up. I saw the light of her eyes as they widened in the dark, though she made no noise, and then Tariq turned, and then Saoud.

"Yashaa," said Saoud. "Yashaa, what have you done?"

TWELVE

WHEN THE LITTLE ROSE was born, my mother was given the care of her wardrobe. My mother's hands spun the yarn that made her receiving blanket, and the thread that stitched together her tiny robes and nightclothes, but when the princess was old enough to require actual clothing, it was my mother's hands that oversaw their design and make.

"Spinning is the start, my Yashaa," she said to me. "That is why a spinner will oversee the princess's clothes. Later, when she is older, she will have a proper wardrobe mistress. But the Little Rose is ours now, and you must always remember that."

It was heady news, even for a three-year-old boy who was more concerned with the frogs around the castle well than he was with the child his mother took such care over. I was not jealous of the Little Rose for taking up my mother's time. Her days had always belonged to the queen, as mine would too someday. Rasima was hardly a harsh taskmistress, and I often accompanied my mother while she went about her work, if there was no one else free to mind me. So it was my hands on which the yarn for the Little Rose was spooled up, and my face she laughed at when I made faces to distract her while my mother measured her or changed her wraps or took a moment's peace from the pair of us. I had no sibling, after all, and had the story gone differently, I might have looked to the Little Rose as sister and princess both.

If there were hard feelings between myself and the princess in those days, it was from the knowledge that someday she would be old enough to know that she was loved by her mother and her father, while I had only my mother. It was her birth, the way the king and queen looked at her when she cooed or giggled, or even puked, that brought to my attention something I had never noted before. The Little Rose had two parents. I had only the one.

"Where is my father?" I asked my mother one night while she spun undyed wool for no particular reason, other than that she liked the work. "Has he died?"

My mother set the spindle down, carefully as always so that her work would not undo itself, and took me in her arms.

"Your father is not here, my Yashaa," she answered me. "I loved him, and he loved me, but he had his own duty to mind, as I do here. He could not stay, and I would not go with him."

"Will I ever meet him?" I asked.

"I don't know," she said. "When you are older, and can walk all day and into the night if you must, we will ask the king if he will outfit you for a journey to find him."

"Leave here?" I said. "Leave you and Tariq? And the Little Rose?"

"If you wish to," she said. "You can always return, remember. Your place here is as assured as mine is, and will always be."

"Even if I can't spin as well as you can?" For this was the deepest fear of my childhood, that I would hold a spindle and spin the thread, and it would not be good enough for the Little Rose or her parents.

"You can always muck out stalls," my mother told me, but she was laughing as she said it, and I knew that she would do everything she could to make sure my thread was the match of hers. It was, after all, as much her pride as it was mine.

And so I practiced. My chubby fingers made lumpy

yarn, almost too thick for the horse blankets it ended up in, though my mother was always sure to point my work out to me as the horse and rider went past. Then I made better yarn, as could be used in new rugs for the cold stone castle floors. By that time the Little Rose had a proper nurse, not a spinner, and it was Tariq who spent the most time with her. When they came to visit us in the spinning room, I was always given charge of them. I was entrusted to make sure they didn't end up falling into the hearth, or into the uncarded wool we kept in bins along the wall; or, at least in the case of the latter, to make sure that if they did so, they did so on purpose.

I thought the world was Kharuf, and Kharuf was the world, and I did not learn otherwise until the Little Rose turned four, and the Maker King brought his son to wish her well on the day of her birth. I stood proudly beside my mother when they rode into the courtyard, horse after horse. Even the prince had his own mount, though he was barely older than I. Each of the horses was tall and brown, and draped in fine gold cloth. I knew they must have stopped just beyond the rise to gird the horses thus, for they bore none of the dust that long travel would have given them. Still, it was an excellent show.

The Maker King dismounted and walked up the stairs to where Qasim and Rasima waited for him. The Little Rose stood behind them, but on her own two feet rather than in the arms of her nurse. The prince followed his father and made a pretty bow to the Little Rose when they were introduced. My mother stood one step down from the queen, in the place of honor her work accorded to her. I watched the Maker King look right through her, as though she wasn't even there, which I did not understand. Surely, after all, the Maker King understood cloth and thread, and the making of it. He wore enough of it.

I looked then to the prince, thinking that we were of an age and would perhaps be sat together, as the Little Rose had sat with Tariq since they were old enough to take spoons at the table. He had dark hair and skin, and cheeks as round as mine, but his expression was already cold in the face of our welcome, as his father's was. He was a child as I was, and yet at the same time he was not. I suddenly hoped we would not have very much to do with one another while he stayed, for he did not look like he would be good company.

As the kings and queen were distracted by the necessary courtesies of formal welcome, and everyone else was distracted watching them, the Little Rose grew bored, and wandered over to where I stood behind my mother's place. I knew from experience that a bored Little Rose was a mischievous one, so when she held out her arms to me, I took her hands without protest, hoping to forestall a scene. She was, after all, old enough to understand dignity; we both knew it was my duty, if not my prescribed task, to help her if she wavered.

The Maker Prince watched us, disdain on his face. Usually, the Little Rose's parents smiled indulgently when she reached for me; but now they didn't look at her at all, and her nurse hurried over to take her away from me. I knew then that I had done something wrong, but I didn't know what. I couldn't see my mother's face, but I could see the face of the Maker King if I dared to look at it, and when I dared, I saw that he was as indignant as his son. I looked back at the flagstones in the courtyard, humiliated and aware, for the first time, that the Little Rose was a princess—*the* princess. That someday, she would be the queen. And though I might inherit my mother's place, if I earned it, I would only ever be a spinner in her court.

I do not remember the rest of the Maker King's visit, except that the tables in the Great Hall were moved, and that Tariq and the Little Rose could not sit together. I spent a lot of time in the kitchen, nursing my hurt feelings with whatever food the cooks would let me sample. It was there, and not from my mother, that I learned the true purpose of the Maker King's visit.

"He has come to offer a marriage contract for the Little Rose," the bread mistress said, as she counted the barley stores with the head brewer. "For the little prince, of course. That wedding will get him his name."

The prince had not endeared himself to anyone in the castle during his stay, so her tone when she spoke of him was not kind.

"Will the king and queen accept it?" the brewer asked. He sounded unhappy at the idea of the match. I knew little of marriage, except that when it transpired the bride invariably went to live with the groom. I did not wish to lose the Little Rose.

"They have asked for time to consider," the bread mistress said. "They will give their answer tonight."

I had skipped most of the formal meals since the Maker King's arrival, and my mother had let me because she understood my discomfort. The prince still stared, though he never spoke to me. I was accustomed to receiving some measure of respect in the hall, for all I was so young, and to giving respect in return. My mother had guessed, rightly enough, that if the prince was disrespectful to my face I would be disrespectful back, and then the Maker King would insist on some kind of punishment, which Qasim would be forced to agree to. During their stay, I took most of my meals in the kitchen.

No force on earth could have kept me from the Great Hall that night, though. If we were to lose the Little Rose to marriage across the mountains, I would hear it from the king's own mouth, not from the kitchen gossip. So I went to wash and dress and joined my mother for the meal.

It was a farewell feast and should have been a sight to behold, except that the head cook cared little for the way the Maker King had sniffed when he'd toured her kitchens, so instead it was merely politely ostentatious. The lower tables were subdued as we ate, and we wondered what the king's answer would be. The Maker King had made the marriage proposal in public, and thus a public answer was necessary. I began to fear the worst.

When the plates were cleared away and the sugared confections were brought out, Qasim and Rasima took to their feet. They faced the Maker King and his son. The Little Rose did not stand with them. Her nurse had, I noticed, rather a strong grip on her.

"My lord," Qasim said, inclining his head to the Maker King. The Maker King did not return the gesture. "You have come on a long journey and honored us with your presence, and with the presence of your son, at the celebration of our daughter's birth. We are grateful for your company, and hope to someday return the favor of a royal visit to your own capital."

The Maker King's face was frozen and blank, but Qasim looked determined.

"You have also offered a marriage alliance between our kingdom and yours, to be fulfilled by our children," Qasim continued. "Forgive an indulgent father, but we had not yet even begun to think of such arrangements for our daughter, and thus are grateful for the time you have accorded us to consider."

Every breath in the hall was held. It was as quiet as I had ever heard anything be. I could feel my heart race in my chest, and my mother's hand gripped my shoulder.

"Our ancestor the King Maker made us separate our kingdoms, as you will recall," Qasim said. "We have consulted our advisors and agree with them. A marriage between our daughter and your son would reunite the kingdoms, and so for the good of Kharuf, we cannot agree to it."

A gasp is a quiet sound when made by one person. When made by dozens in a hall of stone, the echo is rather remarkable. Still, the Maker King remained cold, though his eyes tightened briefly before relaxing.

"Your majesty is as wise as I have been told," he said to my king. "Perhaps if we have younger children someday, we might revisit negotiations?"

Qasim nodded regally, and they all took their seats again. There was a moment of pause, and then the servers who bore the dessert remembered that they were meant to be serving it. With their movement, the hall relaxed. Soon, everything would be back to normal.

The Maker King departed the following day, taking his company with him, and normalcy did indeed return. For one more year, we lived in the castle in peace and comfort, until the Little Rose turned five, and came under a curse. Then the Maker King offered marriage again, on harsher terms and with no pity. And Qasim was forced to accept it; and our long suffering was begun.

THIRTEEN

ILL-CLAD AND BAREFOOT though she was, they knew her for the Little Rose immediately. They knew the same way I had: by her hair. You could not say her summer-wheat hair was lovely, not shorn close and patchy as it was; but it was recognizable, and they recognized her. She would need a better scarf to wrap her head with, or we would be caught the instant someone saw us. Instead of the instant afterward, I supposed, when one of us deferred to her accidentally and gave her away. Tariq was all but making formal prostration at her feet. She could not help but notice.

"You had better call me Zahrah," she said to them. She ran a hand over the patched scarf on her head, and I knew she was thinking the same thing I was. "And forget where I came from."

"We can't do that," Arwa said, leaning toward her the way she leaned toward the fire when the nights in the mountains were cold. Her face shone in the moonlight. "Don't ask us to do that."

Saoud said nothing as he rummaged through Arwa's pack, hunting for her spare shoes. They would be tight on the Little Rose but better than nothing. He would not speak his piece in front of her, not until he was sure of her character. The rest of us had been brought up to love her, but Saoud had been raised to question strangers in the night, and not without reason.

"Did I know you before?" she said to Tariq. I remembered them, racing ahead of the nurse or hanging off my hands, and fought off a wave of jealousy. She had not recognized me.

"Yes, Prin—Zahrah," he choked. "We played together when we were small."

"You were meant to bring back information," Saoud said, dropping the shoes in the Little Rose's lap. His words were only for me, even though everyone else could hear him. "Not the princess herself."

"You didn't see it, Saoud," I said. "You didn't see where they were keeping her. You would have brought her back, too."

He hadn't heard her voice, the quiet assumption that I had come to kill her. He would hear her soon enough, I thought. He would hear, and he would finally understand what it was to be a spinner of Kharuf, to truly be one of us.

Saoud wanted to argue with me, but the moon had come too high in the sky, and it was too bright to go back. It was too late to do anything except run for it.

"When will they miss you?" he asked her. He did not use his gentle voice, but the Little Rose didn't quail.

"Tomorrow morning," she said. "About an hour after sunrise. That's when they come to bring my breakfast and take the blankets away."

"Why do they take the blanket?" Arwa asked.

"To check for threads," said the Little Rose. There was pain in that voice, and a longing so deep I wavered on my feet. "They have to make sure there aren't any loose threads."

"Why—" Arwa began, but Saoud held up a hand. It would have been a flood of questions if she started to ask right now, and we didn't have the time. The moon was high and bright, and, worse, the sun was coming.

"Later, little goat," he said. "Now we have to run."

We didn't run, exactly, but we did move very quickly. The Little Rose had clearly never made such a trek before, but true to her word, she did not give voice to a single complaint. Arwa's spare shoes must have pinched her, and she couldn't have been accustomed to wearing shoes at all, but she followed us. Even Saoud was as impressed as he could be, with his own exhaustion to worry about.

Whatever peace of mind we had bought by spinning was wearing off quickly, and I could feel my own focus begin to fray. We made no attempt at clever misdirection. We had neither the time nor the skill to lay a false trail, and we were too tired to even try. Instead, we made for the mountains by the straightest route we could and hoped for a river to cross. We found it an hour after dawn, right when, presumably, the Little Rose's breakfast was being delivered to her empty room and the alarm at the castle was being raised. It was little more than a brook, but it was wide enough to serve us. We waded upstream for an hour, which Saoud deemed enough to confuse any hounds, and hopefully enough to slow down the experienced human trackers, and then we turned toward the mountains again.

It was slower going after that, as Arwa and Tariq both flagged when their lack of sleep and struggling lungs bogged them down. I was exhausted too, my legs aching to match my arms, when Saoud finally found us a place to camp. It was a little hollow, a dip in the gentle hills that footed against the mountains. It would hide us even in daylight as long as we built no fire, and we were too tired to find fuel for one in any case. Instead we laid out our bedrolls, and slept as close to one another as we could. Saoud and I took the ends of the row without discussion, but the Little Rose hesitated with

127

her blanket in her hands as we finished setting ourselves up.

"Do you want me to sleep somewhere else?" she asked, as polite as she might have been in her father's hall.

"No," said Saoud. "It's too cold. Lie here, between Arwa and Yashaa."

It was dreadfully improper, of course. At least Arwa was yet a child. But Saoud was right. It was cold, and this was hardly the time for gallantry. Arwa, bless her heart, took the blanket and spread it out without a second thought, making a space for the Little Rose between us as though we had been sleeping thus for weeks.

"I'll watch first, if you like," I said to Saoud, thinking to make up for my folly.

"Don't be stupid," he said. "The climb took more from you than the wait did from me. I'll wake you later."

He turned on his blanket so that he was facing away from us, but still gave some heat to Tariq. There was no talking after that, but even though I was exhausted, I couldn't fall asleep. To see the Little Rose so unexpectedly after all this time, and to feel pity for her instead of the hate to which I had become accustomed, made me restless. I could feel her behind me, and the touch reminded me of the hours we had spent together before the curse. My memories were fragile things, but the feel of her was stronger, and my mind raced. I had so many questions, and we had no time.

"Yashaa," she whispered after a while. She said it slowly,

like her memories were finally catching up to her in the wake of her flight. I hoped her father's hounds were much, much farther behind. "I remember a Yashaa."

"Yes, princess," I said, just as quietly. If Saoud heard us, he gave no sign. "I was there."

"Your mother," she said, nearly stuttering over the words. "Does she yet live?"

"She is dying," I said. I made my voice flat and grey. "She was ill when she sent us out on the road, and she was very sick when she sent us away. I do not know if she lives."

"I am sorry," she said.

Rage filled me. My mother struggled to breathe, and I wanted the Little Rose to know what that was like. But also, I didn't. I couldn't. My hate boiled against my pity, and I thought I would drown in them both.

"Save your pity for Arwa and Tariq," I told her. "Your curse killed their parents. At least I still have mine."

She did not reply for a long time, so long that I thought—hoped—that she had fallen asleep. But then she spoke again.

"When we wake," she said, "you must take the blanket. I will carry it when we walk, but first it must be checked for threads."

Fury nearly took me again. She could not even sleep with a frayed blanket, and we were stuck with her care upon the road.

"I am sorry," she said again, "to be a burden. But if there

are threads, I will find them, and if I find them, I will spin them. Yashaa, you promised me."

Saoud gave an odd cough. I didn't know what to think, so I sat up and looked at the Little Rose. The sun was high in the sky now, and I could see that her face, though it was as brown as mine, lacked the glow of stored sunshine. She had been inside that tower room for a very long time.

"What did I promise, princess?" I asked her, as formally as I might have done were I her vassal in truth. "Tell me."

"You know the cruel part of the curse," she said to me. "That my kingdom and my people suffer in my name. You have felt the touch of it, driven as you were from my house and from my lands; and you feel the pain of it, as your mother sickens. But Yashaa, there is a vicious side to it as well. And that viciousness is mine and mine alone."

"Tell us." Tariq was awake. Of course he was. He longed for the truth as much as I was sure I knew it.

"A princess is taught so many things," she said. "How to run a castle and kingdom. How to dance, and how to sing. How to speak to men and women, and learn their troubles. How to solve those troubles, where I can. How to embroider and weave and sew. And, as you know, how to spin."

Her fingers played along the blanket as she spoke, and I saw a thread that was loose upon the hem. Without knowing why, I reached over and pulled it out, throwing the thread up for the breeze to catch. The Little Rose watched it, her eyes hungry, but did not reach after it.

"The gifts I was given for my birthday were meant to highlight those lessons," she continued. "Meant to make me a strong ruler for Kharuf. For each of you."

Oh, how we would have loved her.

"But the curse was for those lessons as well," she said. "Each facet of what I learned would turn my mind into the perfect host. My parents kept me from learning anything, as much as they could, but it doesn't matter. If I spin, the curse will be complete, and the...inhabitation will begin. The demon knew my parents would put off my spinning for as long as they possibly could, and they did, even though the price was high. It guessed eighteen years, long enough for me to become entirely aware of my curse, and what it was doing to my kingdom."

Arwa had tears in her eyes, and Tariq was pale. Even Saoud watched us now, concern on his face. He knew the stories as well as we did. That once there had been a king who was not a man, and he had done terrible things before the Storyteller Queen remade him good.

"So it is selfish," she said. "I do not wish to be taken thus. I want to be queen, my own queen. I want to work and lead, to make things that help everyone in the kingdom, and I can't. Everything that I make, if I make things, would make me a better demon. If I spin, the demon will know that I am ready, and it will come for me. But Yashaa, I swear to you, as awful as that would be for me, it would be awful for the people too. The marriage would still take place, to begin with, tying us to the Maker Kings, and I wouldn't be human anymore."

I reeled, even though I was sitting on the ground and had nowhere to fall. Arwa wrapped her arms around the Little Rose, as though she could protect her from the demon that sought to take her very soul, but the Little Rose's eyes never left mine. In my mind I saw the drawings on the floor of her tower prison—intricate, but easily destroyed by the lightest breeze or the softest brush of cloth. She had sketched in dust with her own fingers, so desperate was she to make. She could not do anything. She could not make anything. Ever.

"I will check the blanket," I said.

It would not be nearly enough, I knew, and I saw that Saoud knew it too, but it was the only place that we could start.

FOURTEEN

WE WAITED UNTIL IT WAS nearly dark before we set out again. Any pursuers would have caught us during the day, as they would be on horseback, and Saoud had rightly guessed that the moon would give us enough light to travel by. As the sun was setting, we had a cold meal, and I inspected what remained of our supplies. It was not much, but it would get us to the mountains; when we were more safely hidden, we would have time enough to hunt and forage if we needed to.

The Little Rose did not help us as we tied up the knots on our packs. I checked the blanket for her, and rolled it up to put in her bag. Arwa had given up her own veil to hide the Little Rose's hair, and wore Saoud's kafiyyah instead.

The Little Rose would need a better cloak in the mountains, but we had no time for that sort of thing now either.

"Should we go?" Saoud said.

I looked out of our hollow and shook my head. The sun still kissed the tops of the higher hills, purple heather against the purple sky. It was enough light for us to be spotted if we moved, but not enough for Saoud to find us another place to hide, were we to need one. Everything in me wanted to run. The restlessness from not spinning was worse than it had been before, and I wanted to be free of the constant pressure on my lungs. Our parents had sickened slowly once they left Kharuf. I hoped we would be so lucky, once we managed to get free of it. I wanted to go, to go now, but I knew better and breathed as evenly as I could to calm down.

"Wait until it's fully dark," I decided.

Saoud sat down beside me and glanced at the Little Rose. He had not spoken much to her, or to me really, for the whole day. I could tell that it was upsetting Arwa. Saoud and the Little Rose were both heroes to her, in vastly different ways, and to have them at odds made her quiet. I didn't much like it either, but I understood. Saoud had no heritage with the Little Rose, no reason to fall naturally into her service. No reason to accept her undeniable burden.

"Why does she trust you?" he said to me, after a long silence. "She remembers Tariq, and vaguely remembers you, but that shouldn't be enough. Explain it to me."

I looked at the Little Rose. It was not my story to tell, though while we waited for the sun to set, there was at least time to tell some secrets.

"It's the gift, Saoud," Arwa said, either not seeing the tension or having no patience for it. I suspected the latter.

The Little Rose was sitting with her legs tucked under the hem of her dress. She stuck her feet out now, and even in the growing darkness, we could see they were nearly a ruin. Blisters lined her toes and the places where Arwa's shoes pinched too tightly. Welts had formed across the backs of her heels, and her ankles were swollen. Soon she would have to walk on them again.

"Did you wonder, Saoud," said the Little Rose, "how I lived in a small room for years and years, and yet kept up with you today? Did you wonder how I could follow Yashaa down the rope, when he is a strong boy and I am only a wisp of a girl?"

"Zahrah," breathed Tariq, who had always believed. "Your poor feet."

She glanced at him fondly, as though they had never been apart, and then looked back at Saoud.

"The phoenix's gift was rebirth," she said. "I tire and I sicken and I ache, and yet I go on. If I were a warrior, strong in body and trained to seek perfection, I would be nearly unstoppable. Alas, I am a girl who was kept in a tower,

135

and my body is weak, except for the fact that it is nearly indestructible."

"My lady, I am sorry," Saoud said, his voice still twisted. "Forgive my ignorance."

"There is nothing to forgive, Saoud," she said. "Or at least, if there is, it is I who ought to ask your forgiveness. I know all of my weaknesses, and still I forced my company upon you. Indeed, I used my gifts to ensure it."

"How then, princess?" he asked, lapsing into formal speech as she had done. That made me feel a little bit better. I didn't know why I couldn't help but treat her as my princess. She made me uncomfortable, stirring memories and feelings I hadn't considered in more than half my lifetime. It made me feel very unbalanced to see Tariq and Arwa treat her almost like she was an old friend.

"The dragon's gift is discernment," said the Little Rose. "I believe with dragons, the ability is used to determine the value of *things*: gold, jewelry, the construction of houses and the like. For me, when I combine it with the unicorn's gift— to see the truth—it lets me gauge the intentions of a person. I knew when I saw Yashaa that he would see me to safety, even though in his own heart he is not so sure of himself. He has many feelings, but in all ways he is honest. And that is why I knew to trust him."

I prayed that it was too dark for them to see how hotly my face burned at her words. I had known since I was six years old that the gifts of the Little Rose were as real as my own nose and teeth, but to hear her explain them—to hear her explain *me*, and so bluntly—was nearly painful.

"And so you trust me?" Saoud said. "Because you trust Yashaa?"

"I trust you," said the Little Rose, "because you love Yashaa."

"Of course he does," said Arwa. "He loves all of us."

Saoud floundered for words for a moment, unused to being so freely talked about. Arwa smiled at him so sweetly that I nearly laughed at the absurdity of everything that had transpired since I climbed the tower, and when Saoud glared at me again, it was with no small measure of amusement.

"Will you be able to walk?" he asked the Little Rose. "Will the shoes even go back on?"

"There's only one way to find out," she said, and began the painful process, with Arwa's help on the laces.

"So, discernment and stamina, and seeing the truth," Saoud said. "What else?"

Tariq helped her to her feet. She took two steps, wincing, and then seemed to bear down on the pain, accepting it and steadying herself in its wake.

"Presumably I will be very good at growing things, should the need arise," she said. "That is from the gnome. The sprite gave me a lightness of spirit, which I have always believed is what keeps me sane."

"What about the piskey?" Saoud asked, and I knew that we had reached the heart of it.

The Little Rose looked at the sky and smiled. She could not have seen very much of it through the window of her tower room, and I wondered if she had missed the stars.

"The piskey offered me escape," she said at last. "Just a little more magic on top of what was already done, but the threads were already spinning when the gift was given. Should I choose to, I can take up a spindle and set myself to spinning thread. In the moment when I reach for the whorl, I will instead prick my finger upon the pointed end. There will be a pain like the sting of a bee, and I will be lost to the waking world before the demon can overtake me."

"Why don't you do it?" Saoud said.

The Little Rose flexed her fingers, hands retreating into the sleeves of her dress.

"You know—you *must* know," she said, desperation in her tone, "what it is to want that which you cannot have."

Saoud, who wanted to belong. Arwa, who wanted her mother. Tariq, who wanted to do his work. And me . . . who wanted more than I could name.

"Yes," Saoud said.

"That is how much I want to spin," she said. "I was born to it. Spinning is my blood, and the blood of my people, from the time before we came across the great desert to settle in this land. I was beginning to learn, you know, when the curse happened. Yashaa was probably already a master of it, but I had other lessons besides. I remember, if I think about it, what it felt like to spin—to feel a work grow under my fingers. I miss it."

It was fully dark now, and we needed to go. We needed to save our talk for when we were more sure of our safety. But I saw her eyes and knew that not even Saoud would interrupt her now.

"I should know so many things," she said. "I should be able to bake bread, even though my kitchens will always have a bread mistress. I should know how to weave a tapestry and write a trade agreement. I should know, but I can't. I was born and bred to do these things, and my heart cries out for them, and I can't. I cannot make anything. Every stitch, every note, every letter, and every dance step would prepare me for the demon's curse, and spinning would seal it. And I cannot take the piskey's gift. I would sleep forever, but the demon would be free—the curse would remain unbroken— and then my kingdom, my people, would be queenless and cursed, both."

The full weight of it settled onto all of us. Arwa wiped her face with her borrowed scarf. Tariq stared into the distance, adding more pieces to the ever-growing story he kept in his mind. I could think of nothing to say or do, but Saoud was already moving.

He knelt before her then, the only one of us unsworn to

her, though I did not know what power was in the oaths of children. Perhaps they were sufficient, as they were made with innocence and heart.

"Princess," he said, "I do not know what I can do, but I am yours. I do not promise this out of pity for you, nor even any particular loyalty to you. I swear it for them, those that you have said I love, because I do. My service is yours, if you will have it."

"I will, Saoud," she said. "And I am glad of it. Guide and guard them, as you have done, and we will follow you."

"The moon is rising," Tariq said, and I could see by its light that there were tears in his eyes.

"We have to go," Saoud said, rising to his feet. "I will lead, then Tariq, then Arwa and Zahrah, and last Yashaa. Do not speak above a whisper. Try to follow the steps of the person in front of you as closely as you can." He hesitated for a moment and then spoke again. "We cannot go back for the spindles. I am sorry."

"It's for the best, I suppose," Tariq said, looking at the Little Rose. "We have nothing she can use to spin."

He spoke so bravely, and I knew his heart was breaking. Arwa's and mine were, too, for those spindles had belonged to our families; if they were lost, all we had was each other. And the Little Rose. I saw even in the dark that she knew it, and she rested a hand on Tariq's shoulder.

"My friend," she said, and was somehow at once both unreachable and ours. "Thank you."

Saoud hefted his pack on his back and looked at me. I nodded, and we set out into the night.

FIFTEEN

IT WAS A HARD MARCH. Though we had not wandered aimlessly before we met the Little Rose, we had been on no real schedule, and thus had not exactly hurried on our way. Now that we feared the hunting dogs of Kharuf were right behind us, with horsemen in the van alongside them, we fairly fled. The blisters that marked the Little Rose's feet burst and bled, but she continued to walk without so much as a whisper of complaint. Even with him knowing the magic behind it, I could tell that Saoud was impressed. Arwa found a plant that would make sure none of the open wounds became infected, but I knew that if we wanted to make a habit of walking, we were going to have to find a better pair of shoes.

At last we reached the steep slopes where no heather grew. We were well north of the pass by now, and did not think of turning toward it. Instead, we climbed the trackless ways over rock and deadfall, pressing through the under-brush, even when there was no clear way before us. Our going was slow, but we had reached the mountains with no sign of pursuers, and the pressure on our lungs had lifted when we crossed the border again, so our pace did not chafe then as it might have otherwise.

"It is possible that my parents will stall as long as they can," the Little Rose admitted on our second night in the mountains. Saoud had commented on the lack of a chase—relieved, but also perplexed, and too weary to think about it—and she looked embarrassed at her answer.

"They won't want you back?" Arwa said, clearly unwilling to believe it.

"Oh, I am sure they do," the Little Rose said. "But they don't know what to do with me when they have me, either."

"Except lock you up," Tariq said darkly.

"I went to that willingly," the Little Rose said. "Or as willingly as I could. It would not solve anything if I was murdered, or if I gave in to temptation and learned to play the harp."

The levity from her was relatively new, and it further increased my discomfort, so I didn't comment on it.

"You really think they'll be happy to let you go?" he said.

"My mother sent us on a quest we had no wish to go on," I reminded him. "Who knows why our parents do anything, except that they still have some strange hope that we will find a future? Even if it is one they cannot share."

"I agree with Yashaa," the Little Rose said. "Even if they do not believe it themselves, I think my parents will spread the story that I have fled over the desert, to whatever freedom I can find there. Or, if they choose to believe that I was kidnapped, the spinners will be among the first suspects— and everyone knows that the desert is where spinners go. If the riders are sent out in force, they will ride south and east for the sand, not west for the stone."

"I hope you're right," Saoud said. "We're going to have enough trouble surviving up here without worrying about unexpected company."

We made even slower progress after that, because Saoud and I called frequent halts while we scouted out the terrain for a place where we could set up a permanent hiding spot. Arwa took advantage of the time to gather all the useful plants she could, and Tariq made what repairs to our gear were possible with his limited tools. The Little Rose sat and watched them, and I knew it must have been a torture for her.

I hated spinning with nearly the same intensity that I loved it. It pulled at my soul and galled it. Even now, when the fire burned at night time, my fingers missed the familiar rhythm of the work. I could not imagine feeling that love, that calling, and being forced to deny myself time and time again. We saw daily evidence of the Little Rose's strength in her feet, but I was starting to gain an appreciation for the pure will that must have comprised her character.

On the fifth day, when Tariq carefully used up the last of the grain we carried for porridge and set it above the cooking fire, Saoud found a valley that would suit us. Its walls were so steep that I suspect he fell into it, rather than spotting it beforehand. On two sides it was sheer rock, cut straighter than the blocks that made the Little Rose's tower. The third side was a waterfall, an unexpected but very welcome blessing. Not only would the falls' pool give us fresh water, but the noise of the water would help hide any noise we might make ourselves. The fourth side was the steep green slope down which we walked after Saoud came to fetch us.

"Bless the Storyteller Queen for these mountains," the Little Rose said.

"Indeed," said Tariq.

"Saoud, I think there is a cave," Arwa said, perched on one of the few outcroppings the valley boasted. "There, behind the cascade."

She was right. The valley was an even better refuge than we had imagined. Now, even if someone found the valley itself, they might never find where we camped—assuming the cave was habitable. Saoud went along the ledge and through the water to find out, and I went behind him.

"It will be dark, even with a fire," he said. "The smoke might not exit well, either. We'll have to be careful."

I nodded, and then remembered he couldn't see me in the dark.

"How far back do you think it goes?" I asked, walking forward with my arms held out before me.

"Hopefully not too far," Saoud said. "Though I doubt a bear could make it down that slope to den here."

My fingers hit hard rock, and I groped sideways to see if the cave changed direction. As far as I could tell, it didn't. We wouldn't know for sure until we lit a fire, but it seemed that we would be all right in here, though we would certainly be cramped. I sniffed the air, and smelled only water and stone. There wasn't even the smell of bat droppings. It was, after such a run of hardship, almost unbelievably good luck.

Saoud and I went back to the mouth of the cave, and waited a moment for our eyes to adjust to the light before we attempted the ledge again. The others were waiting for us, their packs still on their backs, hope on their faces.

"It will suit," Saoud said. "Come. Mind your feet along the ledge."

When we were inside, Arwa pulled a small collection of sticks and dried grass out from under her dress, kept mostly dry by the fabric. She set it on the floor of the cave and waited for Tariq to light it. It took some effort for him to get a spark, and we all held our breath while he worked on it. At last the fire caught, and Saoud carefully fed it the larger branches he had carried in his pack.

In the meager light of the fire, the cave seemed less than welcoming. It was high enough for us to stand straight in, and went back into the mountainside farther than the reach of the light. This spoke more of the feebleness of the light than the size of the cave, I noted; but I could not exactly criticize as they were all we had.

"Come on, Yashaa," Saoud said. "We have to go back to the ridge and pick a lookout spot. Leave the others to set up camp."

I nodded, and followed him out once more. We scrambled back up the slope to the ridgeline, a hard climb, and then walked along it with great care. At last, Saoud found a tree that was to his liking, and we climbed into it with one of the tents. It would not be a comfortable watch, but the view was good, unless something came over the mountain itself for us.

"That would have to be dragons," Saoud said when I pointed this out to him. "In which case, we're cooked whether we see it coming or not."

Neither of us really believed that a dragon would come, nor that it would eat us if it did, but the mountains were generally uninhabited for a reason, and I knew that I would never be fully comfortable here.

"I'm going to take Arwa and Tariq down toward the pass as soon as we're settled here," Saoud said as we worked. "We're going to need more food, the type we can't hunt for, and the Little Rose needs things she can't exactly buy herself."

"You can't buy them and say they're for Arwa," I said. "She's too short."

"We'll say we're buying them large in case she grows," he replied. "Yashaa, you know we must go."

"And I must stay, and deal with the problem I so cleverly brought upon myself." I tried to make light of it, but my reluctance to separate showed in my voice. I didn't want them to go and leave me alone with the Little Rose, and they would be gone for a long time. I had never been without them, and I didn't know if I was ready to spend so much time with her.

"Don't be an ass," Saoud said. "You heard me when I made an idiot of myself and took your problems as mine, from here to the end of time, lest my lady release me."

"Now who's an ass?" I asked, but I felt like laughing true laughter for the first time in days.

"We'll be a matched pair," Saoud said. "I understand royalty likes that sort of thing."

I was still smiling when we slid back into the valley and

made our way along the ledge. They had done good work while we were gone, I saw as soon as I entered the cave. There was a fire pit laid out on the rock floor near the front of the cave, and what remained of our gear was laid out around it to be useful. The Little Rose's blanket had been hung up, blocking off one side of the cave for her privacy and Arwa's. The rest of the bedrolls were rolled near the fire, to save space.

"We'll have to dig a privy somewhere away from the pool," Tariq said. "And then take care using it in the dark."

"Very good," said Saoud. "I will take you up and show you the lookout tomorrow. Tonight, I think we should all sleep here."

Tariq was assembling a supper from the last of the bear meat, and Saoud went to dig the privy. Arwa was sitting next to the fire, with an old shirt in her lap. I watched as she tore it into strips. The Little Rose sat beside her, rubbing her feet and watching closely, and all but stewing in her uselessness. I took a seat across the fire and watched with some confusion.

"Bandages?" I asked, as Arwa took several of the strips, stacked them on top of one another, and began to carefully stitch a seam along the sides.

"Of a sort," said the Little Rose.

"They're too short," I said.

"Some advice, Yashaa," she said, all the dignity she

could muster in her voice, and a desperate need to be taken seriously behind it. "Never ask a girl who cannot make things what she might need so badly she would have to ask a child—sorry, Arwa—to make for her."

"I don't mind being helpful or being a child," Arwa said. "I am happy to make them and not need them yet. It seems a troublesome annoyance. No one's ever explained it before, that's all. My mother never got the chance."

I could tell that the Little Rose was uncomfortable, so I let it drop, and didn't remark on how quickly Arwa tucked her work away when Saoud returned to the cave.

"We'll have to hunt tomorrow," Saoud said. "And probably the day after that, too, unless we are very fortunate."

"And then what?" asked the Little Rose.

"Then they'll leave us here for a time," I said. I did my best to use the voice Saoud's father used when he barked commands at us on the training field. "We need things we cannot get here, and there is no other way."

The Little Rose did not protest, and Arwa and Tariq swallowed any remarks they might have made. Saoud nodded his thanks and began to inspect his knives. Arwa, with a touch of defiance, took out her sewing again as though daring us to comment on it, but no one did.

The Little Rose only stared at the fire, her idle hands clasped tightly in her lap, and said nothing.

iv.

When you make a thing and keep it, you control it utterly. If no hands but yours have touched it, then it is yours. If you make a thing and give it, you relinquish that control, but earn in its place a sort of trust between you and the person to whom you have made your gift. If a thing is made and stolen, then it can be twisted; and this has always been my way.

The thrice-damned Storyteller Witch had tried to change that. She had given so freely that she had nearly died of it, and the creatures she gave to the world kept it safe for her after her power had waned, and even after she died. They took up her watch in our mountain prison, and the poison that plagued us here had no effect upon them. They set themselves in the little valleys and on the slopes, even on the topmost spires of the highest peaks, and hounded us from every side.

Oh, if only the Storyteller Witch's power had been ours. She was the greatest maker-of-things her kind had ever known, even if she did not understand until the end how her magic worked. If she had been stolen and twisted, as her husband was for a time, my kin might have ground the human vermin so far into the sand that they would not crawl out of it until the skies fell. Instead, we could only watch as she raised these mountains from nothing and decorated them with everything our jailors loved.

There were wide glades on sheltered mountainsides where fields of flowers grew. The piskeys and sprites danced upon the wind with floating blossoms underneath their wings. There were deep pools and caves cut from the iron-laced stone where the dragons could lay their eggs, and hatch new fire-breathing menaces, without fear of us finding them in their only vulnerable state. There were grassy fields in hidden valleys where the unicorns could graze by day and sharpen their horns on the stones by night. There were mountaintops where the phoenix could roost. And there was good dark earth, hidden from the wind and scouring rain, where the gnomes could grow whatever they liked, and garden themselves to insensibility.

All of these things the Storyteller Witch gave, and gave with her heart full of love for the creatures she'd made, and the world she set them in. I wanted each of them to burn in fires so hot that their flesh melted from their bones; to scorch the ground so badly that nothing would ever grow there again.

We settled for petty destruction where we could. We fouled the rivers that fed the pools where the dragon eggs were laid. We struck the heads off every flower we could find. We set fire to the grass, and trod upon the gnomic gardens whenever we found them. We gloried in the days when the mountaintops were obscured by clouds too thick for even phoenix fire to pierce. It gave little satisfaction, as the years turned to decades and then to centuries, but at least it was better than nothing.

The creatures did not fight back. They did not have to. With their powers combined, they were more than a match for us, so they had only to stand firm. I took my lessons from the wind and rain: two forces that seemingly affected the mountains little, but in truth accumulated their damage over the span of years. I could match that span. I did not foul rivers, I diverted them. I did not pick the flowers, I found insects to devour them. Little by little, I wore away at the very earth the gnomes could turn to their use, until their gardens were few and far between.

This was the way I was able to leave the prison of the Storyteller Witch's making. It galled me to take so much time and expend effort in such a ludicrous way, but it worked. I was not free forever, and I could not meddle overmuch in the affairs of the lowlands without attracting the attention of my jailors, but I could begin; and, in beginning, I regained my strength.

There was a cost, of course. There is always a cost. The long years I'd spent wedging open the cracks in the mountain prison had not gone unnoticed. Weaker fae than I were struck down, or cast into ore-lined caves to suffer the long pain of iron sickness, but I evaded capture and swore further revenge in the names of my destroyed kin. Once I began to focus my efforts on the kingdoms of the King Maker and his descendants, those cracks were filled once more. Flowers bloomed again, and water ran clear and crystal over the smoothed-out stone. It was a careful balance, and one I fought to maintain as my plans for freedom coalesced. And it was enough.

At last, I needed only the Little Rose to grow into the queen I would have for my own use. Though her life was nothing to mine, those years were the longest of my long wait. I could not spy on her as much as I wished to, to my abject frustration, and was forced to rely on the clumsy maneuvers of the Maker King and his abhorrent son. At last though, she was nearly ready to be mine. I needed only for the magic of my curse to complete itself in her, and then I would be victorious.

I had also done my best to avoid temptation. When I had cursed the Little Rose, I could have taken her back to the mountains with me then, and raised her to suit my purposes exactly. I could have made sure that her mind was perfect, rather than leave it to chance and the whims of her tutors. I might have raised a monster, prepared in every way for the horrors I would use her body to unleash; but I chose a different path. If I had had the Little Rose on hand, I might have taken her the moment she showed promise, my weariness at my isolation driving me to recklessness. So instead I separated myself from her—pushed her away—and made sure that when our paths did cross, it would be time for her *life and soul to become my tools forever.*

When she disappeared, I laid waste to every flowered glade I could find, and cared not if every piskey in the whole cursed range watched me do it. Then I went to see the Maker King, for there was work to do.

SIXTEEN

I WAS DOUBLY GLAD OF THE WATERFALL after Saoud and the others took their leave of us, because when they had gone, the silence that settled between the Little Rose and me was nearly intolerable. With Arwa and Tariq to buffer us, we had at least maintained some level of courtly niceties, and Saoud had kept us all grounded in the reality of our situation. Without them, I found I did not know what to say to her, and so as a result I said nothing. I had held her in my mind as a princess for so long that, when faced with her as a person, I couldn't reconcile the two. Cursed or no, and whether or not she had shoes, she would always be a princess. And I was a spinner, or at least I might be; so

I spent my time debating with myself about what our next steps should be.

She let that stand for three days. Three days of echoing quiet around the pool, around the cooking fire, broken only when I bid her good night and ascended to the lookout post that Saoud and I had constructed. I tended to the camp and cooked our food. She gathered kindling and, when I was busy or distracted, she soaked the strips of cloth that Arwa had sewn for her in the pool. She clearly did not want to be disturbed, and so I did not disturb her. On the fourth morning, she took the bowl of bitter vetch from me when I offered it to her and then grabbed my hand before I could pull away.

"Yashaa, this will not do," she said.

"I'm sorry, princess," I told her. "It's too early for wild wheat, even if Arwa had been able to find some before she left."

"I don't mean the food, Yashaa," she said, aggravated. "Or the camp, or anything else like that."

"I'm not sure I understand, then," I said. "But if you tell me, I will—"

"Oh, be quiet," she snapped, and then immediately softened. It was an odd contrast. When she was angry, she might have been my friend. Kind, she was a princess to her fingertips. "Or rather, *don't* be quiet. You've barely said anything to me since the others left. I'm sorry you are stuck here with only me for company, and I do regret that I forced you

157

to take me with you in the first place, but I couldn't think of another way out of the castle."

"Princess, all of that is fine," I said. "What do you want me to talk about?"

She took a deep breath, as though she wanted to say all manner of things and couldn't decide which to say first, and I knew that I still irked her in some fashion. Apparently she decided not to hold it against me, however, because she took a bite of her vetch and chewed without any indication of the pent-up anger she'd exhibited only a moment before.

"Tell me about Qamih," she said. "I know very little about it, and nothing at all that doesn't in some way relate to the Maker King. Tell me about the people there, and how they have treated you since you left Kharuf."

Now it was my turn to chew. I was a fair hand at camp rations, but not even Tariq could do very much with bitter vetch. I forced it down, and marshaled my thoughts.

"I have only the faintest memories of Kharuf, before we came back to you," I said to her. "I remember the smell of the heather more than anything else—anything outside the castle, in any case. It always seemed to be a gentler land to me than Qamih, though that might be because it was my home, and because my mother always speaks of it with such fond longing."

"I will remind you," said the Little Rose, with a smile. "Only, tell me first of Qamih."

"It's wider, somehow," I said to her. "I have walked it from one end to the other when I was a child, and though I know its borders, it feels like it goes on forever. It is bounded by the sea, as you know, and there are great flats where clay is harvested like a sharecrop. There are forests, too, and broad fields where wheat and barley are farmed."

"It doesn't sound so bad," she said.

"We were not welcome for very long in any of the towns," I said. "They have guild laws in Qamih, and their own spinners and weavers, and they did not want anyone from Kharuf encroaching on their territory. It was nearly impossible to gain admittance to a guild, save through marriage, and few of the guild members would marry an outsider. My mother did not seek a suitor, in any case, and neither did Arwa's mother, though she was younger and had not given her heart to Arwa's father, as my mother gave hers to mine."

"Did your father die?" she asked, concern writ in the lines around her eyes.

"No," I said. "Or at least if he did, my mother never heard of it. He went back over the Silk Road into the desert before I was born, because he has his tasks there, as my mother had hers in Kharuf."

"I have always known that my marriage would not be for love," the Little Rose said. "I had hoped that others would

159

not feel so constrained by their duties. But I suppose it is the way of the world."

"My mother told me that she loved Queen Rasima and her position in your parents' court too much to leave it, and that my father felt similarly about his own path," I told her. "They chose between two loves, not for lack of it."

"I'm not sure that's any better," she mused, and I nodded my acknowledgement of the truth in her words.

"In any case," I said, "my mother did not marry, and so there was no position for her in the guild. We wandered until Arwa was well into her walking years, and then we set up a permanent camp at the first crossroads beyond the mountain pass, coming from the Kharuf side, of course. We met Saoud's father there, and he agreed to teach us staff fighting and knife work."

"And your mother could talk to the wool traders, and hear news of Kharuf," the Little Rose guessed.

"Yes," I said. "Though she rarely passed any such information to me. She was determined that I would grow up and become a guild member in Qamih, so that when you wed, you would have at least one ally on the west side of the mountains."

"I am flattered by your mother's foresight," said the Little Rose. "Did you resent me?"

"Of course I did, princess," I told her. "You had cost me my home, and your curse was killing my mother. I watched

Tariq's father breathe himself to death."

I had not meant to speak so harshly. In the days since the others left, I had let no moment go by without reminding myself of who she was, even though my own feelings for her were complicated by long misunderstanding. I had tried to be polite, even though whatever court training I had ever had was long since faded from my memory. And then to say that!

"It's all right, Yashaa," she said. "That is how curses work. They poison everything."

"The demon was not content with just hurting you," I said. "It hurt others in your name, and because I did not know it, or how to hurt it back, I turned on you instead. I thought it was your selfishness, or perhaps the selfishness of your parents, that kept the curse intact. I know better now, and I am sorry."

"There has been too much suffering in my name," the Little Rose said. "I hate it too, and if I could end it, I would; but now I am as much trapped by the piskey's gift as by the demon's curse."

Her words hung there, like the pot we hung over the fire to cook in, and then I looked straight into her eyes for the first time since I had first beheld her in the tower.

"There must be a way," I said.

"What?" she said.

"There must be a way to avoid the piskey's gift *and*

keep you from being taken over by the demon," I repeated. "Look at what we know of the demons already, what we've learned since we started exchanging information. The Storyteller Queen was human, and she was able to roust evil from her own husband, who murdered every girl he married before her. If we can find out how she did it, we could do it too."

"There is no one left alive who knows that," the Little Rose protested. "You were brought up on stories less than ten years old, and look how they misled you. How are we to tell what is true and what is myth, if we start to ask questions about her? Even Tariq doesn't know that, and he knows the stories better than the rest of us combined. Who else would we ask?"

I was silent a long time, listening to the waterfall. Saoud had said that we would see anything coming from our lookout point—anything except a dragon, which would fly over the mountaintop instead of climbing the side of it. There were demons here, yes, but there were other creatures too, and they didn't die the way humans did. Their memories were long.

"We need to ask a piskey," I told her. It had seemed impossible when I had said it before, but now that we had the Little Rose with us, now that we were in the mountains where the piskeys lived—now that I had had some time to think about it, and discard all the other, even more terrible ideas I had considered—it seemed more plausible. There were two parts to the magic that bound the Little Rose, and if we couldn't find the demon, we could at least try to find the creature who was less likely to kill us on sight. "If possible, we need to find the piskey who was at your birthday party, but I think any one of them would do. They were there when the Storyteller Queen told the greatest of her tales. They were part of it. And they were there when you were cursed, so they must know how to help us."

"That is a terrible plan," said the Little Rose.

"That's exactly what Saoud said before I climbed your tower," I admitted. "So at least you will know I am consistent."

She laughed, and for the first time I heard the sprite's gift at work. She had said the sprite's gift kept her sane; her world was a flat and empty place, with dark horrors lurking at every edge of it. And yet she did not shrink from it, nor wilt under the weight. I wondered if it would also keep the sanity of those around her.

"Very well, Yashaa," she said. "We will leave this valley, and go in search of creatures that only a few living beings have ever beheld."

"Your feet have only just healed," I pointed out. "Would you prefer to wait for the others to return before we try?"

"And spend more days sitting across the fire from your quiet contemplation?" she said. "I think not, Yashaa. The tower was prison enough that I don't need to repeat the experience here with you."

I was horrified, and then I realized that she spoke in jest. Or at least partially so. The past few days had proven that I was, at best, poor company.

"As you command, princess," I said. "Hopefully we'll be able to find better food while we seek enlightenment."

"That would be quite appreciated," she told me. "I know I said earlier that your cooking was adequate, but I am afraid I was lying when I said it."

"I know, princess," I said. "I am the despair of my mother's teachings on all fronts."

She laughed again, and I was overcome by the desire to make her laugh forever. If this was the service that my mother had so loved before the demon's curse had ruined it, I felt at last that I understood some part of her calling to stay so long in the court of the king and queen who ruled Kharuf. My mother had risked illness and suffering, and I had always thought it was a folly, but now I knew better. I would serve the Little Rose, not because I had once hated her and now wished to make amends, but because I wanted to; and I would serve her at risk to myself if I had to.

The Little Rose took the bowls to the pool and set to washing them. It was a task she could do, because unlike the cooking itself, it did not result in the creation of anything new. Likewise, she could collect wood, though she could not make a fire, even if she had known how. It was a poor freedom, several steps below the life we had made for ourselves at the crossroads, but it was hers; and as I watched her make the most of it, I felt a stirring in my soul I thought might be hope.

SEVENTEEN

BY THE TIME WE WERE ready to start our search the next morning, the Little Rose and I had reached an unspoken accord. I would pretend that it did not trouble me to speak to her as I spoke to Saoud, and she would pretend she didn't notice every time I was troubled by it. It became easier as I practiced, though I could not bring myself to call her "Zahrah," nor could I think of her as anything but a princess. But I could talk to her, and since conversation was one of the few things she could make without fear of consequence, I knew it was a service as important as any I might otherwise provide.

I concealed all evidence of our camp in the valley. There

was only the smallest chance that anyone would find us in the mountains, but I didn't want to take it. We had, after all, essentially kidnapped a princess. The grass was thick and lush enough that we had not left tracks, and everything we had could be fit into the cave. The Little Rose gathered sticks and rocks so that I might leave a message for Saoud on the cave floor, where I was sure it would not be disturbed, telling him that we had gone for food and would return. I doubted very much that he and the others would make it back before we did, because we were not planning to be gone overnight; but on the off chance that they did, I had no wish for them to worry overmuch.

So, on the fifth day after we had found our small haven, we left it. I carried a small pack, because while we did not intend to be abroad for very long, I wanted to prepare for as many contingencies as I could. The Little Rose had her shoes in her hands, because the grass was soft; the less she wore them, the better for her feet. Keeping that in mind, I directed us up the slope, rather than down it. Arwa had reported a glade nearby, and I thought that would be as good a place as any to start looking for food, as well as the more difficult object of our explorations.

"Do you have any idea where the creatures might be?" I asked the Little Rose when I finished explaining my intentions.

"Only stories," she said ruefully. "But I suppose they have gotten us this far."

As we climbed, I told her about the bear we had fought. I didn't want to frighten her, but she needed to know that the woods around us concealed danger in more forms than she might imagine.

"Can you climb trees?" I asked.

"I never have," she said. "But I have never climbed down a rope to escape from a tower either, and I managed that well enough."

"Climbing up is easier most of the time, in any case," I assured her. "If there is a need, you must find a tree and climb it."

"And leave you to defend me?" she asked.

"No, I will be right behind you," I said. She smiled. "At least until I have assessed the situation."

"How did you know it was a demon in the bear?" she asked, her smile fading.

We had reached a rocky outcropping. I watched as she looked at the terrain, then at the shoes in her hand. She decided to take her chances, and we continued on.

"Its eyes," I said. "There was something very strange about its eyes. I had never seen a bear before, but I have seen plenty of animals, and there was something not quite animal when the bear looked at us. Also, it seemed too intelligent. It didn't react to pain as it should have."

"Wonderful," she said, stumbling slightly on a ledge.

I caught her without thinking about it, my hands on her waist and shoulder, and set her on her feet again. I would have done the same for Arwa, or Tariq when he was younger, but with the Little Rose it was different. My fingers knew that the cloth of her dress, plain and unadorned, was of a finer weave than anything Arwa had worn in years, but there was something else when I touched her . . . something I could not name. I felt my cheeks flush and I did not like it.

"Yashaa?" she said when she realized I had stopped walking. "Do you see something?"

"No, princess," I said. I shook my head, and the world righted itself around me. "I'm sorry. Sometimes I drift into my own thoughts. I will be more careful."

"I can see the world as well as you can, Yashaa," she said. "You don't have to be on constant alert. I may not know what I see when I see it, but I will know its intent, and that will suffice if you are woolgathering."

She was teasing, I reminded myself. She was teasing because she was my companion on the road, and that was what companions did. I had done it with Saoud since we were old enough to know our own minds. Yet the difference between her teasing and Saoud's nagged at me, and I could only nod at her and keep walking.

At last we crested a small rise and saw Arwa's glade

stretching out before us. There were flowers everywhere, blossoms swaying gently in the breeze, and a ring of trees bounding the margins like sentinels protecting a garden.

"It's beautiful." There was a wistful note in her voice when she said it, but her face was lit by the sun, and I saw joy and wonder in her expression.

"Come," I said to her. "I will tell you which of them are poisonous."

In the end, I set her to collecting bitter vetch, as it could not easily be mistaken for something that would kill us. I apologized, as much for the end result of the job as for the tedium of it, but she only smiled and reminded me that once Tariq came back, our diet was bound to improve. I laughed and went to set snares for rabbits along the tree line.

It was, I decided, reassuring to have a plan again, even if that plan was less than solid. I hoped to have made some progress on it by the time Saoud returned, as he would be highly skeptical of it; but at the same time, I knew it would be easier with Tariq to help us. Talking with Tariq always seemed to straighten out details. I tried to recall the clues that would help us find the creatures we sought. I knew that piskeys liked flowers, and there were certainly flowers here. I would watch for the golden dust, like that which Arwa had found, because I didn't know if piskeys left any other trail.

"Yashaa!" called the Little Rose, and I could tell that she had tried her best not to sound alarmed when she shouted. I ran to her side anyway.

"What?" I asked.

She had made good progress, collecting the vetch in that damned blanket and dragging it behind her as she moved along the upper edge of the glade. Now she was at the far side of it, looking over the edge into a hollow I had not seen when we first arrived.

"It's a garden," she said.

I looked, and saw that she spoke the truth. This was no wildflower garden like the glade, with flowers and trees. This was a vegetable garden, with plants I knew to be food planted in straight furrows. This part of the glade was completely hidden until you were very close to it. Arwa had only spent a brief time scouting, and she must have only seen the wildflowers, and maybe some of the bees.

"Look at how small it is," the Little Rose said, and for a moment I was confused. The garden was large enough to feed a family of four for the winter. But then I saw what she meant.

There was a fence around the edges of the garden, too fragile to be of any use at keeping the rabbits out, but definitely made by hands that had loved it. Knotted reeds held the small wooden crosspieces in place, and each tiny fence post was set in the ground quite deliberately. It was

171

as though a child had made it.

"The stories say that the mountains are where the gnomes build their gardens," I said, my voice cracking on the words. "That sometimes they come down into the world to help farmers who need them, but their greatest joy is gardening in the mountain air."

"The gnome who came to my birthday party went to the garden when she visited." The Little Rose's voice was as awe-filled as mine. "That garden still prospers, though we have little enough to plant it with."

"We should leave this place," I said. "It is not for us."

"No, it is," she said.

"We should at least step away from the garden." I took her elbow and forced away the flood of strange emotion that accompanied the touch. "We don't want to disturb it."

"The gnome won't mind." She sounded very sure. She saw my discomfort and laid her hand on my arm. "Yashaa, gnomes are the kindest of the Storyteller Queen's creatures. Their payment is help."

"How can we possibly help?" I asked. "The creature isn't even here for us to ask."

"Look," she said, and pointed farther down the fence line. I saw a place where the reeds had failed, either due to a determined interloper or because of the weather, leaving a rather large gap. "We can fix the fence. That will be our gift."

She went to gather the greens she had discarded earlier,

and I returned to the tree line for the appropriate wood. It still made me nervous, but the Little Rose was so sure. And so help me, there were pomegranates along the back of the gnome's garden.

When I came back, she handed me the shoots and sticks, and I did my best to replicate the gnomic work. I could manage the new fence posts, digging carefully so as not to disturb any of the plants, but when it came time to tie the knots, my spinner's fingers failed me. They were too broad, and I tore the stalks instead.

"Give it to me," said the Little Rose, and there was iron in her voice, and some of the anguish that had been there when she spoke of others suffering for her sake.

"Princess," I said, even though I knew she wouldn't heed the warning, "this will be making."

"I am aware, Yashaa." I was already moving to obey her; such was her grace.

I should have argued more. We didn't really need the food out of the garden. It wasn't spinning, which would have been the end of her, but it was making, and we knew that even something as small as a few knots would start to open the pathway for the demon. But she sounded so sure, and even though I had lived away from her for almost a decade, I still followed her orders out of habit. She wanted to make something, wanted to take her own risks, and so I helped her.

I watched as her delicate hands manipulated the stalks into knots, holding each crosspiece up against its post. Though she was unpracticed, her hands were steady, and there was a calm to her countenance that I had never seen before. In the tower, I would not have called her beautiful. Now, in this sunny garden with mud under her nails and her veil sliding off her shorn head, she was lovely.

When the fence was mended, she stepped lightly over it. She walked carefully between the rows, bare feet sinking into the turned dirt with every step. She was cautious and measured, taking very little but immediately going to that which would be the most useful to us. This was the dragon's gift made manifest: to see a thing and know its worth. She carried her small harvest in her veil, leaving her head uncovered in the sun, and before long she came back to me with a smile on her face. She threw me a pomegranate, and I caught it.

I looked at the fence then, and felt the oddest sense of pride. Here was a thing we had made together. Out of everyone who had known the Little Rose in Kharuf, who had helped to raise her after the curse, who had served her as princess and lady, I was probably the only one who could say that I had made something with her. I felt a chill, though there was no wind or any sign of a cloud in the sky. The fence had been the price of the garden, but I did not know the price of the fence.

"We'll come back tomorrow to see if we have caught anything's attention," I told her.

"All right," she said, nodding. We both remembered that the gnomes were shy.

The fruit was perfect.

EIGHTEEN

WE DID NOT SPEAK on our way back to the valley. It was mostly downhill anyway, and the Little Rose was concentrating on walking without dropping anything that she carried. I had the pack and the bigger of the bundles, but she was not particularly well balanced with her burdens, and the sloping ground was potentially treacherous under her bare feet. By the time we slid down next to the pool for a drink, it was nearly sunset; or at least it was in our narrow cutout of the mountain. The Little Rose filled the cooking pot with water. I cleared aside the message I had left for Saoud, but kept the materials, so that I could leave another the next time we left the cave.

"Will you tell me about Kharuf?" I asked, when she had set the pot above the fire and cleared the way so I could make our supper. "My mother's stories were mostly about you."

"Of course," she said, and took a seat across from where I worked. She ran her fingers along the hem of her veil for a moment before she remembered herself and forcibly returned her hands to her lap.

"Something old, if you please," I said. "So, perhaps not about Kharuf, but about how Kharuf was made."

She nodded, took a moment to settle and consider her words, and then began.

"When my ancestress, the sister of the Storyteller Queen, led her people through the desert, she had more than just her kin in her company." I set the lid on the cooking pot and sat back to listen. This was about my family too, however far removed. "She had to leave her sister behind, you see, because the queen had a qasr and the desert to rule, and children to raise to the ruling of them. The Storyteller Queen was older than most when her sons and daughters were born, because the King-Who-Was-Good would not go to her bed until she trusted him, and it took her a long time to come to that. Her sister's children were old enough to make the journey, and so all but one of them did. They brought with them the kin of those they hoped to marry, who followed the queen's sister because they trusted in the power of her leadership, and thus their caravan was long."

I had heard variations of this tale before, as they had told it in Qamih as well, but the Little Rose told it with a style to which I was unaccustomed. I had not known, for example, about the children of the Storyteller Queen. The men in Qamih who spoke the words did not really care where the heirs had come from, only that there were heirs to be had. I leaned back on my hands and let the words of the story flow over me.

"They had camels beyond counting, given by the Storyteller Queen's father, who was the greatest of merchants before he died," the Little Rose continued. "And they had with them sheep and goats and cattle as well, with the promise that the King-Who-Was-Good would send horses when they had a place to be stabled."

She paused, and I could not read the expression in her eyes. This was her history, and mine, but she bore the physical marking that connected her without any possibility for denial to those who had trekked across the sand, and perhaps that made the story all the closer to her heart.

"With such vast herds, it was difficult to mind them," the Little Rose said. "Even with all the herd masters to direct, and the children to do the daily tasks, there was not enough fodder and not enough water in the wadis. Some in the caravan wished to turn back or wait until fortune provided better circumstances.

"But my ancestress remembered the night of her

wedding and the creatures her sister had made. She knew that fortune cannot always be trusted, as it cares little for time, and she knew that circumstances can be changed, if the work is good enough. Lastly, she knew that her sister's creatures had gone ahead of her, and so she knew that there had to be a way. So she spoke words of encouragement to her kin, and led them on. She made sure they journeyed in an orderly fashion. There was no great hurry, so they took care with every step of their march. Each night's camp was laid out with precision, and each day they made sure to line their path with desert stones. Every time they crossed a dry wadi bed, my ancestress made a note of the flood markings and put up markers to show how high the water would come.

"In this way was the trade road—which we call the Silk Road—built, with places for caravans to stop, and a way laid clear to the qasr of the King-Who-Was-Good," the Little Rose said. "And because of the power of making, the flying creatures came down from the mountains to see the work. They saw too that the herds were in want of food and water. Now, the dragons and the unicorns and phoenix could not offer much in the way of help, but the sprites had a particular fondness for goats, and the piskeys had no small measure of pity for the sheep, so they convinced the gnomes, who could not fly, to help. They carried them down from the mountains and set them in the shade of the oleanders that lined the wadi beds. The gnomes looked into the ground there, and called up what water the earth could spare. The herds could drink, and the plants could grow, and thus the great trek of my ancestress was saved from disaster."

I lifted the lid of the cooking pot to stir the vetch. I knew why she had picked that story to tell.

"Did the sister of the Storyteller Queen give the gnomes a gift for their work?" I asked. "Or did that part of the arrangement come later?"

"I know you do not trust magic, Yashaa, and why should you?" she said. She was reasonable. I always wanted to do what she advised, even when it went against my nature. "You have only ever seen magic's price, and it has cost you the lives of those you love."

I could not deny that.

"But I have seen both sides," she said. "I, who have been gifted and cursed both, and feel the two forces constantly at war within my own mind. I promise, Yashaa, it is worth the price sometimes."

"Worth it?" I said. "Arwa was an orphan at ten, Tariq at twelve. Speak to them of worth. Your own people starve because the money they once spent on food must now be spent on cloth. They choose between warm winters and full bellies, and that is your fault."

"And your mother is dying." Her voice was like ice. "I know this, Yashaa. Do not forget, I have had nothing to do for most of my life except sit idle in a tower where I can see my kingdom and not help it. My suffering is different from yours, and maybe it is less, but it is mine, and I will not listen to you belittle it."

All of the friendliness between us was gone.

"I only meant," she said after a long moment, "that I will keep fighting this war within myself, and that we will keep looking for something to satisfy the price. I would like to look in the garden."

"We?" I asked, still unwilling to forgive her, even though as soon as she spoke I wanted to.

"We," she said. "I will not be driven out, nor will I abandon you."

"That's not what I meant," I said. "Today you made a fence. Have you made anything since your curse?"

As soon as I said the words, I regretted them. I remembered the dust drawings on the tower floor, and the terrible hunger with which she had watched Arwa sew.

"Nothing beautiful," she said. "Nothing great. But Yashaa, I have been afraid for too long. Perhaps we have held the demon at bay all these years, but it has done no real good. I have done nothing for so long, Yashaa. I want to try doing *something* instead."

"We lost the spindles," I reminded her.

"Not those," she said, and a shudder ran through her. I knew that for all her bold words, she was still afraid of what

181

she might do if presented with that temptation. "Not spinning. But other things."

"Like what?" I asked.

"Cooking," she said. "Digging the privy. Making flower
chains. I don't know. The things you would only expect of
the youngest, most talentless child."

"I wouldn't let a child near the fire," I told her. The edge
was gone from my words. Despite my misgivings I had for-
given her, though she had not asked for it, and I had not
really wanted to. "And we have a privy."

"Something else then," she said.

It was almost, but not quite, an order. Perhaps that's
what ruling meant: giving people enough of an idea that
they finished it themselves and thought it had been their
own in the first place. It worked, even though I knew she
was doing it.

"You said you never learned dancing?" I asked.

"No," she said. "My father took no chances. You make
patterns when you dance, after all."

"It will still be a pattern," I told her, "but Arwa left her
staff, and I will teach you how to use it. If we start with
that, and if you feel it is all right, then we can move on to
something else."

"Why staff fighting?" she asked.

"Because that is where you start," I told her. "And
because you don't need to wear shoes."

That contented her, and she passed me the empty bowls from where they had been drying. I was focused on the cooking pot, on not spilling any of the food we had gathered, but not so focused that I didn't see when she pressed a hand to her temple. She rubbed her head the way my mother did, when the summer storms came to the clay flats in Qamih and brought a sort of aching pressure with them. I was not subject to the same aches, even with the head wound the demon bear had given me; but I knew what a headache looked like, and I couldn't think why the Little Rose should have one.

And then, of course, I could. The phoenix's gift made it possible for her to walk all night when she hadn't walked so much as a mile before, but it could not take away the pain of it, and it could not take away the pain now. We had only done a gentle climb today, and the sun had not been overly hot. She had drunk enough water, and she could not have been overexerted by her work gathering the vetch.

But she had made a fence. She had used that part of her mind she had so long resisted using, and now it ached, like muscles set to an unfamiliar task. I remembered the ache of my arms and legs when I had first begun training to fight with a staff, and again when Saoud and I had learned to fight with knives. Perhaps the same thing was going on inside her head, as her mind expanded and then turned to rest. If the demon sought to build a fortress inside her, the weight of the stones was certain to hurt her, until she became accustomed to carrying them. It was yet more physical proof of the magic that wove its tangled way through our lives.

She caught my eye, and lowered her hand.

"It's nothing, Yashaa," she said, determined as ever. "Only more than I am used to."

Her words had a power of their own, I had come to realize. She would say a thing, and I would do it. It worked with the others as well, but I had spent the most time with her. I had wondered if it might be magic of some kind, that I would do what she said, but I knew better now, or at least I knew that her words put no spell on me but that which I chose to take. Her power was not in magic, because she had said that it was nothing, and I knew, beyond a shadow of a doubt, that she lied.

NINETEEN

THE NEXT DAY, I woke early and took a stick from the woodpile. It was the length of my forearm, narrower at one end than the other. It had been meant for kindling, but I would put it to another use. I went down to the pool and scooped up a bit of mud off the bottom. It was mealy stuff, and would make no vessels fit for even the lowest of tables, but it would do for my purpose now. I rolled the mud between my fingers, squeezing out most of the water, and then fastened it to the wider end of the stick. It wasn't a lot of weight, but it would do.

I had kept up the practice of checking the Little Rose's blanket for loose threads. I even checked her dresses and veils when she wasn't wearing them, and had by now accumulated a collection of scraps. This morning, I would spin them all together. I sat cross-legged by the pool and missed my mother as I set the whorl spinning experimentally. The wet mud held, barely, and I set out the scraps on my knee so that they were in easy reach.

Sitting on the ground to spin is not the easiest way to do it, but there was no other seat, and I had no distaff to hold the pieces if I stood. After only a few minutes, my shoulders ached from holding the spindle up so high, but I had a short length of ugly thread. I was almost ashamed of it, except I knew that it was all that I could give, and I hoped that the recipient would see its worth.

"Good morning," said the Little Rose, sitting in the wet grass beside me.

"Good morning, princess," I said. "I haven't started breakfast yet. I wanted to do this first."

"You don't need to hide spinning from me, Yashaa," she said. "I can't do it, but I still like to watch good work done."

"This is hardly good work," I said, examining the thread as I wound it around the spindle.

It was varicolored, but not in an attractive way, and though it did not have lumps in it, there were definitely places where it looked stretched. I picked off the mud-whorl, and did my best to remove any flecks of dirt from the thread itself, but it was still far from the sort of thing that would make my mother proud of me.

"It's not very good," I told her. "But I hope it will suit."

"Is it for the gnome?" she asked. Her bare feet moved back and forth through the grass. Even after all the days she had spent out of the tower, the ground was yet a wonder to her.

"It is," I said. "Though I am nearly ashamed of it, the thread will be stronger than the reeds we used yesterday. This will make the fence stronger. Or," I amended, "at least parts of the fence. There isn't enough for the whole thing."

"It's a wonderful gift, Yashaa," she said. "Shall we go and give it?"

"Breakfast first?" I asked, even though she was already standing and looking at the slope in a measuring sort of way.

"Here," she said, and tossed me half of a pomegranate.

I caught it, and we began to climb. Now that we knew where we were going, it took us far less time to reach the glade. The Little Rose didn't bring her shoes at all, and soon we were close enough to smell the flowers. I went first to check the snares, which were empty. Upon short reflection, I removed them entirely. I no longer had a wish to kill anything that happened into this glade. That done, I went back toward the gnome's garden, where the Little Rose was waiting.

"Look," she said, awe writ on her face.

There was a basket, small enough that I could lift it with

one hand. It must have been made by someone far smaller than I, though, because it had two handles. It was carefully woven and just as carefully filled. There were grains and fruit, the nicer sorts we had been too fearful to take the day before. There was no vetch at all. It could not have been a clearer expression of thanks had the gnome itself appeared to speak to us. I stuck the shaft of my makeshift spindle into the ground, the thread side pointing up so that the gnome would be able to see it, and picked up the basket.

"Do you feel better about magic this morning, Yashaa?" the Little Rose asked. She set down her own offering, flowers that didn't grow in the glade, and looked at me.

"No," I said. "Not really."

She waited. Even her silence had power.

"I'm a spinner, princess," I told her. "I spun thread for your mother. I spin thread for you because you can't do it for yourself. And so the gnome gets thread, and I get misgivings about the whole process, but it is my duty, and so I do the work."

"I don't understand you sometimes, Yashaa," she said.

"If it is a comfort," I told her, "I never understand you at all."

She laughed, and I watched her dance through the flowers. There was no reason or direction to her steps, no trace of the court dances she ought to have known. Instead, she spun seemingly at random, as much carried on the wind as the blossoms that surrounded her in the air. Her skirts and veil flared around her, and for just a moment, I wondered what she would look like with her hair grown out, its summer-wheat color spread against the blue of the sky and the green of the grasses.

"Do you dance, Yashaa?" she asked, having caught me staring.

"No," I told her. "Well—just the staff dances that Saoud's father teaches us. That's what I was going to teach you, if you like."

"There's never been a pretty girl in a traveling caravan that caught your eye?" she pressed. I was not entirely sure what answer she was after, so I settled on the truth.

"No, princess," I said. "There has never been."

She flopped into the grass. Had I thought her less dignified, I might have said she was pouting.

"You are a terrible disappointment, Yashaa," she said to me. Her voice was quite serious, but her eyes still danced.

"Oh?" I said, sitting beside her.

"Yes," she said. "I have always known that my wedding would not be for love. At best, it is hoped I will love my children. No one ever has anything good to say about the Maker King's son. So I have spent my life listening to stories of shepherdesses and spinners, of traveling dancers and merchants, of all the sorts of people who get to marry for love. It helps me remember why I must get married at all."

"I will confess I have not thought very much about marriage," I said. "Though, I suppose one of us will marry Arwa. Probably Saoud, because then her children will be of Qamih, and they won't starve. She might even be able to join the guild."

The Little Rose looked at me, and I knew that I had spoiled her game. She wanted me to tell her of some dream I chased, but I couldn't do it. The only dream I had ever chased was her, and they had not been particularly good dreams.

"I suppose only the very lucky marry for love," the Little Rose said.

"My mother used to say that the king and queen were lucky," I told her. "They had only met twice before their wedding, and yet they did their duty to the kingdom, and wed. And then they grew to be fond of one another."

"It's true," the Little Rose said. "I am terribly jealous."

"Is the Maker King's son really as bad as I remember?" I asked. "I mean, we hear little of him at the crossroad camp, and there is much about my childhood that I have remembered incorrectly."

"He is, and worse," she said. "I am sure of it, though mercifully I haven't seen him since we were very small. There's always talk, you see. The servants in the castle love me, in their way, and they gossip about how terrible it is that I must wed him. I understand that some of it must be exaggerated, but there is so much of it, Yashaa, and it's quite consistent. I fear that it must be close to the truth indeed."

"My mother doesn't share your fear," I said. "When she sent us out, she wanted us to go to the Maker King's court and swear to serve the prince after he had married you."

"I'm very glad you didn't," she said. "I should have hated to see you for the first time at my wedding, only to learn that you were sworn to my husband, and not to me."

"I think it was the only way my mother could think of to get us into your service at all," I said. "She never imagined, I think, that we would simply walk to your tower. I'm not sure if she will be furious with me for risking Tariq and Arwa like that, or proud."

"You risked yourself, too," the Little Rose pointed out. "You still risk yourself."

"I don't mean the risk of your father's guards or army," I said. "When Tariq crossed in Kharuf, the first thing he did was nearly cough up his lungs on the riverbank. It's the curse, you see. It doesn't affect us in Qamih, but Tariq has done the most spinning of all of us, and so when we came back, he felt it the worst."

"But you felt it too?" She spoke so quietly I could hardly hear her.

"It was a pressure on my lungs," I told her. "And, worse, I have never wanted to spin so badly as I did when I could not. It was difficult to think straight or focus on anything.

Saoud had to mind us, like we were sheep."

"How did you manage to climb into the tower?" she asked, but I could see in her face that she already knew the answer. "Yashaa, tell me you didn't."

"I did," I told her. "It was the only way. It's the only way that Saoud was able to take Arwa and Tariq with him to get supplies, though they won't have to move quickly, which will make it easier to breathe. Saoud will make sure they don't spin, and will keep them focused when they become distracted by their desire to work thread. We do what we have to, princess, even when it is hard. We always have."

She beheaded a bright orange flower whose name I didn't know, rather viciously I thought. I picked up the fallen blossom and tucked it into the corner of her veil, by her ear, where she would be able to smell the scent of it.

"I hate the curse," she said, her voice quiet again. "I hate that I have caused so much misery, and I hate that I can't even end it by ending myself."

"We are going to find that piskey," I said. "Or one who can help us. And we'll find a way to break the curse. I swear, I will see it done."

It was difficult to imagine dark and cruel magic in the glade, with the sunlight shining on us and the scent of flowers in the air. But when I listened, I could hear the deeper thrum of the mountains underneath me, and then it was easy to remember that the very ground we sat on had been built to be a prison and a paradise both.

"Come, princess," I said. "We should go. The gnome will have work to do, and it might not want us to see it yet."

I pulled her to her feet, and we went back down the slope.

TWENTY

I LEFT THE LITTLE ROSE standing by the pool, and crossed the ledge behind the waterfall to put away the basket. I sorted out the food and took inventory. It was not a great amount, but it was rationed such that we would get two or three meals out of it. We would not have to eat plain vetch until our very bodies started sprouting it. I wondered briefly if I ought to keep some of it for when the others returned, but I had no way of knowing when that would be, and I didn't want anything to spoil. Besides, with luck they would be bringing food as well. I secured everything and then went back through the falls and along the ledge. I was not at all prepared for the sight that met my eyes.

The Little Rose had left her veil and overdress on the bank and gone into the pool to swim. Or at least float. I wasn't sure if she was able to swim, or if she had ever had the chance to learn. In any case, she had no fear of the water. I noticed that her hair was several inches long now. It must grow very quickly. Of course, Arwa never cut hers at all, and the rest of us simply hacked off the ends whenever our hair grew past our shoulder blades. Perhaps short hair grew faster. It was still uneven and pale against her scalp, but it wasn't as awful-looking as when I'd first seen her in the tower.

I meant to turn and go back into the cave so that she could have her privacy, but she saw me and waved.

"Do you swim, Yashaa?" she called.

Our ancestors had come from the desert, where even a bath was a great luxury. There was more water here, in Kharuf and in Qamih—there was even an ocean if you went far enough to the west—but I had not done a lot of swimming, even though I knew how.

"Only to bathe," I replied. "And I did that this morning."

"You know, I think I've figured out what's wrong with you, Yashaa," she said. It was that voice again, the voice that teased in such a way that I knew she was very serious. I sighed. Arwa was never this much trouble.

"And what is that, princess?" I asked. I sat down on the bank so she would know that there was no chance of convincing me to get in the water. I took out my knife and began to sharpen it on a whetstone.

"You never have any fun," she said. She held up both hands in defense. "And before you pout at me, let me remind you that while I know your life has been very hard, I've spent the better part of seven years locked in a room with barely a window, much less a functioning door, and I had absolutely nothing to do with my time."

"I like the staff dances," I told her. "They are useful and enjoyable. Does that pass royal muster?"

"Barely," she allowed. "In the future I will, as your liege-lord, endeavor to find activities that will suit your incredibly narrow definition of the term."

"You have my gratitude, princess," I said. In this imaginary court of hers, I would be happy to serve in whatever position she allowed, as long as the others had their places too, and I could be of use. "What besides swimming do you do for fun?"

"Needle you, of course," she said. She kicked water at me and didn't seem to mind at all that it fell well short of its target. "You are delightful."

I made a mockery of a bow to her, as well as I could from my seated position, and she laughed again.

"I also liked talking with Arwa," she said. "Saoud and Tariq are as formal as you, but Arwa was good at making me feel comfortable."

"We all want you to be comfortable, princess," I said.

"I know that," she said. "And I am glad. But Arwa talked to me like I was just a person. When the rest of you talk, it is impossible for me to forget that I am a princess, and cursed."

"I can never forget that," I told her. "Please do not ask me to try."

"I won't," she said. "Not now that I know you better. Not even to needle you."

"I appreciate it," I said. "Your lips are turning purple, and we're about to lose the sun. You should come out."

"All right," she said. "Turn around."

I did of course, and stared at the rock wall of the valley while she changed. I could hear the sound that her soaked underdress made when it hit the grass, and the soft whisper of the overdress as she pulled it back on.

"You can look, Yashaa," she said, and I turned.

She hadn't put her veil back on yet, and her hair dripped trails across her forehead faster than she could wipe them away. She was looking at the knife, and all of the ease that she had carried in the pool dripped off her, like the water.

"Yashaa," she said, "would you cut my hair?"

I stared at her. There was barely any hair to cut. Even with my knife at its sharpest, I could not possibly do a good job of it. Worse, I might cut her.

"I can't," I told her when I could speak.

"Please, Yashaa," she said. I heard the effort it took for

her not to make the words a plea, and I hated myself for having denied her.

"Why?" I said. "I mean, why must it be cut? It's still short, isn't it? And if you keep your veil on, no one will recognize you by it."

"It's not the veil, Yashaa," she said. "It's the hair. If it gets long enough for me to braid, I will braid it. I do want to make things, but I want to do it on purpose. I want to be able to control it."

And then I understood. Even her own body betrayed her to the foul demon's curse.

"Come and sit, then," I said, and she sat down in front of me.

I put the whetstone aside, and tested the edge of my knife against my finger. It was as sharp as I could get it, and it was the best blade I carried. If Saoud were here, his throwing knives might have done a better job; but he was not. I sucked the blood from my thumb while she settled herself, and then I put a hand on her shoulder to steady her.

"You must tell me if you're going to move," I said. "This knife is a far cry from the razor they must have had at the castle."

"I will," she said, and stilled.

Her hair was finer than mine, I learned, as I ran my fingers through it. It slid away from me when I tried to grasp it, finer than the finest thread I could have spun. I did not know if even my mother could have worked with it, and she was the greatest spinner I had ever known. I leaned forward and used both hands: one to hold the knife, and the other to try gathering up her hair.

It would have to be done in small parts, I realized immediately. This was not going to be a quick job. I set my teeth and cut away from her skull to spare her from any accidental slips of the blade. I cut my own fingers twice before I got the hang of it. It was slow work, and she did not move while I did it. I crossed the even dome of her skull, taking more care around her ears, and finally traced the back of her head, where the muscles in her neck were quivering from the effort to stay motionless.

At last I was done, and I brushed the knife blade in the grass.

"Thank you, Yashaa," she said. She wrapped the veil around her head so quickly, I thought she might get her hands caught in it.

"You're welcome, princess," I said. Her shoulders slumped, just a little bit, but then straightened again as she got to her feet.

"I'll go and make sure we have enough water for dinner, then," she said, and fairly fled across the ledge before I could even get to my feet.

She didn't speak to me for the rest of the evening. I knew I had not offended her, but I wondered if perhaps she might be upset at how she was forced to air all of her weaknesses before me. That could not be an easy way to live. Even if she knew I would never press an advantage on her, she must find it difficult to trust that it was so, trust it all the way to her bones. Worse, if the Maker King's son was as awful as she thought, then letting her guard down at all—even around trusted companions—would only lead to future danger.

She had told me that she loved Arwa's informality with her, and I had thought she might have been, however indirectly, asking me to follow the younger girl's example. Now, though, I was less sure of it. I could be kind to her and remind her who she was at the same time; moreover, I could remind her that it was all right if she stayed guarded around me forever. It was not my first choice, but it would help her after she married. It was probably the only thing I could give her. If she ever left us, I would never see her again. We had, for all intents and purposes, kidnapped her. It was not as though we could expect an invitation to her wedding.

And if we stayed in the mountains? If a piskey flew right in front of us tomorrow and stopped to talk, and it had all the answers we needed, then we could break the curse and return to Kharuf in triumphant glory. Ah, but I discarded that thought as soon as I had it. We had seen no evidence of piskeys in the mountains, and we were too isolated here; there was no way to gather new information, and we had no idea what her parents were doing to find her. No, in all likelihood the Little Rose would have to leave the mountains, and break the curse far from the shelter we had found here. It was not going to be so easy to be in her service.

We needed distance, again—the distance we had given one another before we met that night in the tower, when I had been but a shadowed memory, and she had been the princess I would never see properly enthroned. So when she went to bed that night, I climbed back up to the lookout perch that Saoud and I had built and took up the watch there. It was dark and quiet. Only the stars were out above me, shining bright in the blackness of the sky. Saoud's father had told us that the stars moved, the same as our own sun did, and that they were very far away. I wanted to be far away, too, far from the Little Rose and her curse. Maybe if I took my mother there, she would get better.

But I knew I couldn't. I had promised my mother to help what remained of Kharuf's spinners, and I had promised the Little Rose that I would help her break her curse, no matter how dark the magic got. I was held by both of those promises.

I heard a noise below me, and drew my knife. It could be anything: animal, demon, creature. Friend or foe. I breathed the way Saoud's father had taught us, slowly and taking care not to hiss. And then my heart lightened.

Saoud stepped into view, a large pack on his back, and Arwa and Tariq were behind him. My worries did not disappear, but they shifted. Tariq would have ideas, Saoud would have plans, Arwa would make them work.

"Yashaa?" said Saoud. "Are you there?"

"Yes," I said, and swung down from the tree. I threw my arms around his neck. He returned the embrace, but there was a slowness to it that gave me pause.

"What?" I said. "What is it?"

"Let's go down," said Saoud. I reached for Arwa and Tariq, and they reached back. "The Little Rose should hear this, too."

V.

To set a trap, one must be sure to lay out the proper bait. It is possible to snare a rabbit or perhaps a mink through common luck and timing, but if smarter prey is the object of the hunt, then some thought must be given to its catching. The trap I laid for the Maker King was exquisite. It took me decades to place each part, and in the end, I baited it with a rose.

The Maker King, despite his shortcomings, cared about his own kingdom because it was the source of his power. That I could admire, because as much as I hated the mountains where I was imprisoned, I understood their importance, and could use their rockslides and avalanches to my own needs as required. I knew that, above all else, the Maker King wanted his people to name him, as they had named his father and his father's father, and back through the generations to the King Maker, the first of the Maker Kings. I used that to lay my trap. I reminded him that there had once been only one kingdom, and wondered what people would name the man who put the kingdoms back together. The Maker King, after all, had a son.

Prince Maram was a terrible sort. I supposed he looked well enough in the human way, and that, with his nobility, seemed to buy him a great deal of leeway. As a boy, he'd had broad shoulders even when he shirked the practice field, and the sort of features that human girls found easy to look upon. I saw further than that fine-boned face, though, into his heart and mind, and knew that he would be even better an instrument for me than his father. Unlike the Maker King, Maram did not care about his people at all. He loved only himself and longed to possess everything he touched; and that which he could not possess, he sought to ruin for anyone else.

The animals kept as pets by the castle folk learned to avoid him almost as soon as he could walk. The lapdogs would cower behind their mistresses' feet when they saw him, while the cats simply exited as soon as he came into view. The hunting dogs he spoiled, treating them to lavish food, so that they would forget all the times he had cuffed them, and would mind him when he gave them commands. Only the horses and hawks had his respect, presumably because they were the only beasts in Qamih who might actually harm him unless he took care. Still, he did not go very often into the stables, and it was reported by the grooms that when he returned from riding, his *mounts often had bloodied sides from his spurs.*

Maram was a terror to his nurses, a plague to his tutors, and a horror to any of the castle children assigned to be his companions. To his father, he was the perfect son, and indeed, he played the part so well that it was easy for his father to brush aside the terrible things he had been accused of doing. After all, it was always his word, the word of a prince, against the word of someone lesser. In any case, his father needed him because it was Maram's wedding to the Little Rose that would give the Maker King his name, the name that would finally grant him his place in his family's legacy.

I had visited Maram infrequently since the day I had ensured his marriage would take place as I wished it. He believed he would be marrying the Little Rose, a mere girl he would always be able to control, and I wanted to be sure that he always believed that. With her disappearance, however, and with the general ineptitude of the search for her in Kharuf, I required his help.

I found him in his chambers, hovering over a selection of knives. They were made of iron, which infuriated me, but as long as I stayed on the opposite side of the room from them, it would be well enough.

"Maram," I said, and he jumped.

"Lady," he said, bowing floridly from the waist. He had met me only once before, though I had watched him for a long time. Clearly I had made an impression. He was profoundly odious. When he bedded the Little Rose, I decided, I would withdraw from her almost entirely,

and keep only enough of her to be sure she could not regain control of her own body. "How may I serve you?"

"Your princess has been kidnapped," I told him. "And the vagabonds have taken her into the mountains where her own people cannot track them."

"How terrible," he said. "My poor little rose."

"Indeed," I said. "I require you to seek her there and restore her to her parents."

"Why?" he asked. His impertinence made me fume, but I kept control. I could destroy him after I destroyed the rest of his kingdom, and as many humans as I was able to find.

"She is to be your wife," I reminded him.

"Is she?" he asked. "After being kidnapped by some sort of unsavory characters?"

"If you kill all of them, she will agree to whatever story you tell her," I said. I didn't much care for the Little Rose's reputation. I only needed her alive and contained. "She needs to preserve her reputation as much as you do. It doesn't matter if it is the truth, only that people believe it, and they already believe all sorts of lies about you. Imagine how romantic your people, and hers, will find it if you hasten to her rescue."

"You wound me, Lady," he said. "But at the same time, I do feel stirred to action. I will go, as you have said. Shall I take a war party with me, or will it be more romantic if I ride alone?"

His mockery would stand only as long as it took for me to spring my trap, and then I would tear him to shreds.

"It matters not, princeling," I told him. "Ride however you see fit. Only, ride quickly."

He bowed again, and I was gone before he could stand up to gaze at the empty place where I had been.

TWENTY-ONE

THE FIRST THING ARWA pulled out of her pack was a pair of shoes. They were soft-soled, which meant they couldn't be new. That was probably for the best. New shoes were almost as uncomfortable as small shoes, and if Saoud's face was any indication, the Little Rose was going to have to get accustomed to wearing them quickly. They were sturdy, though, and the laces were simple enough that the Little Rose didn't hesitate before tying them.

"Here," said Tariq, and passed her another veil.

She had been wearing Arwa's, which was enough for the mountains, but it would be noticeably small on her head if we met people on the road in daylight. A woman of the Little

Rose's age customarily wore one that was large enough to reach her waist. It was not enforced, as a rule, but if Saoud wanted us to escape notice, a girl with a small veil would stick in a person's memory. The Little Rose changed quickly, as she had done by the pool earlier, but we all still saw her head and her newly cut hair. When I turned back to Saoud, he was looking at me with a measuring expression on his face, but he didn't say anything.

"What about a dress?" the Little Rose said, spreading her skirt. "This one is clearly of a different style than Arwa's, and the cloth is better."

"We couldn't find one," Saoud said. "We had to cut our trip short."

"If you wear a pair of Tariq's trousers and a tunic from Yashaa, you will look enough like me to pass, I think," Arwa said. "We will have to alter the tunic, but I can do that tonight."

"I will do it," Tariq said. "You are still more concerned with straight lines and even stitches than speed, little goat, and this must be fast work."

"I have to practice!" Arwa protested. Saoud hid a smile.

"We'll find something for you to practice on," he promised. "And you'll need to set the pins for Tariq anyway."

Tariq disappeared into his workbag, while Arwa led the Little Rose behind their privacy screen and began the task of preparing a new outfit for her. Saoud took stock of the cave, noting the basket, but passing over it for now. Clearly there were larger concerns, and I wanted to know what they were.

"Can you hear us, princess, if we talk now?" I asked, having selected my best tunic and given it to Tariq.

"Yes," she replied. I could hear the whisper of fabric as she changed.

"We made it to the first village easily enough," Saoud said. "Their market was very poor, and we couldn't find the sort of supplies we needed. Also, we didn't want to buy things that were obviously meant for use in the mountains, or on a long trip. Word is spreading of the Little Rose's apparent kidnapping, you see, and it would be suspicious."

"We feared as much," I said. I watched Tariq lay out his needle and awl and then turn his attention back to what thread he had left.

"We may have underestimated them," Saoud said darkly. He had never been good at sitting idly, and had taken out his knives to check for damage. I passed him my whetstone.

"What sort of pursuit have my parents arranged?" asked the Little Rose.

"Stay still!" said Arwa, and the Little Rose murmured an apology.

"Messengers were sent to every village, if what we heard is to be believed," Tariq said, without looking away from the trousers he held up in front of him. They were clean and nearly new, and would probably fit the Little Rose with minor adjustments.

"I believe it," said Saoud. "And there is worse news."

Arwa came out from behind the screen with the pinned-up tunic and switched it for the trousers. Tariq set to work, needle and awl moving together like two halves of the same whole through the heavy cloth of my tunic. My mother had made it, of course. I hoped she knew, somehow, that the Little Rose would wear it now.

"The Prince of Qamih is coming to Kharuf," Saoud said. "To rescue his beloved bride."

"What?" exclaimed the Little Rose, bursting out from behind the screen. Arwa, who had apparently been marking the hem of the trousers, was bowled over. The Little Rose stumbled on the extra fabric Arwa hadn't pinned up yet, but caught herself and let the skirt of her underdress swirl around her legs.

"The Maker King's son is riding to your rescue," Saoud repeated, his voice dry and his face carefully blank. "The merchants from Qamih are besotted with the very idea of it, though your own people are slightly more reserved in their hopes."

"I will not go with him," the Little Rose declared. "He is to have me when I am eighteen and not a moment before."

"We know, Zahrah," Tariq said. I was still amazed that

211

he could use her name at all, let alone at a time like this; despite her attire and circumstance, everything about her gave her away as our princess. "We won't let him."

"How?" she said, letting Arwa take her back behind the screen, and then helping the shorter girl rehang the blanket.

"We're going to run," said Saoud. "Now, before he crosses the pass."

"Where can we possibly go?" I asked, but in my heart I knew his answer. There was only one road for spinners, in the end.

"The desert," Saoud said. "We'll cross the northern part of Kharuf, and find our way into the desert. There are oases there that aren't on the Silk Road, and that is where people will look for us. We will find a safe place, and we will stay there as we stay here."

"How long will that hide us for?" the Little Rose asked.

"Long enough for us to come up with a way to break the curse," I told her. "Or long enough to learn that we can't."

Saoud looked at me, not comprehending, and I explained about the gnome and the garden.

"How will we find the Storyteller Queen's creatures if we leave the mountains?" asked Arwa, emerging from behind the screen with the trousers in her hands. The Little Rose was behind her, clad again in her dress.

"There is nothing certain in magic," I told them, even though they knew it. "But there is hope there."

"When must we leave?" The Little Rose loosened the laces on her left shoe, and retied the knot. I watched her carefully for any sign that the headache had returned. You could make a carpet out of knots, after all, so tying her shoes might count toward her curse.

"Tomorrow?" Saoud said it like a question, looking at Tariq.

"The day after," he said. "And that's if you spare Arwa to help me sew."

"Tariq is right," I said. "They can't stay up all night sewing and then walk all day, even if it is downhill."

"Fine," Saoud said. "But I want you to show me the glade."

The Little Rose watched as we made plans and worked on repairs. We did not resent her inaction, of course, but I found that she made me anxious, watching us as she did. If she found us wanting as protectors, she might leave us. Worse, she could turn us in. I was certain she wouldn't, not after the days we had spent here, but I could understand that she might want to, even if it meant a return to her tower and prison of a marriage bargain.

"We should stop for now," Saoud said, though there was still plenty to do. "We can work tomorrow, but sleep is important too."

"I'll take the watch," I said. "I haven't walked as much as you have in the past few days."

"I'll come with you," Saoud said. "I can relieve you later, and there is room for two in the lookout."

We bid good night to the others, and watched Tariq bank the fire to ensure that he would actually sleep. He could sew in the dark, I knew, but not well, and I was reasonably certain he would insist on his best work for the Little Rose, even if it was only alterations on a secondhand tunic. Then I followed Saoud up the slope, and we climbed into the tree to keep watch.

It was as dark as it ever got in the mountains. There was no moon, and the stars gave only enough light for the black peaks to shine in muted reflection of the light. This was the rest of the Storyteller Queen's gift, of course; the creatures to protect us when they could, and the iron ore to weaken the demons and to give us weapons with which to fight them. I felt my own knife, the weight of it hanging from my belt, a comfort against the darkness, even though I knew that in a fight against a sword it would be next to useless. The Maker King's son was rumored to be good with a sword.

"You cut her hair," Saoud said, after a silence that was so long I thought he had fallen asleep.

"She asked," I replied. "She said when it gets too long, she braids it. She shouldn't, of course, so she asked me to cut it off."

"We thought about getting henna for her," Saoud said. "But Arwa said that disguising her hair would only make it more obvious, even if we did Arwa's too. She's better with just the veil."

He was silent for another stretch, and I looked out at the stars.

"Do you really think we can break the curse?" he said. We'd had too few quiet moments, he and I. I knew what it meant, his asking now; he thought we might have a chance. Before, his silence had shown his doubt. Now he had hope, even as the rest of us did.

"I don't know," I said. "I want to. For my mother, and for her."

"My father always told me that someday, you and your mother would return to your roots, and I would be reminded that I would never be one of you." I couldn't see Saoud's face in the dark, which meant he couldn't see mine. I wanted him to. I wanted him to see my expression when I spoke.

"But you are," I said to him. "You always have been, I think. At least since we learned to fight together."

"Yashaa." I don't know what Saoud intended to say, but I interrupted him before he could say it.

"No, you listen," I said. "You have been my brother for as long as I have known you. You stood beside me while I learned, even if it was a lesson you didn't share. Your father taught me, and my mother taught you, even if her lessons were hard and cold. And you have sworn your service, by your own choice, to the princess I was born to. That, if nothing else, spins us into the same thread."

Saoud laughed, or sighed perhaps. It was a quiet sound in the dark, and because I couldn't see him, I couldn't read it properly. But I hoped I had given him peace.

"Good night, Yashaa," he said to me. "Wake me up for a turn at watch, or I'll make you carry my pack when we set out."

He slept in truth then, while I waited up with the stars.

TWENTY-TWO

SAOUD LET ME SLEEP until one hour past sunrise. He must have gone down to the cave to check in with the others, because when he shook me awake, it was to tell me we would head straight for the glade, and the water skin he handed me was still dripping. He also had flatbread and olives. The bread was stale, but I didn't care. I had been eating porridge or vetch for days, with the exception of the gnome's gift from the day before, and even stale bread was a welcome change.

"Come on, then," I said, when I had spit out the last olive pit and put the stopper back in the skin. "It's not very far."

Saoud was a quieter companion than the Little Rose. He was content to follow where I walked, and was not easily diverted to look at interesting trees or unfamiliar flowers. Of course, Saoud had spent enough time abroad in the world that he could walk and admire the view at the same time.

We reached the glade just as the sun was cresting the trees that sheltered it, and so Saoud saw it at its best: sun-drenched and green, with the light breeze stirring the flowers as though to welcome us specifically.

"I see what you mean about this place, Yashaa," he said. "And what the Little Rose means as well. This is good magic."

We sat in the sun like children, as though we had no cares or burdens, or reason to flee the pursuit of a prince with a questionable reputation at best. Saoud unrolled the map his father had given him, which had guided our steps through the mountains until we'd strayed off of the known paths to hide. Saoud had added his own markings, and I guessed that they were the villages he and the others had visited when they had gone down without us.

"This village had no bread at all," he said, pointing to the mark that was closest to where he would have come out of the mountains. "They were eating what game they could catch, but to make bread, they'll have to go into their seed for next season."

"Will they have to eat the sheep?" I asked. It was only ever considered as a last resort. Kharuf needed wool more than it needed meat, but if there were no alternatives, then desperate measures had to be taken.

"Not until the winter, at least." Saoud knew enough about sheep to know that made little difference. The sheep had been shorn only a few weeks ago. They would not yet have enough wool to merit a second shearing. Saoud pointed to another mark. "This village had bread, but little else," he said, and moved to the next mark. "Here was where we were finally able to trade, but we had to be careful because we were closer to the main trade routes, and rumors travel more quickly than goods these days."

I nodded. If they had bought obvious desert gear and henna, it would have been more than enough of a clue for the prince tracking us to at least send men after us, if not follow us himself.

"If we stay north, we should be able to avoid all but the most resilient shepherds," Saoud said, tracing a finger along the route he wanted us to take.

I looked at it. Saoud's father had not spent much time in Kharuf, so his map was not particularly accurate. However, it was unlikely that any villages up in the northern regions had survived this long, and the terrain itself was only slightly rougher than the heathered slopes to the south. We could not walk entirely due east, but we would be able to accomplish nearly that, unless we ran into a river that hadn't made it onto the map.

The desert was represented on the map by a single

delineation, separating the place where grazing for sheep was easy from the place where grazing them was hard. This was the land the Storyteller Queen had called the scrub desert. It was possible to live there, if you had water, and so that would be our chief concern.

"It is going to be a long walk," I said. "But if you think it is safer than staying here, then we will do it."

"The things I heard, Yashaa," Saoud replied, "they made my blood run cold."

"The prince is that bad?" I asked. I trusted the Little Rose's opinion of him, but thought perhaps her gossip might be out of date.

"Not just the prince," Saoud said. "They say the demon who cursed the Little Rose rides with him, or at the very least directs him."

"Why would it do that?" I asked.

"It wants the ruination of Kharuf," he reminded me. "And marrying the Little Rose to the Maker King's son is the best way to ensure it. Qamih already bleeds Kharuf dry. After the wedding, when the Little Rose is legally required to share her rule of the kingdom, Prince Maram will have all the power. He will be able to make it so that Kharuf is on fire if he wants to, and the villagers seem to think he might."

"My mother thought the wedding might save Kharuf," I said.

"Yashaa, your mother dreamed more than Tariq does,"

Saoud said quietly. "She always had hope, even when there seemed to be none, and when she got sick, she only hoped harder. Tariq thinks about the stories like they are pieces that he has gathered, and he looks at them from all angles. I know your mother is a good woman, but she was wrong about this."

I was quiet. Though there was no cloud above us, I felt that the light of the sun had dimmed.

"I don't mean that she was foolish, or naïve," Saoud continued. "But she wanted to believe so hard that I think she made it true. Except she only made it true for herself. You and Arwa and Tariq will have to find your own truth, and it will not be so pretty as hers."

"You will be with us, too," I said. "It's your truth as much as it is ours."

"I know, Yashaa," he said. "But I have a different path, even though we have walked together for so long."

"Come," I said, having had as much truth as I could stand. "I will show you the garden."

I pulled him up after me, and led him across the glade to the little hollow where the garden was. Already, the reeds that held the fence posts to the crosspieces were being replaced by the string I had made. I had taken a spool of Tariq's thread the night before, telling him what it was for, and left it now.

"Look," said Saoud, and I went to where he was standing

on the far border of the garden.

I had not expected another gift, from the gnome or otherwise, and yet here before us was just that. There was a basket of food, larger than the first one, as though the creatures knew there were five of us now instead of two. Beside it were two small wooden boxes with clever catches on the lids, so they would stay closed even if they were packed away and carried on someone's back. Saoud picked one up and opened it. Carefully he licked the tip of his finger and tasted the contents.

"Salt," he said, and made a face. I passed him the water skin so he could wash his mouth out.

"It will be useful in the desert," I said. Saoud's father hadn't been the one to tell us about that particular method of survival. My mother had known it, from the days when she still thought she might someday take the Silk Road herself.

"Indeed," said Saoud. "And it is expensive."

"I have left a spool of Tariq's good thread," I told him. "Do you have anything else?"

I had only my knife and the clothes I was wearing. Saoud was much the same, except he also had the hoops he was wearing in his ears. They were small and not worth a great deal, but they were his and he loved them. He reached under his kafiyyah and began to twist one of them off.

"Oh, no," I said. "I didn't mean that. They're from your father."

"It's all right, Yashaa," he said. "I will keep one and leave the other. I don't craft things the way you do, so it is the best thing I can offer. And when I remember the one I still have, I will remember this place."

He walked back around the garden, and set the hoop down on top of the spool of thread. I stepped closer and looped it through the thread itself so that it wouldn't get lost if the spool was somehow disturbed, and we carried the gift from the gnome back through the glade.

A creature stood there, the first living thing I had seen in some days that was not a far-off bird or my own friends. It was very short and very white, and it stood on two legs, though it carried itself as though it could also stand on four. It had two little horns on its head, gossamer wings on its back, and a long face that smiled at us. It was not the sort of smile I was used to. It wasn't joyful or glad or kind. Rather, it simply was, and it did not need us to judge it. It was both reassuring and deeply unsettling.

We stood there, frozen to the spot, while it regarded us. It seemed to decide that we were worthy of it, for it inclined its head as though in greeting. Neither of us spoke. I could not have said words to it, even if speaking then would have solved every problem I had ever faced. It didn't speak either, which I took as a mercy; but its smile grew in intensity, and I found that somehow, the wider it smiled, the more comforted I was. Then it laughed, and my heart soared to hear it.

The sprite, for it could not be anything else, wavered in the sunlight, and then vanished before our very eyes. We stood still for a few long moments, though I could not have said what we waited for, and then we turned together and left the glade.

"This plan of yours," said Saoud, after we were well on our way. "You plan to talk to one of those things."

"Maybe not a sprite," I said. "Or a unicorn or a phoenix or a dragon."

We both shuddered.

"It was overwhelming, even though it was small," Saoud said.

"Yes," I said. "But I think a gnome or a piskey might be a little bit more approachable."

"What makes you say that?" he asked.

"I have no idea," I admitted. "I only hope they are, because otherwise I am not sure how we are ever going to talk to one."

"Maybe the Little Rose will have an easier time of it," Saoud said. "They seem to like her already."

"We can hope," I replied.

We didn't talk the rest of the way back to the hidden valley that had been our haven. I had not stayed there very long, and I had felt lonely, angry, or desolate when I did, but somehow I was reluctant to leave this place, even though I knew we would be safer in the desert. I had begun to know the Little Rose here, and thought about how my life would follow the course of hers, whatever course that might be. That gave me peace, and it was a peace I was sad to relinquish for a dash across Kharuf to the unknown sands beyond it.

So I took each chance I had to memorize the grass and the stone and the way the sunlight gleamed off the ore that still hid in the rocks where the Storyteller Queen had put it, and I hoped that it would be enough to sustain me on my road.

TWENTY-THREE

IT TOOK A DAY TO REACH the gentle foothills that hemmed the mountains to the north of the main trade pass. Moving downhill and over mostly familiar ground, we were able to make good time. We could have pressed on, but Saoud wanted to camp for one last night in the shelter of the hills before going back into Kharuf. He remembered, after all, the manic nature that had all but overcome us there, and wanted to be sure we would face it as well rested as possible.

"Come on, Yashaa," he said, holding my staff in one hand and his in the other. "It's been too long since we practiced."

It was easy to fall into the rhythms of staff patterns with him, to block each of his strikes and mirror his movements with my own. We did the straight-line patterns first, and then he nodded and we began the circular forms. Stepping carefully, we moved around each other. We didn't need to watch our feet—the ground was even enough—and I hardly even needed to watch Saoud; I knew where he would step next in the pattern.

I felt all the discomfort of the past weeks slide away as we trained. All the oddness of the Little Rose, the danger and magic of the mountains, and the almost certain peril we would face in Kharuf seemed to fall into the pattern beside me, and then they were ordered into something I could manage. Only that last argument with my mother refused to fall in line, and I pushed it away so it would not be a distraction.

"Are you ready?" Saoud said. We had done the full circuit twice, and he was grinning.

"Come and get me," I replied.

He stepped outside of the pattern then, staff flying in a flurry of movement. I answered his motion with my own, stepping into his strikes to get past his guard. Fighting with Saoud was like breathing. He came at my left side, which I had momentarily exposed when I'd raised my staff to block him. I saw it in his chest and shoulders, his slight overcommitment to the move. Years of practice, and he still thought I was weaker on the left than I was. I stepped into the blow instead of dodging it, turning so that Saoud's staff cut the air next to the place where my shoulder had been. I saw

227

realization on his face, a brief flicker of rueful acknowledgement that I had him again, and then I neatly hooked my staff behind his knee and brought him down.

"It's not about hitting at all," the Little Rose said, as I helped Saoud back up and we bowed to each other. "You use the staff to put your opponent out of place, and then you press your advantage when you have them on the ground of your choosing."

Saoud looked impressed.

"That's true, Zahrah," Arwa said. "Saoud's father says that that is the first lesson of staff fighting. He would be pleased to have you as a student if you learned that so quickly. Have you seen staff fighting before?"

"Not really," she said. "But this was an excellent example of it, I think."

"Tariq," Saoud said. "It's your turn."

Tariq took my place, and they squared off. We watched them execute the same patterns, only slower, and the Little Rose followed each rise and fall of Saoud's shoulders, not his staff. Then it was Arwa's turn, and the pace slowed further, though Saoud still moved deliberately against her.

"Saoud's father calls himself our dancing master," I said. "Saoud is nearly as good a teacher as he is, though he'll tell you that it's only because his father started the work."

"Do you teach?" she asked.

"No, princess," I told her. "I train with Arwa sometimes,

because it teaches me patience, but I learn as much as she does when we do it."

"You said you would show me," she said. There was a delighted sparkle in her eyes when she spoke. I thought she must be desperate for any sort of activity after a life of idleness.

"Saoud is better at it," I said. "I expected them to be gone for longer, and for us to have to find something to do to pass the time."

"Show me," she said.

I hesitated, remembering her headache after we had repaired the fence.

"Tariq," I said, "give the princess your staff."

He passed it over with some measure of reluctance and followed us to a patch of ground where we would be clear of Arwa and Saoud. I showed the Little Rose how to stand, and marveled at the quickness with which she mastered the starting pose. It was not an entirely natural way to stand, and most newcomers to the fighting style leaned too far forward. The Little Rose found her balance immediately, and even the placement of her hands on the staff was perfect.

"You said you had never done this before," I said.

Saoud's father had finally got so fed up with my tendency to put my hands too close together that he had made me carry a stick around for days at a time, so that I would become accustomed to the proper distance. Even Saoud hadn't mastered it right away. Yet here stood the Little Rose, feet and hands expertly spread.

"The sprite's gift includes dancing," she reminded me. "Maybe this is it."

"If you say so, princess," I said. Magic, it seemed, would follow me everywhere. "Here is the low block."

I demonstrated the move and then practiced it with her. To the relief of my dignity, while her form was excellent, her strength did not match mine. When I switched her to the low strike, she grasped it much more quickly, and I realized it was because I had used the move on her to teach her the block. I had forgotten to count for her, so that she would know the rhythm of the strikes, but she seemed to know the rhythm innately and matched her movements to mine without effort. Except for the disparity of force, it was almost exactly like sparring with Saoud.

She was smiling and breathing hard when I held up my staff to signal a stop. Saoud and Arwa had finished and had both come over to watch. Saoud's face was troubled.

"I was careful," I told him. "You know I can hold back, you've seen me do it."

He only shook his head, and went back toward the fire.

"How do you feel, princess?" I asked. She wasn't holding her head, but the headache had taken a while to appear the first time.

"It's wonderful," she said. "It's much better than the fence."

That worried me.

"Don't look at me like that, Yashaa," she said. It was unmistakably a command, and I straightened as she spoke it. "Remember, the most enduring part of a rose is the thorns."

"Of course, princess," I said automatically.

Tariq took his staff back and commended the Little Rose on her first efforts. Arwa followed them back toward the fire, chattering in her excitement at having another girl to train with, since we boys were far too cautious with her. I caught Saoud's eye. He smiled briefly but immediately looked away, and I knew that he was still troubled. I couldn't face him yet, so I stayed off by myself, listening to the sounds of the night as they came alive around me.

These were the sounds I had known all my life. The insects and night birds, the creaking of trees. I knew that I had, at one point, known only the sounds of a stone castle in the night, but I did not remember them. My life had been a long march and a meager camp, but the constants in it had been fireside spinning, and the sounds of night. I wondered for the first time what night sounded like in the desert. With the lack of greenery, the insects must be different. And surely there were no trees at all.

I called my thoughts back from that far distance and

focused on the rolling plain directly before me, though I could hardly see it in the dark. First we would have to get through Kharuf—where we would be hunted, where food would be scarce, and where there would be nothing to break the wind as it bore down on us. Then we would worry about the desert.

"Yashaa!" Tariq shouted from near the cookfire, and I turned to run toward him.

We had gone down the slope a ways to find a place to spar, so the camp was uphill from us. As soon as I turned, I froze, for I saw why Tariq had shouted for me.

The Storyteller Queen had made a chain of discrete mountains, most with a single peak, though they were joined together by lower hills everywhere except the pass. Therefore, I could see quite clearly that it was the peak of the mountain on which we stood that had called Tariq's attention. Its neighbors were all black-topped with the dark of night and with their own dark stone. Our mountain blazed with light, burning golden, as if the iron ore that laced its very bones glowed in the dark. I shook myself, and raced toward the others.

"It can't be a forest fire," Saoud said when I drew near. "There aren't any trees up there."

"Is it a dragon?" Arwa said, her voice very small in the dark depth of the night.

"No," Tariq said. "Dragon fire can't burn stone without

232

some kindling to start it, and there's none up there. It's phoenix fire."

Saoud and I had told the others about the sprite we'd seen in the glade, of course. Tariq's eyes had gleamed when we'd described it, but the Little Rose had looked sad.

"Does it want us to stay?" she asked. "Is it trying to warn us about something?"

"I don't know," Tariq said. "Phoenix fire is very rare."

"Wonderful," said Saoud. "Maybe it would like to fly to the Maker King's son and tell him exactly where we are."

"Saoud," Arwa chastened him. By the dim light of the campfire, I could tell he was abashed.

"Phoenix fire means a good start in most of the stories," Tariq said.

"What does it mean in the rest of them?" I asked. If I had known how useful Tariq's father's tales would be, I might have paid them more attention. As it was, I had no problems relying on Tariq, and listening better to what he said now.

"A good end," said the Little Rose.

"I suppose we shall be happy with either," Saoud said. It was as close to an apology as we, or the phoenix, were likely to get. He smiled at me across the fire, and I knew that whatever trouble had been between us, he had decided to let it go. Perhaps that wasn't the beginning or ending the phoenix had intended, but I would take it.

"Come on," I said. "I'll watch first, but the rest of you should sleep."

The noises of the night never changed, even though the phoenix-fire glow above us didn't dim as the night drew on. No other animals were disturbed by it, and I hoped against hope that it meant the sight of the fire had been for us alone.

TWENTY-FOUR

WE WALKED FOR TWO DAYS across the heathered slopes of Kharuf without seeing so much as a sheep on the horizon, but we took no chances. We set up camp at night in whatever concealment we could find, digging the fire pit as deep as we could and burying it again as soon as we were done cooking. Even the Little Rose took her turn at watch now, though she didn't usually watch for very long. She still didn't trust herself with the blanket on her own, and it was too cold for her to sit up without it. She usually took the first turn, as a result, but it spared us all a couple of hours to reorder our thoughts after a long day's march.

Saoud's father had told us that there was more to

trekking than simply taking the steps. You had to plan food and water, which were both easy enough for now, and you could only move as fast as your slowest companion. Usually that was Arwa, who absolutely hated the idea of us slowing our pace to match hers, but with the Little Rose's gift for stamina, it was complicated. She could, as we had seen, walk farther than anyone should be able to, but it cost her to do it. Saoud talked with her, reminding her that we must reach the desert fit to keep going, if we had to, and she conceded the point. Though it chafed her more than it chafed Arwa, she called a halt when she needed it, and it was she who set our pace across Kharuf.

On the second day, just after we set out, Tariq stopped in his tracks and put his hand to his chest. I reached for my water skin, sure he would need a drink after he had finished coughing, but then I realized he wasn't coughing. None of us were. I still had a tickle in the back of my throat, but that was all. Saoud walked back to us, and I saw the question in his eyes.

"We're all right," I said. Then, again: "We're all right."

"How is that possible?" Tariq said. "The first time we came into Kharuf, I nearly left a lung on the riverbank. Arwa?"

"I'm fine too," she said, breathing deeply to confirm it.

"What's different this time?" Saoud said.

"We ate food from the gnome's garden," Tariq said. "But I don't think that's it."

236

"Could it be because the princess has started to make things?" Saoud asked. We all flinched away from the implication that her making could ease our illness.

"No," said Tariq. "That doesn't feel right, either."

"Feel right?" Saoud said.

"No, Tariq, think," I said. "Or don't think. However you figure things out, no matter how strange it seems, follow the thread of it."

"Our parents got sick, but they weren't immediately incapacitated," he said, speaking slowly. "They were able to hang on for months before they had to leave."

Once I would have interrupted him with an angry remark about King Qasim, but now I knew better, and held my tongue.

"They didn't have the gnome's food, and Zahrah wasn't making anything," he continued. "But she was there."

He looked directly at me, his eyes bright.

"Yashaa, your mother was completely devoted to her princess and to her king and queen. It was like they were a focus, some bit of magic that no one even knew about. Not a spell or anything, just . . . a connection." He turned to look at the Little Rose. "It's you. That's why we're better this time. It won't save us, not forever, but you'll help us get through."

The Little Rose's eyes were bright, too.

"Come on," Saoud said, his gentle voice drawing us forward again. "We should take every advantage we can."

On the third day, we came to what had at one time been a village. The wooden walls of the huts and houses had collapsed, but the foundations were still there. Heather grew everywhere, topping the low and rotting walls, and crowding over the paths that had once been the village roadways.

"Find the well," Saoud said to Arwa. "And see if it has been fouled."

She nodded and went off. It was a small enough village that even if she strayed beyond our sight, we would still be able to hear her. We busied ourselves checking the other houses, in case anything of value remained in them. The settlement had not been quickly abandoned. This was one of Kharuf's forgotten places. With spinning forbidden, the people who lived here had nothing to support themselves with. They had gone south, to where the land was marginally better for farming. If they were lucky, they got there early enough that land was still available. Most were not so fortunate. The few people who had remained in the north were shepherds, and only needed help during the annual shearing.

The Little Rose stood in the middle of what I guessed had once been the town square. The remains of a raised platform rotted there, and the houses that faced it had stone foundations and dugout cellars, like the ones shops needed for storage.

"This is my fault," she said. "Everything is always my fault."

"And now you are working to fix it, princess," I reminded her. "And we are here to help you do it."

"It's been years, Yashaa," she said. "So many have suffered and died."

"They won't blame you," I said.

"You did." The accusation was quiet, and it stung because it was the truth. If she had been Arwa, I would have put an arm around her shoulders. But she was the Little Rose.

"I was sick during your birthday party, did you know that?" I said. "I had the sheep pox, so I had to stay away from you and Tariq, because you hadn't caught it yet."

"Most of what children remember is told to them," she said. "No one ever wanted to talk to me about that night, but I made them. I don't want to make you, but if you would do it anyway, I would listen."

"It was beautiful," I said. "The most beautiful night I have never seen. I didn't even get to see the hall when it was empty, before the guests arrived. But when it was full of light and song? Before the demon came...princess, I imagined that night for years."

"Is it a happy memory?" she asked.

Behind me, I was aware that Saoud and Tariq had come into the square. I expected them to join us, but instead Saoud took Tariq by the shoulder and led him into another abandoned house. I wondered briefly what he had spotted there.

"No," I told her. "It is an angry one. It has been angry since I made it, lying in my bed all those years ago and barely able to hear the music. It was torturous, princess, to be so close to it and miss it entirely. Your mother sent me a plate she had made up herself, and I barely ate it, I was so furious with my own circumstances."

"Children can be vicious," she said. She looked away from the platform and smiled at me. "What made you change your mind?"

"You did," I said. "I carried that anger with me for so long. Every time my mother tried to tell me what she had seen that night in the Great Hall, I twisted her words to match my rage, and I focused all of it on you. I thought you were selfish and spoiled. I thought my mother's love of you had ruined her, and I thought your parents were terrible rulers for letting your safekeeping outweigh the safety of their subjects.

"But then I climbed a tower," I said. "And I saw you at the top of it. And I understood."

"What did you understand?" She took a step closer to me and looked like she was about to take another.

"That you aren't just the Little Rose," I said. "You aren't a far-off person that I can ignore, and you never will be. I understood that you are my princess, and even if your court cannot have spinners, I would still be in it."

She froze, her weight half pushing toward the step she was about to take, and seemed to shut in on herself.

"I would never keep you in a place you could not spin," she said, so quietly I had to lean in to hear her speak.

"I think that's why I would stay," I told her.

She had wanted something from me before, I was sure of it, and I was just as sure I had not given it to her. Before I could ask, Arwa came running into the square at her usual carefree pace.

"The well is still good!" she announced. "It's not even overgrown, like so many of the houses are."

Saoud and Tariq came out of the house behind us empty-handed, and we followed Arwa back to the well. Saoud fell into step beside me. I knew that he had overheard everything I had just told the Little Rose. I had made promises to them both, and that had been a foolish thing to do. Saoud did not rebuke me, and I was glad, for I had not yet had the time to muster a defense.

The well was more than good. It was nearly untouched. Even the rope and bucket were still there. Only a slight crack in the mortar that held the stones of the cover together betrayed the well's age.

"Wait," said the Little Rose and I, speaking in the same breath. She looked at me, as though the conversation in the square hadn't taken place, and I knew we were of a common mind.

"It's like the gnome's garden," the Little Rose told Arwa. "There are creatures here."

"Listen," said Tariq, and we heard it.

The wooden walls of the village houses had been held in place by wattle and daub. Nails might have been used around the windows, to fasten the coverings down, but they were still a luxury. The technique meant that wall collapse left pockets of decayed plant matter between the planks. With the summer sun and the shelter of the wind, it was warm enough for bees.

Once I heard the buzz of them, I wondered how I had missed it. They must be in every wall, returning now to the safety of their hives as the day drew to an end. There would be hundreds of them, thousands likely, and where there were that many bees...

"Piskeys," breathed Tariq.

"We should go," Saoud said. We all gaped at him in protest. "Not far," he said. "Just to the edge of the village. We'll camp there, and see if we can come up with a way to fix the well cover. In the morning we'll do the work, and then if the piskeys come out, we will ask them."

We retreated to the western side, and found a place to pitch the tents. Tariq and I worked quickly to set them up, and Arwa went to dig a privy without being told.

"Yashaa," said Saoud, "come. Let's see if we can find where the villagers got their mud from."

I went with him, and before it was fully dark, we found a good-sized pond. It was shallow and on a path from the village that had once been well-trod, so we guessed that it was the source of both the reeds used for the wattle and the mud used for the daub. It was too dark to gather any great quantity, but at least we knew where it was, and were able to take a small amount back in my drinking cup.

I gave it to Tariq when we returned, and he ground it between his fingers.

"This should do," he said. "It will have to bake in the sun for a few days, but it's still warm enough for that. We'll make the cover out of reeds. It won't be as strong as the stone cover, obviously, but it will suit, and it will be easier for the piskeys to maintain, if they have to."

"The reeds won't be dry," said the Little Rose. "Won't they just rot?"

"We can take them from the edge of the pond," I said, "where the summer heat has dried the bed of it a little. It won't be perfect, but it will be better than something with holes in it that might crack at any moment."

Arwa passed out our dinner. It was the last of the food from the gnome's garden. After this, it would be back to vetch. At least Tariq was better at cooking it than I was, and we still had the supplies they had brought back from their short excursion south.

The buzzing, which had all but stopped as the night

grew dark, intensified again. I listened and realized that the pitch of the noise had shifted. It was lighter somehow, and the movement of it was more carefree than a honeybee, driven to its task, would be.

"There," said Saoud, as the first small shower of gold dust appeared in the sky by the village edge.

The noise grew closer, and though we couldn't see them fully, we knew by the trailing golden lights that the piskeys were dancing in the village below. The sight of their stately patterns further calmed the itch I had been feeling since we'd come back to Kharuf. Even if it was less oppressive this time, thanks to the influence of the Little Rose, I knew what it would do to my body if I did the work. The dance was beautiful, and we watched it for hours until we finally dragged ourselves inside the tents and went to sleep.

TWENTY-FIVE

IN THE MORNING, SAOUD TOOK the Little Rose with him and went out to see if there was anything in the area that he could hunt. It was odd for them to go off together, but I supposed that watching Saoud hunt would be more interesting than watching us weave mud and reeds all day. I didn't know if they would catch anything, but I supposed there were rabbits everywhere, and a bit of fresh meat would suit us all well. I didn't regret my decision not to trap when we were in the mountains, but now that we were away from them I remembered what hunger felt like, and I had not grown any fonder of it. In truth, I saw it as a mercy: Arwa and Tariq and I would spend most of the day weaving, which would mean boredom to Saoud but outright torture for the Little Rose to watch.

Arwa and Tariq went to cut reeds and fetch as much of the mud as our cooking pot could hold, while I went back into the village and tried to find a wooden frame of the right size, if any such thing remained intact. With the new day's sun on the heather, the buzzing this morning was impossible to miss, and there were bees flying everywhere back and forth between clumps of flowers and their hives. Since they were usually territorial, I knew that the piskeys must be influencing the bees directly to have so many in one place. They were busy at their work, as I planned to be, and I knew that if I didn't disturb them, they would leave me alone.

I found the ruins of a house that was less overgrown by heather than its neighbors, and didn't appear to have a hive concealed anywhere in what remained of its structure. I sifted through the ruins of the collapsed roofing material until I found what I was after: the planks that had once framed the window of the house. Windows were a sign of luxury in wattle and daub, so once upon a time, this house had been well done by. I was thankful for it now.

I shook the frame experimentally, and it didn't fall to pieces in my hands. I tested the joints at the corners. The edges had been fitted together, not fastened, and therefore were much more stable. Whoever built this house had cared for it a great deal. The fact that they had been forced to leave it, for almost certain poverty in the south, turned my stomach.

By the time I returned to the campsite, the pile of reeds was large enough to get started. Arwa was the best weaver of us, having learned from her mother before her death. She selected the largest reeds and used them to set the warp. She took some care with the knots, both because the reeds were fragile and because, unlike a normal weaving, this one would stay on the frame when we were done with it. The warp she set was very tight. We wanted this to be as waterproof as we could make it before we added the daub, because we wanted the finished project to be light enough to be easily moved.

At last Arwa decided the warp was good enough, and turned to look at the reeds Tariq and I had selected for the weft. It didn't particularly matter if these reeds were too short to reach across the frame, because they could be fastened to the warp itself if need be. The daub would cover over those spots.

They would have continued until the work was done, but I made them stop for lunch when I realized how high the sun had risen. None of us had coughed all morning, which was a relief.

"It's such a blessing not to feel so ill this time," Arwa said. "I didn't like it, and I liked the compulsion to spin even less. Even though spinning did help for a little bit."

"In any case, we've no spindles anymore," I said, thinking of my own buried leagues away, possibly beyond my reach forever. "And Saoud would stop us if we tried to spin using his kindling."

Tariq and Arwa exchanged a glance, and Arwa shook her head slightly.

"Come on," Tariq said, setting his bowl down. "We can leave the dishes. I want to be finished with the weaving before Saoud and Zahrah return."

We all had slices on our fingertips by the time we were done, and I had a welt across my palm that would itch as it healed, even though it wasn't very deep. The reeds were tricky to weave, but they held their place, so at least once we did the work we wouldn't have to do it again. I covered them with a thin coat of the daub, hoping it was enough to seal the reeds from the weather, while not making the whole thing too heavy for the piskeys to lift.

I left Arwa and Tariq to tidy up, and took the frame down to the well. This was the most complicated piece of craftwork that I had done, or helped to do, in a long while, and I was much more pleased by it than I was willing to admit to the others. Arwa was a true master, I thought, though there would never be a weaver in Qamih who would certify her, at least not unless she married Saoud. And Tariq's patience was admirable, not to mention his ability to adapt his work to any task. Our parents had prepared us so well for a court that didn't exist, and now we could only hope that one day soon it would.

At the same time, the whispers of doubt nagged at me. I was a good spinner, better than Tariq if I set my mind to it and practiced, but what did I know of running the spinning room as my mother had done? I had fought her lessons so hard that she'd had no chance to show me the practical details of it, the non-craft work that went into keeping the whole operation spinning neatly. Saoud could serve as a guard, and Arwa and Tariq seemed well on their way to settling into their own craft-path, but I was aimless. Useless. Even if we broke the curse, my service to the Little Rose would be limited by my own childish stubbornness.

If we were successful, and if we were successful soon, then maybe my mother would still be alive to teach me. This time, I promised myself, I would not be so dismissive of her. I would listen and I would learn.

And if we were not successful—if we had to spend the rest of our days hiding in the desert, or running across the world to keep away from the Maker King's son, then I would spin what I could and help Saoud keep us safe. It was a poor second choice. It would mean that I would never see my mother again. That Kharuf would die. That the Little Rose would live out her days on the edges of an idleness so profound, I could only understand it because I had seen how it made her suffer. It would be a poorer court, of course, but we would serve her. We would serve her.

When I reached the well, I wrestled the stone cover aside, being careful not to further damage it. I didn't want rocks or mortar to fall into the well if I could help it. Then I took the bucket and lowered it into the deep. The water that came back to me was crystal clear. I set it to the side as well, and covered the hole with our screen. It was a bit large, covering the well along with a good patch of the surrounding grass, but it was sturdy enough. Unlike a cairn of rocks, it would not provide a hiding place for snakes. I broke four stones off of the old cover and used them to weigh down the edges of the screen. I didn't think the wind could lift it, but there was no point in being incautious.

Then I turned around. I was alone, save for the buzzing of the bees, but I felt much the same way I had in the mountain glade. There was a presence here.

"We are going to leave tomorrow," I said to the nothing in front of me. It felt foolish, but I knew my words were heard. "If you test the well cover tonight and it's too heavy, or if you don't like it, please tell us. We can spare another day to set it right."

We couldn't, really. Saoud had said as much. But I had to make the offer.

"It should be easy enough to maintain," I continued. "It

just needs new daub from time to time. The reeds should be fine for a while."

The buzzing sound grew louder around me. I could feel it in my teeth, as though the gaps between my very bones vibrated with the noise. It was an answer, even though I couldn't understand it, and I nodded to show I understood.

I would have gone back to the camp then, to wait for Saoud and the Little Rose to come back. There was dinner to prepare, and even though we checked our gear nightly for damage, and hadn't done anything that would damage it, I found the ritual of sorting through our things calming. It reminded me of who we were, where we had come from, and what we hoped to do. We would have to scrub the cooking pot well before we ate; the mud we'd filled it with had a faint smell that would not make our meal any more palatable than it already was, and I had no fondness for grit in my teeth. I would have told Arwa and Tariq that they had done good work that day, and asked Saoud to tell us about what he had seen, even if it had been nothing but more and more heather on the rolling hills of Kharuf.

I would have done all of that, but instead, when I turned away from the well and the bees, the Little Rose was there. She was so far inside my guard that if she'd been holding her staff, she would have had me in the dirt before I could draw breath. She said nothing, only stared for a moment that seemed both long and short, standing in the afternoon sun with the sound of the bees and the smell of the heather all around us.

And then she kissed me, full on the mouth.

vi.

I could not bring myself to travel with Prince Maram, though I was less than confident in his ability to complete the task I had given him. He had never been tested in real battle, living as he did in the peace his grandfathers had made, and his skill as a hunter was nothing particularly special. I might have taken hold of his horse, or perhaps the horse of one of his riding companions, in order to monitor him, but I was reluctant to do so; Maram was free with the spur. Even leaving that pain aside, I had not yet lowered myself to join with a common animal, and I swore I never would. My spies might take bears and birds and common dogs, but I had my dignity. I would have the Little Rose or nothing.

I was limited to visiting the prince's camp for short periods of time in the evening, after he had given up his pursuit for the day. He was not moving as quickly as I wanted him to. He usually rode with less regard for the well-being of the mounts, but the others he rode with were holding him back. I seethed but said nothing. Maram was petulant and contrary, and if I commanded him, he would only seek to countermand me.

While I was not harrying the prince, I scoured the southern parts of Kharuf, looking for my lost rose. I haunted villages and raised horrors to loosen the tongues of merchants on the road. No one had seen her. No one had seen anyone suspicious at all. I widened the scope of my hunt, venturing north into the abandoned wastes. This, I thought, would be an easy path to take. Since the abandonment of most of the northern villages, for which I was largely responsible, it should have been simple enough to track anyone. People leave trails. They set fires. They make marks.

What I found instead were bees. Bees and sheep. The sheep had fouled the areas around the old roads, their tracks stamping out any evidence that other creatures had passed. The bees swarmed any time I tried to walk upon the ground itself, pushing me back into the sky, where my view of the earth was obscured.

It could not have been more obvious if the Storyteller Witch had come back to tell me herself.

The Little Rose was close. She was ahead of me, but she was close. And the creatures were trying to shield her from me so she could flee into the desert.

I gave myself up to the wind, and hurtled across the sky to the *foothills where the prince's men were camped. Their tents were disorderly, pitched without regard for where their companions would sleep, and already there were discarded tools and food littering the ground. They were set up at the crossroads of two routes, where a permanent, if poor, trading camp was established. When I arrived at the prince's tent, he was polishing his sword by a cooking fire and looking out over the trading camp, as though he were imagining what it might look like if it were on fire.*

It galled me that I had to use a creature who didn't even feel loyalty to his own kind. One of my own kind had done that once—had put himself above the rest of us, and sought glory and power. For a time it had gone well, but when he was brought down, we had all been brought down with him, and now we suffered. That I would make the Maker King's son suffer, too, was my great solace.

"I have found her," I told him, not bothering to make any courtesies to him before I spoke. I cared little for his rank or feelings.

"That is wonderful news," said the prince. "I have found out who has taken her."

That was a surprise. I hadn't expected him to have done anything useful at all.

"Do explain," I said.

"An old spinner came to see me when we were pitching the tents," he said. "She had come to beg news of her son, who she had sent to petition me. She hoped to hear that he was well, that his petition had been heard and considered justly. She hoped he would have a place in

255

my court when I married the Little Rose, because he was a spinner from Kharuf.

"Imagine, then," he said, "that poor mother's grief when she learned I had not ever seen her son. That he had never come to me, or to court at all, and that her hopes for him had been dashed before they had even truly gained their bearings."

"And you think he has the Little Rose," I said.

"These people from Kharuf, they have nothing but their memories," the prince said. "We have made sure of that. I asked her how old her son was, and she told me he has only eighteen winters. He would remember the Little Rose, you see. He would remember her and her castle."

I considered the words. The Maker King's son was wrong about the people of Kharuf, but he was close enough to the mark that he might have struck upon something by accident. They had more than their memories. They had their pride, and they had their love for their princess.

"Were there others with him?" I asked.

"A boy of his own age, another boy a few years younger, and a slip of a girl," the prince said.

His grin turned vicious, and if I had bothered to give myself a true face, mine would have as well. Even with all the protection the damned Storyteller Witch could muster for them, five children were nothing. Nothing but easy prey.

TWENTY-SIX

WEARING SHOES, THE LITTLE ROSE stood at eye level with my chin. To kiss me, she had to stand on her toes and propel herself forward and upward. I was not at all prepared for this sort of attack, which pulled me away from my center of balance and onto my heels, but I did manage to catch her before she overbalanced us or caused us to fall through the screen and into the well. Her nose pressed against mine, and she stepped on my foot. When she moved finally away again, it was a long moment before I realized that I held her by her waist, preventing her from moving any farther. I dropped my hands immediately.

"That was terrible," she said, looking at the space over

my shoulder. "I have to go and murder Saoud."

"What?" I said. It was, perhaps, not the most helpful of questions, but it seemed to encompass everything I wanted to know.

"He said I would have to tell you." She was still looking over my shoulder.

"You didn't tell me anything," I pointed out.

"I have been trying to tell you for days, Yashaa. I thought . . . I don't know what I thought."

"Princess," I said, and her eyes flashed with anger. She managed to look straight at me, and I saw fire there.

"My name is Zahrah," she snapped. "The others use it, even Saoud. Why can't you?"

I didn't know. She was the Little Rose. She was my Little Rose, and she was my princess. Her name wasn't mine to say. At least, I had thought it wasn't.

"You were Tariq's friend, back when we lived in your father's castle," I said. "And Arwa has worshipped you since before you met her. I thought I was different. I was older, and I remembered too much of how life used to be. I thought—I thought that I was meant to live without you. Then we met again, and I thought I was meant to live behind you. To have a place in your house, if you would have me, and to do my work there."

"Your work," she said, and the fire in her voice was gone. She laughed, a sad echo of her usual joy. "You meant every word you ever said to me. You meant exactly what you said."

"Of course I did," I told her. "What did you think I meant?"

"In the stories, the bold rescuer is always gallant," she said. "He swoops in and sets it all to right."

"I am not your rescuer, princess." I said the word without meaning to, but she didn't flare up at me again. "If anything, you are going to rescue us."

"I know that, Yashaa," she said. "It's only that for so long, all I had were my dreams."

"All I had were my memories," I told her. "So perhaps I can understand. Tell me whatever it was Saoud told you to say."

She blushed, and straightened her veil.

"He said that you were hopeless." She was looking at the space next to my ear again, words grating out of her like they were being pulled behind a square-wheeled cart. "He said that his father told him how it was with men and women, but he didn't think that anyone ever told you. He said that I would have to tell you what I felt. But the problem is that I'm not certain what I'm feeling either, so when I saw you—when I heard you telling the piskeys about the well cover—it was like I forgot how words worked."

"And so the kiss," I said.

"And so the kiss," she said. "It turns out that remembering stories doesn't make you good at that."

I laughed and realized that there were bees everywhere around us. They flew close but did not touch us.

"I thought you were flattering me," the Little Rose said. "When you told me that you never fancied another girl. I thought you said it to make me feel better. But you really never have."

"I haven't," I said. "Did you ever dream of the Maker King's son and hope that he was different from the stories you'd been told?"

"No," she said. Her face closed up, and she was solemn again. It was almost more than I could bear.

"Tell me about your dream, Zahrah," I said. I took her hand and led her to a place where there was soft heather and no bees, and we sat. "It can't possibly be more foolish than what we're doing now."

"I must marry," she began. "I know that much. And I suppose because I have always been trothplighted to the Maker King's son, I imagined having the freedom to choose on my own."

"That doesn't seem unreasonable," I said.

"Yashaa, it is the most unreasonable," she said gently. "I lived in a tower. I barely knew the maids who brought my meals to me, though I could sometimes overhear their gossip. I could see the guards or riders coming over the hills, but I knew nothing of them."

"When I came through your window, what did you

260

think of me?" I asked, though the possible answers made me fearful.

"I thought you had come to murder me, of course," she said. "That's why they had to put me in the tower in the first place. To keep me safe from others, and safe from myself. Except you hadn't," she said. I noticed that she was sitting in such a way that there was no possibility I might accidentally touch her. "You wanted information. You wanted to know the story, too, and I thought that if I played the pretty princess for you, you would take me with you."

"I knew you manipulated me," I told her. "I didn't care."

"That doesn't make me feel better about it," she said. "That might actually make me feel worse. Every time you said anything, I thought we were growing closer."

"We were," I said. Because we had been. "I'm sorry."

"It is for the better, I think," she said. "It was a silly girl's dream."

"To imagine a land you could rule safely, with someone whose reputation you trusted beside you?" I said. "That doesn't seem silly to me. It seems like what your parents have, for the most part."

"Yashaa," she said, "you're still doing it."

"Doing what?" I asked.

"'Someone whose reputation you trusted'?" she repeated. "If you were any more courtly, I think you'd split down the middle."

261

"I am nothing of the sort," I protested. "I grew up in the dirt, princess. I don't know anything about how to live at court, not anymore. I never learned how to run the spinning room. I never even wanted to. Then I met you, and I saw what service was supposed to be."

"I don't want service, Yashaa," she said. "Not from you."

I knew what she meant. I knew what she was trying to tell me. But I couldn't keep my disappointment from my face when she said the words. I had been directionless for too long and had only just made peace with my circumstances. I needed time to readjust. I watched her face fall.

"I'm sorry, Yashaa," she said. "I shouldn't have done any of this."

She moved to stand up, and I grabbed for her hand and missed it. I caught her veil instead and pulled it off her head. I let go and she scrambled to fix it, covering the mess I had made of cutting off her hair.

"Wait," I said. "Zahrah, please."

She stilled.

"I will try," I told her. "I will try to understand. I will think about what I say before I say it, and make sure that I say what I mean."

"You have always said what you meant, Yashaa," she told me. "I only misunderstood you."

"But I know that now," I said. A thousand things that she had said and done in the past few days suddenly burned in my memory, lit by new light. "I know it. Please, let me try."

"Yashaa," she said. "I don't want you to do this because you think it is your duty."

"You told me you don't want my service, even though I thought that was all I had to offer you," I told her. "Let me do that anyway, and if something else grows beside it, so much the better."

She breathed a great sigh, and I saw Zahrah for the first time. The Little Rose wasn't gone, but she was centered in new ground, and it was a ground I could see clearly and understand. It was the start of something new, but something that would be the better for what had come before. It was something that would be strong, even if we stumbled through the beginning of it.

"Do you want me to kiss you again?" I asked. My heart raced at the thought of it, though I couldn't have given good words as to the reason why. "I think it's the only way we're going to get better at it."

She turned her face toward mine, and I learned that kissing is much easier when you are closer in height, and when you have the advantage of warning, and when neither of you is knocking the other off their feet. It was still very strange, but it was no stranger than climbing down a tower with a princess above you, and no stranger than searching the wide world for one specific piskey. This time when we parted, I felt the loss of her closeness and a surge of the want for it. That was something even I could recognize from stories.

"That was better," she said, laughter in her eyes.

"Indeed," I said, nearly breathless.

In the face of my attempt at solemnity, she cracked, and her laughter joined the buzzing of the bees in the air around us. I could have watched her forever, but I was trying to remember that she wanted me to do more than watch.

"Come on," I said, and pulled her to her feet. "I didn't even ask if you caught anything."

"Rabbits," she said. "Three of them."

"Saoud will have them all dressed and half cooked by the time we get back," I told her. "And we'll be stuck with the washing up."

"I think it was worth it," she said. She looked down at the well cover. "You did good work. I didn't realize it could be made so quickly."

"It won't last forever," I told her. "But it will last long enough. And it is a good gift for the piskeys here."

"Do you think they will give us something?" she asked.

"I am nearly certain they have heard every word we've spoken since we got here," I told her. "In which case, they know about the piskey we seek. Maybe they have a way of communicating."

"That would be wonderful," she said. She looked around and raised her voice. "And very much appreciated."

There were four stones on the well cover, one holding down each corner. I had picked them because they had flat tops, and because they were broader than they were deep; I hoped that this would make them the best at securing the screen. On the top of one of them, next to the bucket I had filled, was a large green leaf laid out like a table linen. On top of that, there was a honeycomb.

"Everything is appreciated," I said, stooping to pick it up. It was awkward to carry, because I also had the bucket, but I managed.

Zahrah had not let go of my hand.

TWENTY-SEVEN

THE LOOK THAT SAOUD GAVE ME when we reached the campfire spoke volumes. I watched as he struggled to appear annoyed with us, before giving up and all but collapsing under the weight of his laughter. Tariq and Arwa stared at him, but Zahrah laughed too, and I couldn't help but smile.

"You are no help at all," I told him, and he laughed even harder.

Zahrah had to explain the joke to the others, because I couldn't, and when she was done, Tariq only raised his eyebrows at me, while Arwa sighed and said that she had known all along.

"Well, at least *somebody* knew," Saoud managed to croak, regaining some measure of control over himself.

"Be nice to him, Saoud," Zahrah said. "He has a honeycomb from the bees."

I cut it into pieces and passed them out while we waited for the rabbits to finish roasting. They were not particularly well fed, I noticed, but they were a welcome change, and the honeycomb was even more welcome. It was a meager feast, but I was happy for it, and happy for other things besides.

Arwa went to get more water from the well, and Zahrah went with her. Tariq made himself busy at, as far as I could tell, nothing. Saoud stared into the fire, and for the first time in as long as I could remember, I couldn't read his face.

"Thank you," I said. "For figuring everything out and fixing it for me. I don't think I ever would have."

"You would have," he said. "Someday. But it would have been too late."

"Your confidence is stirring," I told him. Then I sighed. "I wonder how many things my mother tried to tell me and I didn't hear them, because I turned her words to my own understanding of them."

"I don't think it matters," Saoud said. "You had other teachers, and you're not closed-minded. You still learn, and you're willing to learn from anyone. If Arwa had been the one to hit you over the head with this, you would have listened to her."

"Arwa is very clever," I reminded him. "And she knows all sorts of things that I don't. I would be foolish not to listen to her."

"Arwa is barely twelve," Saoud said. "Do you think that there are many who would take her seriously?"

I counted the days in my head and realized that we had missed Arwa's birthday. She hadn't said anything. I couldn't even count the honeycomb as a gift for her, because I had given it to everyone.

"And now you're upset that you missed her birthday," Saoud said. "Which we all did."

"I remembered," Tariq said. "But too late."

"That's not my point, Yashaa," Saoud said. "My father worried about us, all of us, because we lived in that camp and never left it. We learned about Kharuf and we tried to learn about Qamih, but we never went out and tried to do anything. My father left me behind because it was safe, and because he needed to travel more quickly than I could go when I was a child. When I grew older, he left me behind because of you, all three of you. But he hoped that we wouldn't stagnate at the crossroads."

"We weren't sick, like our parents were," Tariq said. "But we would have stayed at least until Yashaa's mother died."

"And look at the mess I've made," I said.

"It's a good mess, I think," Saoud said. "It's a mess that might lead somewhere good, somewhere better. We're willing to chance it with you."

"Still?" Now it was my turn to stare at the fire.

"Of course, idiot," Saoud said. "Do you think a person can only be one thing?"

"My mother is," I told him. "She loved my father, and he loved her, but they had their tasks, and they did them."

"You are luckier than she was, then," Tariq said. "Your task and heart are in the same place."

"And you share your heart," Saoud said. "You always have. You can share it now."

I looked away from the fire. My eyes were dazzled by the light, but they cleared soon enough, and I saw the truth in Saoud's face. We were brothers still. Tariq passed me a knife and the smallest cooking pot, and I set to stripping the rabbit bones so we could boil them for broth.

"What did she say to you, anyway?" Saoud asked. "To get your attention?"

I smiled at him in a manner I hoped was truly infuriating. "She didn't say anything at all."

Saoud groaned and then laughed again, and then Arwa and Zahrah came back and we turned to more serious discussion.

In the morning, while the rabbit stock was warming, Saoud went to bury the skins. I took my staff and Arwa's, and led Zahrah through the practice patterns again. She remembered them perfectly, and I only needed to make minor adjustments to her form. I found it was difficult to pay attention to what Zahrah was doing when she was trying to hit me, so I gave her Tariq's staff, which was heavier, and called Arwa over to take my place.

The girls faced one another and then began the easiest of the staff patterns they knew. I watched them circle, and for a moment I saw them as they might be one day—not moving through the patterns of a staff exercise, but the patterns of a dance. They would wear long dresses, like the ones my mother and Tariq's father used to make, instead of the tunics they had now. Their skirts would swirl around them like the lightest spindle whorls, and instead of drawing wool into yarn, they would draw the eyes of everyone in the room.

Everyone. Like the king and queen of Kharuf. Like the Maker King's son, or whoever replaced him if that betrothal was broken along with the curse.

"Yashaa?" Zahrah held up a hand to call a halt, and looked at me with worry on her face. "You look so sad."

"I was dreaming," I told her. "It was a foolish dream."

"I thought we had agreed to dream of foolish things," she said.

"We did," I said. "Perhaps this one was too real, too close to what might come to pass someday."

"What did you see?" Arwa said. I looked at her. Saoud had said I listened well. Maybe it was time to talk.

"I saw you and Zahrah, dancing in the Great Hall in

the king's castle in Kharuf," I told her. "I don't remember it perfectly, the hall, but I remember the light, and the way sound echoes through it, getting quieter but never fading entirely. It's a good place for dancing. Proper dancing, not the staff patterns you're practicing."

"That's not sad," Arwa said. "That's wonderful. Were you dancing with us?"

When she spoke, I saw understanding bloom in Zahrah's eyes. She knew that I had seen the princess again, that I still could not see myself beside her, only behind her.

"He will need to practice," Zahrah said. "But so will I! Imagine if my parents threw a ball, and the only dances we knew were staff patterns? We will all learn together."

"Or we can learn desert dances," Arwa said. "If we have to stay there instead."

"Someday," said Zahrah, "I will learn whatever I want, and I won't be afraid of it."

"You should eat breakfast first, then," Saoud called. He had returned and Tariq was ladling out the bowls.

We ate and then struck the tents. We were nearly out of ways to put off leaving when I realized the buzz of the bees had been slowly increasing. It was an odd sound, that buzzing. Even though we had only been in the ruined village for a short time, I still had learned to ignore the sound. It was almost like I only heard it when the bees wanted my attention. Or perhaps when something else did.

"Wait," I said. "Saoud, we have to wait a few more minutes."

He nodded, clearly able to hear it himself, and we all sat down in the grass. There had been no dancing in the sky last night, nor any sign that the piskeys had heard what I'd said when I'd laid down the well cover beyond a feeling that they had. Now, in the daylight, we wouldn't be able to see the golden light of their wings so clearly, but perhaps we might see something else.

"There!" said Tariq, his voice reverent, and I saw.

There were four of them, flying in a stately way that looked like a royal procession. I knew that if they wanted to, they could flit through the air so quickly we wouldn't be able to count them. They wanted us to see them—to know that they were approaching. Arwa took off her veil and spread it out on the grass before Zahrah's feet. The piskeys alighted on it, though they did not sit. Instead they leaned on the golden staves they carried, like tiny shepherds—or bee-herds, I supposed.

"Good morning," said Zahrah. No, it was the Little Rose who spoke to them now. Regal bearing shone in every inch of her. "Thank you for the honeycomb. Our travel fare is rough, and can be tedious after many days on the road."

"You are quite welcome," said the piskey who stood the closest to her. "We are likewise grateful for your repair of the well cover. It will be easier for us to manage than the stone one was."

"You have Yashaa to thank for that," the Little Rose said. "And Arwa and Tariq. They are wonderful crafters."

"And you are not, princess?" said the piskey.

"I cannot," she told them. "If I do, my mind becomes a stronger place for the demon who wants to steal it for its own use."

"You could spin," said the piskey. "That would end it for you."

"It would end it for me," said the Little Rose. "But my curse would go on, and my people would suffer."

"The trouble with magic," said the piskey, "is that even those creatures who make it are bound by it, and the binding becomes so muddled by life and living that it is difficult to unravel."

"We have noticed as much," I said. I was surprised that I had the courage to speak at all.

"What happens when you make things, child?" the piskey said.

"I haven't made very many," the Little Rose admitted, and she was Zahrah again: unsure and vulnerable, but no less determined. "It hurts to hold back. I want to learn and make and do, but I have not let myself, and others have helped by not letting me either."

"But you have slipped up," said the piskey shrewdly.

"You have fallen through the cracks of your own prison."

"Yes," said Zahrah. "I helped fix a fence."

She looked at me, and then back at the piskeys.

"It hurt even more," she said. "My head ached for hours, so much that I could barely think straight."

This was not the time for it, but later I was going to have words with her about this. I had known she was in some pain, but not that much. I never would have let her risk the staff patterns.

"But there was an exultation afterwards," she said, and I saw the mirror of it in her face. "It felt like a part of me was finally completed. But it didn't bring me closer to breaking the curse. We need you to tell us how."

The piskeys looked at one another, and then their leader sighed.

"The thread tangled as soon as my gift to you was spun into it," it said. We all straightened. This was the very piskey we sought. "I saw it, and I did not know how to set it right. We have spent these years trying to untangle the knot ourselves, but all we have for you are guesses and suggestions, not answers."

"We will accept those," Zahrah said. "And I, at least, will accept them gladly."

"I will too," Tariq said. "I am not afraid to do some of the thinking for myself and to try to put the pieces together for my princess."

The smallest piskey fluttered around his head, showering his dark hair with gold dust.

"The demon is coming, child," the leader of the piskeys said to Zahrah, and it was as though our fate was sealed with its words. "But there is hope. You must be completed or you will never have the chance to know peace. Never rule. Never see your kingdom safe."

"How can I?" she asked.

"You must learn," it said. "You must make, and you must do. I'm not sure which of them will plague you more, and I am sorry, for you will suffer the cost of it. It is the faerie's curse. But remember my gift, too. You may find the right time to use it, once your own mind has begun to open up."

There was pain in the piskey's face. Regret and longing to make something right, where it could offer no help. It had already tried, as it had told us, the day the Little Rose turned five, and the knot had only tied itself all the tighter.

The Little Rose bowed to the piskey, and then the four creatures took wing, leaving a golden trail of dust on Arwa's veil.

TWENTY-EIGHT

WE DIDN'T SPEAK VERY MUCH that day. I could have said it was because we were making up for our late start, but we all knew the truth. The piskey had all but said that the only way to break the curse was to play right into the demon's hands. Yet we still marched away from our pursuers, away from the castle where Zahrah, at least, would have been home with her parents while the horrors swooped down on her. I supposed that couldn't be much in the way of comfort.

When we finally stopped, it was two hours before dark. We set up the tents and lit a small fire, once Tariq had dug a pit for it. I noticed that the heather here was scrubbier, and flowers were few and far between. We must have been getting closer to the desert, though I could hardly see the point of reaching it now.

"I will go back," said Zahrah, as though she had read my thoughts. "They will put me back in the tower, and I will go insane there, but I will do it."

She looked straight at me for the last part, and I knew that while she would miss the others, she would miss me the most. It wasn't a particularly happy realization.

"You still have to marry the Maker King's son," Saoud said. "That hasn't changed either."

She considered her options—home, with its myriad prisons, or the dangerous freedom that was life with us—and then something hardened in her.

"If the demon is going to have me," Zahrah said, "I want to be *me* first, all of me. As I was meant to."

She looked at all of us, the children who had grown up on stories of her, and who had come to love her when the stories were made into a real person who could stand before us. Even Arwa was fearless, or perhaps she was the most fearless of us all, for I couldn't deny that I felt cold doubt in my bones, though I wouldn't give in to it.

"Help me," she said.

It wasn't the princess who ordered. It wasn't the Little Rose who manipulated. It was Zahrah, and she was asking. Anything I might have said stuck in my throat.

"The first thing you made wasn't a fence, Zahrah,"

Tariq said, coming to our rescue. "It was your ties to us. It was our friendship and our loyalty. Of course we will help you."

"Usually we start with spinning," I said. "But we can't do that."

"I spun as a child," Zahrah reminded us. "And I sewed once, too. I made the cloth bags my mother used to wrap the gifts she gave to the creatures who came to my birthday."

"I remember," I said. "I was appalled that such messy stitches made it past my mother's watchful gaze. I was never allowed to do such work."

She stuck her tongue out at me. She was much more fun now that she was a girl and not a rose.

"Here," said Arwa, passing over her sewing kit. "There's got to be something that needs hemming."

In the end, we settled for hemming the last of Saoud's spare tunics for Tariq, who had grown again.

"We had to replace his shoes, too," Saoud said, while we watched Arwa show Zahrah how to set the pins, and Tariq stood there as a clotheshorse. "I did it when we got Zahrah's. Do you remember growing that much so quickly?"

"We must have," I said. "I only remember that it hurt."

"I trip a lot," Tariq said. "And sometimes when I'm sewing, my fingers forget what they're doing. But eventually I'll be back to normal."

The girls finished the hem, and Tariq changed back into his old shirt. Later, I was sure, he would take it apart to use for something else. It was fraying a little bit, but there was a lot of usable fabric.

"Your turn, Yashaa," Arwa said.

I went to sit with them and began the task of helping Zahrah remember how to work the awl and needle. Tariq was the best at it, but he moved so quickly it was sometimes difficult to follow his movements, and he wasn't very good at slowing down. He watched us for a moment before turning his attention to Saoud.

"Rabbits?" he asked.

"If we're lucky," Saoud replied. "Come on, before they pin you to the ground."

I missed hunting, to be honest. I didn't have Saoud's gift for it, but I was competent enough, and I could make better snares than he could. We had been a good team. This was the part of my spirit that had never taken to spinning and craft, despite my mother's hopes. The part of me that liked to move more than just my hands, and was not content to sit in a room with thread and wool and the easy rhythm of work to fill my time.

If I wasn't a spinner for Zahrah, I didn't know how I would spend my time. There would be others to hunt and guard, and she would have better people to give her lessons. She needed to learn things I didn't know how to do, for a start. Plus, there was the ruling of her kingdom to think of. I couldn't help her with that.

Or perhaps I could. Saoud said that I listened, even to people like Arwa who often went unheeded. Perhaps that would be my task. I could work, and I could listen, and I could help the Little Rose, if I was married to her.

I stuck the needle into my thumb and cried out.

"Yashaa!" said Arwa.

"I'm sorry," I said, and turned away because I didn't want to bleed on the tunic. I scrambled for an excuse. "It's been a while since I did this."

Married! To Zahrah! The thought was both laughable and desperately appealing. Of course that was how the story ended. We break the curse and both of us are heroes, and then we wed. The thought was so ridiculous I could barely think it, and it was so necessary that I wanted it with all my heart. I looked at her as furtively as I could. She was sewing slowly, with Arwa guiding her. Her brow must have been furrowed in concentration, because her veil was slipping forward.

She had thought of this before I had, I knew it. She had thought of it from the start. Once she had seen a grand and gallant tale, but now she saw a quiet, oddly feasible future. It was still a dream, but it was closer than it had been when we were in the mountain valley, and closer than it had been when I crawled through the window of her tower.

If we did this, if we were successful, we would marry. We wouldn't have the abandoned love of my mother and father. We wouldn't have the arrangement-made-good of her own parents. We would have ourselves, and we would make something of that, too.

"Yashaa, has it stopped?" Arwa said.

I made a show of examining my hand and wiping my thumb in the grass.

"More or less," I told her. "I'm safe to return to work."

"Is the work safe for you?" Zahrah asked.

"I can only hope," I told her. "Because otherwise it's going to take so long to hem this tunic that Tariq will have outgrown it before he even tries it on again."

It was like a great weight had been lifted from me, knowing the full end of my own dream. It would be different work than I had learned, and different than what my mother had planned, but it would still be good. And if we didn't break the curse, well, then we were all going to need new dreams anyway.

I looked at the stitches that Zahrah had done. They were even, at least, though they were larger than anything we might have done. I watched her sew two handspans' worth of stitches, and then I called a halt.

"I can keep going," she said. "I'm getting faster, I think."

"I want to see the headache you get before we turn you loose on our alterations," I said. "You told me it was nothing in the mountains, and I knew you were lying, but you concealed more than I thought."

"The phoenix's gift lets me recover," she admitted ruefully. "It does not precisely ease my recovery. I thought it would get easier, but so far it hasn't. I do feel better eventually, but every time it's like I am adding on more weight."

"It's like that when you practice anything, at first," I told her. "Eventually, you'll have all the weight you need, and then you'll get better at bearing it."

"I hope so," she said.

Arwa and I continued to sew, and while we worked we told Zahrah the craft knowledge that our mothers had told us when we were small. We told her about the different kinds of sheep, and the ways to herd and shear them. We told her which plants could be used in place of wool, though they were not commonly found in Kharuf. We told her which trees make the best needles and spindles, and how to find the best pieces of finished wood if you were setting the frame for a loom.

I don't know if she remembered any of it from when she was small, but it was wonderful to talk to her like that. She asked good questions and didn't fidget, the way we had when we had been forced to sit still. Perhaps it was because she wasn't a child. We talked until the hem was nearly done and we were sewing mostly by firelight.

"Saoud and Tariq should be back soon," I said. "Even

if they haven't caught anything, it will soon be too dark to continue."

"I'll start boiling water, in any case." Zahrah stood up to get the pot, but made it no further than her feet before she collapsed back onto the ground.

"Zahrah!" said Arwa, dropping the tunic and crawling to her side. "Yashaa, help me."

But there was nothing I could do. It was the headache, the same as she'd had in the mountains, and this time it was worse. Her eyes ran with tears if she so much as looked at the fire, and I imagined she felt the light of it in her skull the way I had felt the needle in my thumb, only multiplied a hundredfold. I sent Arwa to soak a veil in cool water and pulled Zahrah into my arms.

"You were right," she said, grimacing through the words. "Yashaa, it feels like my head will explode."

"It won't," I told her.

"It's magic," she said. "How can you know?"

"The demon needs your head, Zahrah," I said. "That means it won't explode."

It was cold comfort at best, and I knew it, but it was the truth. I held her until Arwa came back, and then we helped her to sit up so we could wrap the cool cloth around her head. She vomited twice, and again when Saoud and Tariq came back with a rabbit and she smelled the blood. She didn't even try to eat, so I put her to bed.

"Stay," she said. "Please."

Arwa could sleep in the tent with Tariq. Zahrah's reputation was already ruined. It could do no harm.

"All right," I said, and I held her until she finally fell asleep.

TWENTY-NINE

OUR TENTS WERE ALL THE SAME, so I was awake for a few moments before I remembered where I was. I had slept fitfully at first, worried that Zahrah would vomit again, but once she was asleep she didn't stir at all, and eventually I had drifted off and stayed asleep. Saoud had not come to wake me for a watch, probably thinking he would wake Zahrah if he did so. I hoped that when she did wake up, her headache would be gone.

The ground was hard underneath the tent, and we had reached the season when damp rose through the dropcloth, making the mornings cold. Usually I slept wrapped in my bedroll and was warm enough, but this morning, with the press of Zahrah's body against mine, it was actually almost comfortable. Or at least it was until I shifted, and realized that the ground was not the only thing that was hard.

It wasn't an alien feeling, of course, but usually I was alone when it happened, and I could push it out of my mind. With Zahrah so close, all I could think of was getting out of the tent before she woke up and noticed. I moved as carefully as I could and exited the tent with all possible speed, though I did make sure that she was still tucked underneath the blanket.

It was barely dawn. The sky was grey except for the east, where pinks and oranges were beginning to bleed over the mountaintops. The heather blossoms were still closed, though I knew they would soon unfurl, and everything was quiet. Saoud sat near the fire pit, feeding kindling into the small flames, and he looked up when he heard me approach.

"Here," he said, passing me a piece of the rabbit he'd caught yesterday. I had missed supper, so I tore into it. "How is she?"

He did his best not to sound anxious, but I knew he wanted to be on the move again as soon as we possibly could.

"She slept all night," I told him. "And she didn't vomit any more. She might be all right to walk today if she drinks enough water, but we have to be careful."

"She'll keep going, even if it hurts," Saoud said, and nodded. We both would have done the same, of course, but eventually our bodies would have given out. I didn't know if Zahrah's would, and I was not in a hurry to learn.

I finished the rabbit and shifted my weight uncomfortably. Saoud looked at me, and I could tell he was trying not to laugh. He knew perfectly well what had happened, and I was torn between wanting to hit him and wanting him to explain what on earth his father had told him about these matters. He decided for me.

"Shall we spar?" he asked.

"Yes," I said, and saw that the staves were already beside him.

He did laugh at my discomfiture then, but I forgave him because he let me skip the pattern warm-ups and go straight to actual fighting. It was messier than usual, and I struggled to concentrate, but as we lunged at one another I felt myself relax into it. By the time Tariq and Arwa came out to the fire, I had recovered my form enough to dump Saoud on the ground. He was still laughing at me, but I decided to take the win.

He got up and we began again. This time my movements were more precise, approaching the measured rhythms I had practiced. I was able to read his intentions, and I took fewer hits. When I knocked him down for a second time, I felt that this round I had earned it. I pulled Saoud to his feet, and we ceded the ground to Tariq and Arwa so that they could have their turn.

"Better?" he said, as we returned to the fire to check on breakfast.

"Yes," I said. I paused, considering my words, but decided to plow through them. "I think she wants to marry me, if things go aright."

"Yes, Yashaa," Saoud said. "That is exactly what she wants."

He did me the favor of not speaking the words like he was talking to a small child, but I knew that he might as well have.

"I didn't prepare for that," I told him. "I didn't expect it."

"She knows that, Yashaa," he said. They had covered a lot of ground while they were hunting, apparently, including much of my future. "And she knows that you'd marry her out of duty, even though that's not why you'll actually do it."

"If this works out, I hope we find your father," I told him. "I mean, I hope we find him anyway, but I need to ask him some questions."

It was just as well Saoud was already sitting down, because he laughed so hard that I thought he might stop breathing. I ignored him and turned my attention to the pot of vetch that was now threatening to boil over on the cooking fire. I saw Zahrah come out of the tent, and smiled at her in what I hoped was not too foolish a manner. She came over and sat down beside me—close, but not as close as I might have hoped.

"Good morning," she said, her voice quiet. Saoud pretended he couldn't hear her. "Thank you for watching over me last night."

"Of course," I said. "Are you feeling better?"

"I'm hungry," she said. "Yes, I do feel better. I thought I would feel weak and useless this morning, but I don't. I'm stronger, and I'm not sure that's a good thing."

"Is it the phoenix's gift?" I asked. Saoud coughed, and we both looked at him.

"I think it might be that you slept for so long," he said. "We haven't had a restful time of it lately, and you've been keeping watch too. It's possible that you just needed sleep."

"Whatever the case, I am ready to keep going," she said. "Both the trek and the sewing."

"I'm glad to hear it," I said.

She went to take a turn against Arwa, and I saw that she hadn't exaggerated how much better she was feeling. Last night she had hardly been able to stand, and now she could circle Arwa and hold her staff steady as she moved. If she was always able to sleep off the effects of her evening's work like that, then we might not need to slow our pace much at all.

By the time we had eaten and struck the tents, the sun was clear of the mountains. We walked carefully today, wary that we would soon come to the border of Kharuf. We were not sure how it was guarded, or if it was marked. Kharuf ran into the desert, which was technically beyond the rule of Qasim and Rasima, but it wasn't claimed by the desert kings either, at least not in any material way this far north of the Silk Road. We weren't sure if the curse would follow us into the desert or not. We would have to wait and see.

The heather grew sparse and yellowed around us, and was replaced by short plants with spiky leaves we didn't recognize. We came to a dry wadi bed when the sun had more than halfway completed its descent from the sky. Here at least there was the smell of oleander, which I knew. We followed the wadi until we found a pool of clear water, and decided to stay there until we knew which way to go next. The map Saoud had from his father went no further than the border, such as it was, and we couldn't go into the desert until we knew which way to find water.

The pool was sheltered from view, but Saoud took no risks by camping close to it. Instead, we went several hundred steps down the wadi until he found a cave hollowed out by floodwaters where we could be concealed. He checked the cave carefully, looking for traces of snakes or burials, and found none. This was good news in that it meant we could stay there, but discouraging all the same: if no one had ever lived here long enough to bury their dead, there was little chance we would be able to stay long ourselves.

There was nothing to burn, which was just as well. Fire in the desert was visible for a long way at night, and it was not the season for random brush fires. We had dry rations enough, though they were uninteresting, and even if it was a long walk to water we would not go thirsty. Still, I could not escape the feeling that we were exposed here, more exposed than we had been thus far, and it made me uncomfortable.

I set the thought aside when Zahrah took up Arwa's needle again and began to sew. This time I was free to watch her work without worrying about instructing her. As I had seen when she repaired the fence, there was a calmness to her when she crafted. It was as though all of the pieces of her, carded and rolled when she was five, were finally being pulled from the distaff and spun into something useful and good. I tried not to think about who it was useful and good for, of course, because that is where the demon lurked. Instead I saw the girl my mother had loved, and the one in whom we had put all of our hopes. And she was beautiful.

Zahrah stitched three handspans' worth and then set the work aside to wait. We tried not to make it too obvious that we were waiting, too. This time we were better prepared. She had eaten lightly before she began, the better to avoid last night's terrible dry heaving, and I knew that she had made sure to drink water steadily all day. Her bed was ready, behind the screen she and Arwa had hung up when we were organizing the cave, and she had taken the precaution of setting the cooking pot nearby, just in case she could not make it to the mouth of the cave.

"Do you want to go outside?" I asked. "I can carry you back in, if need be."

"Thank you, Yashaa," she said, and took the hand I offered to pull her to her feet. She didn't let it go when she was standing.

We walked along the wadi bed until we found a slope I deemed gentle enough to carry her back down if I had to. We climbed out and looked over the desert. The sunset here lit the sand with brilliant colors. It was as though we looked at all the beauty in the world, and yet I knew the world went on from where we were. In the direction of the sunset was Kharuf and Qamih, home and hunter, and the desert king ruled somewhere beyond our sight to the east and south, and some of the spinners from Kharuf were at his court.

The sky darkened, and Zahrah did not wilt. We waited, and the air cooled. The stars came out above us, shining as brightly and steadily as they ever had, and she was still beside me, her hand in mine, her breath a calm wave in the center of a brewing storm.

"Yashaa, we should go back," she said when the night was fully dark. "The others will worry, and my head is starting to ache, though it is less tonight than it was yesterday."

"All right," I said. She kissed my cheek, and we stood. And froze.

We saw campfires, more than ten, spaced out like sentinels in the night. This was not a caravan, with its large central fire. This was not a lone shepherd keeping warm against the dark of night. This was the Maker King's son, and the others who rode with him, and we were finally caught.

THIRTY

WE COULDN'T RUN. EVEN IF we knew the way to another source of water, we were traveling on foot. They would surely have horses, and a better idea of the land. We would only be able to go as far as our water skins could take us.

"This is not the cave I might have chosen for hiding," Saoud said. "It's not deep enough, and if we seal up the entrance, it will be obvious that the stones didn't fall there naturally."

"What if we made it look like a tomb?" Tariq suggested.

"It's too risky," I said. "It will be clear that the construction is new. And the Maker King's son probably doesn't care about the desert gods or the desert dead. He might take a look inside, just because he can."

"So what do we do?" Arwa asked.

"I could go to him," Zahrah suggested. I could tell her head was pounding, but she hadn't vomited again, and her voice was steady.

"No!" That came from all of us at once, and was louder than we intended it. We all hushed ourselves immediately.

"No, Zahrah," said Saoud. "We have not come this far to let you go alone now."

"We'll get as much water as we can," I said, "and go to the back of the cave. We'll be as quiet as possible and hope for the best."

"That is a terrible plan," Saoud said. He smiled in spite of the seriousness of the moment. "But your terrible plans have done well by us this far."

"This is the worst of them, I think," I said. "We will be at the mercy of whoever searches this part of the wadi."

"Do you think they are really searching, or merely tracking?" Tariq asked.

"They are camped in such a way that I think they are truly searching," I said. "They must have a general idea of where we are."

"We haven't been able to make good time," Saoud said, though he did Zahrah the courtesy of not looking at her when he said it. "We haven't laid false trails, or done much to obscure the real one."

"That's true." I said. "And now we must make the best of it. Tariq, get everything that can hold water and put it near the front of the cave. Save a pot with a good lid."

"I don't think I'll throw up," said Zahrah. She sounded almost sure of it, rather than merely determined to hold it together.

"It's not for that, Zahrah," I said. "We won't be able to leave the cave tomorrow for anything, and we might have to stay under cover for more than a day."

"Oh," she said, and understanding dawned. It was going to be an uncomfortable time.

Tariq got the vessels and selected the one to use as a privy. Arwa took it to the back of the cave and did her best to set it up so that it would be both useful and discreet. The rest of us fetched water, using the night to cover our walks back and forth to the pool. The wadi bed was rocky, not sandy, which was a mercy: we would not leave tracks. On the third trip, Saoud found a shallower cave, closer to the pool. He dug a fire pit there, though he did not light a fire, and then buried it again. Without ashes, it would not bear up under close scrutiny, but he also took the time to strew the ground with footprints, and impressions where five people might have sat around the fire. Finally, he left his whetstone and two of Tariq's empty thread spools.

"You can come back for it," I told him. "They probably won't take it."

The whetstone had been a gift from his father.

"It's all right," he said. "After all, you all left your spindles behind."

At last, we had collected all the water we could, and we withdrew to the cave to wait for sunrise. The others slept, but Saoud and I were watchful, even though there was nothing to watch but the mouth of our hiding spot, and jumped at every noise. As the sky grew lighter, we heard the wadi toads begin to croak, and we knew that the prince's men would soon be striking their own camp and taking up their hunt again. Zahrah stirred beside me but did not wake, and I put my arm around her shoulder. It was colder now, and I didn't want her to wake up because she was chilled. Sleep was the only real defense against the terrible wait that would be our day.

She sighed but didn't wake, and I rested my chin on the top of her head.

"Sleep if you can, Yashaa," Saoud said, so quietly I could scarcely hear him over the chorus of toads outside. "I will watch for a bit."

I thought I would be unable to drift off, but found instead that I was almost unspeakably weary. Zahrah was a comforting weight beside me, and I fell asleep between one worry and the next.

It was fully daylight when I woke, though I could not have said how much time had passed. Arwa and Tariq were both awake, and when I moved I knew that Zahrah was awake too, and had only been staying still to spare my rest. Saoud was nodding off, Tariq having taken over the watch, and once he saw that I was conscious, he let himself go.

My neck was stiff, but I couldn't stretch it properly. I knew that my legs would probably cramp up soon enough. It didn't really matter. If we were caught, it wasn't as though we could run. I rolled my shoulders as best as I could, feeling every knot and every place where the cave wall dug into my back. Arwa was leaning over to whisper something to Zahrah, but the words were so quiet I couldn't hear them. Whatever Arwa said, Zahrah nodded and turned a little more toward the younger girl. I pulled my arm back from where it had rested on her shoulder and ignored the creak my elbow made when I bent it after so many hours in the same position.

Arwa removed her veil and shook out her hair. She hadn't been able to wash her hair in days, but it was protected from the dust of the road, so it was probably cleaner than mine. I had forgotten how long it was, because she had always been so careful to tie it up. It fell nearly to her waist, and I thought she might have been able to sit on it, had she tilted her head back a little bit. She unbraided it slowly, showing Zahrah how it went, even though the movements were reversed, and then slowly braided a smaller portion of it, so that Zahrah could see.

I remembered what Zahrah had said the day I cut her hair—that if it grew too long, she would braid it. Braiding was making. You could turn braided cloth into a rug with a bit of sewing, and braided threads could be stitched onto a hem for decoration. Zahrah couldn't braid her own hair, and wouldn't be able to for some time thanks to the latest trim, but she could braid Arwa's.

Her first attempt was clumsy, the plaits wide and gaping, and one of her strands was much shorter than the other two, which resulted in a larger tail than was generally considered fashionable. I laughed quietly as she began again, this time taking care to separate the strands so that they were all of even length. The second attempt was more tightly woven, and I tapped her on the shoulder to let her know that I thought she had done well.

"You're not helping, Yashaa," she breathed, so quietly that I had to lean forward to hear her.

"You're doing fine," I whispered back, close to her ear. Her own veil was still anchored on her head, so I couldn't see her face. I wished I could. I had learned that I liked to watch her work.

She made six more small braids in Arwa's hair before she stopped. Each one was neater than the one that had come before it. When she was done the sixth, she carefully unwove all of them. Arwa's hair, used to braiding, held its shape even without a tie, so all but the loosest of Zahrah's attempts had stayed in.

Arwa quickly rebraided her hair into a single plait and wrapped her veil around her head again. We had not spent much time on the exercise, but I could feel Zahrah relax against me, and I knew that she was feeling momentarily better for having done something, even if it was only busy-work. Arwa was more settled too, and Tariq, who had been spooling and unspooling his own store of thread, also looked calmer.

Saoud slept on, and we waited...and waited. As wretched as the waiting was, I knew that any action would be worse. It would mean we had been found, and I would endure all the monotony in the world if we could avoid that.

When Saoud woke, we decided it must be close enough to midday to eat something and drink a ration of the water we had hoarded. Though I wasn't hungry before I started eating, I found that as soon as my portion was gone, I was famished. I took another drink of water instead. We had enough food for two days in the cave and water for three days after that, and it would do me no good to want more of it now.

Zahrah was holding her head.

"Do you need more water?" I whispered as quietly as I could. Saoud looked on with concern.

"No," she said. "This time it's different. The headache from sewing was an ache that started in my back, and went to my neck and my teeth and the place behind my face. This is like a stabbing needle, right in both of my eyes. It's sharper. Like something is trying to catch me by surprise and open me up."

She spoke the words as they came to her, describing what she felt, but in the instant after she said them aloud, we both understood them. For the first time, I saw true fear in her eyes, and I knew that I probably looked the same way.

"Saoud," I whispered. "I think the demon queen rides with the Maker King's son."

We all carried iron knives and pins. The demon could not take them from us, but the prince's men could. Even Zahrah would be unprotected if they found us now. I was still scouring my brain for an idea when I heard something and froze. The others froze, too. I'm not even sure any of us breathed.

The croaking of the wadi toads had faded hours ago, and there had been little noise beside that ever since, but there was a sound now. It was the scrabbling step of feet on loose wadi stones, and it was coming closer.

Zahrah groped for my hand but dropped it as soon as she had caught it. I knew why. If we were found, she could not show fondness for any of us. They would use it against her, or they would use her against us. Instead we sat, trembling and waiting and hoping.

And then there was a shadow in front of the cave, and it swallowed up any hope we might have had left.

vii.

The key to a good plan is patience. Any idiot can cobble together an idea, taking pieces of knowledge and power and foresight and laying them out so that the order of them finds itself, but more than that is required for true excellence. I have watched countless schemes fall apart within sight of their end because the one who had charge of them lost patience. Men were out of place, the weather did not cooperate, tools or weapons failed, and without them, all was scuttled.

Even my own kind were not immune. I had seen my lesser kin go down from the mountains too early, before their power had rekindled. They tried to make bargains and manipulate humans, but they over-extended themselves and could not pay the price that magic always requires. I had paid it in small sums, stretched over decades of waiting, and as a result, I was strong.

I could tell that she was close. We followed the trail that the piskeys had made by accident, but before we went too far, I knew that she was before us. I could feel her—the part of her mind that I had ensured would always stay empty until I chose to fill it. It called to me, as I had known it would. The gaping space where I would make my beginning with her, before I reached out and took the rest of her by force. It was every bit the temptation I had feared it would be, but I was not afraid.

This was what my kinsman had felt, all those years ago in the desert. He had taken the king and used that power to get more, but he had still been tempted by the Storyteller Witch, and by the magic she had brought to their marriage bed. He had not been strong enough to kill her, to take from her if she would not give, and to leave her body in the sand like he had left hundreds before her. So he reached too far. He failed. And he took the rest of us with him when he fell. I would not make his mistakes.

The hunting parties rode out the morning we reached the first wadi bed, but the prince commanded that the camp be left standing. He knew that his prize was close, though he did not know what winning it would cost him. Magic is a tangled knot pulled tightly in each direction, and some of the threads are hidden by the others. The Maker King's son could not see the complexity before him. That suited my purposes too.

And so I waited one last time while the horses went out and men scoured the desert. I could have gone with them, could have found the Little Rose before they did, but they had earned this chase and catch. And I had earned the fear that the Little Rose would feel when she was finally caught. If I had raised her, she would have been perfect, but she would have been a pawn. Now she would be frightened and angry, and she would try to fight me. It would be all the better when I caught and crushed her, leaving her screaming in her own mind while I did horrors in her name, or sent her to her husband's bed.

The sun rose, and I took a form that men could see. I went to the prince's tent and demanded entrance. His remaining guards let me in without mustering any defense, even though they were plainly surprised by my appearance. Their master thought it a lark, I supposed, for a demon to surprise his own men. I felt my distaste for the lot of them surge, and was glad that soon enough I would grind them all back into the sand from whence they had come.

At last there were shouts from the wadi, and the prince was called to see what had been found. I could have gone then, to look at her, and see her face when she was trapped. But I had not come so far to waste this moment on a whim. She would see me for the second time in her life, and she would be on her knees before me. It would take time to arrange, time for the prince to secure her and bring her back to his camp, but it was time I did not fear to spend. I had waited this long, and I could wait a little bit more.

THIRTY-ONE

THEY TOOK ZAHRAH OUT FIRST, lightly pulling her with one man at each of her elbows. I felt Saoud move to restrain me if he had to, but I offered no resistance, since Zahrah didn't either. She could have made them drag her, but they seemed willing to treat her respectfully, and so she let them. That was the first thing I learned about our captors. The second thing I learned was that they were less certain what to do with the rest of us. They had clearly been expecting to rescue a kidnapped princess, and likely thought they would find her in the clutches of bandits or some such. To find us so young and vulnerable in a cave perplexed them, and so they hesitated.

Several long minutes passed, and we stayed sitting on the floor of the cave. We didn't move, and they did not come in to take away our things. I saw Arwa dig into her pack and shuffle something around. Without Zahrah between us, there was a space for her to move. I couldn't see what she was doing, and she was too far away to stop without drawing the attention she was clearly trying to avoid. It took her only a moment, and then she was sitting still again, waiting.

I turned back to the men at the cave mouth. They were soldiers in Qamih colors, and they carried short swords at their waists. They had the look of men who had traveled far—worn boots and the slight bowlegged stance that comes from sitting astride a horse for hours at a time—but they did not look overly weary. I knew their camp was close, but apparently they had not ridden hard to catch us. It was useless to lament the days we had wasted in Kharuf. We had stopped with purpose every time, and it was not as though going farther into the desert would have solved anything, but still I felt like we should have done more. We were all Zahrah had, and we had failed her.

I thought how, only a short time ago, I had dreamed that someday soon we would break the curse and Zahrah would be a princess in truth, instead of a dark secret that everyone pretended would live without worry for the rest of her days. I had dreamed that I might marry her and take up a place in her court, as my mother had planned, though it would not be the place she had thought I would have. It was so foolish now, and I realized that it had always been foolish. Dreaming had done me no good, as it did us no good now. There was only the reality of capture, and the uncertainties of what punishment we would endure at the hands of the Maker King's son. I hoped for Zahrah's sake, and for Arwa's, that the rumors of his character weren't true. And yet, he had chased us across the heathered slopes of Kharuf. We were probably not so fortunate.

There was a stir at the cave mouth, and a man's figure came into sight.

"Get them out of there," he said. "It's too stuffy in that cave for me to go in. Bring the villains out to face me, as they ought."

My first impression of Prince Maram was that he had not earned his reputation as a fighter. He was broad-shouldered, of course, and well-muscled enough, but the sword he carried was too delicate for real combat, and his hands had no sign of any of the calluses that would have been formed by extended use of weapons. He dressed very well in silks that were far too expensive for the conditions he wore them in. They would be ruined, certainly, by the day's end, but he seemed to have no care of that. It angered me, who had seen the suffering of those who starved to buy the most basic homespun wool, to see him have so little regard for his clothes.

The prince made a disgusted sound when he saw us, waving his hand before his face as though the air of the cave offended him. I'll admit that after several hours of sitting in close quarters there was a bit of an odor, but it was hardly as bad as he made it out to be. I wondered how he could bear the scent of his horse at all, or if he rode with some sort of scented handkerchief to protect his frail sensibilities.

They took Saoud out first, hauling him ungracefully to his feet and forcing him to his knees as soon as he was clear of the overhang. Then it was my turn, and then Tariq's. Arwa caused them some problems, because in the dim light of the cave they hadn't seen her veil or realized that she was a girl until they picked her up. The guard who set her beside me looked at her almost apologetically. Too late, I wondered if we should have tried to pass Arwa off as Zahrah's hand-maiden, but as soon as I thought about it I realized that between her clothes and her bearing, Arwa was clearly one of us. We were all blinking as our eyes adjusted to the light.

"My princess," Maram said, and I realized that Zahrah was standing just behind him.

There were still guards standing at each of her elbows, though they no longer supported her. She was straight-backed, and had covered her face with her veil, which she had never done in front of us before. I noticed that they had taken her shoes. He didn't know then, the Maker King's son, how far she could go in bare feet.

"Your captors, my love," he said to her, bowing slightly from the waist. "Now you can see that you have nothing further to fear from them."

Zahrah said nothing and did not so much as move her head, though her shoulders trembled a little bit. She had put the veil up as a defense, so that Maram could not read her face. I hoped he merely thought she was being modest in front of her fiancé and so many of his men. I couldn't see her either, but I knew she would be fuming. It was rage that shook her, not fear.

"What shall we do with them, your highness?" asked the guard who had carried Arwa. I sensed a great reluctance in his tone, and fear coursed through me. This man was expecting to receive a terrible order, and he would hate it, but he would carry it out.

The Maker King's son looked at us for a long moment, as though he expected us to beg. We wouldn't, of course; and I knew Zahrah wouldn't either.

"Bring them," he said. "We will return with these miscreants to the castle of King Qasim."

I let out a whisper of a breath, but did not dare show more relief than that. We would not die here in the sand.

"But do not worry, my love," Maram continued. "We will take them to your father, and then we will have them executed at your command, so that all your subjects will know how much you love me."

He knew. His vicious grin gave it all away. He knew that we had not kidnapped Zahrah, that she had come with us of her own accord. And he knew that she cared for us, though I could not imagine he knew why or how much. That didn't matter to him. He had five creatures to torment, using our pain against each other, and when he was done he would get to keep her to torment further. Saoud couldn't reach for me with the guards behind us, but he did lean into my shoulder as much as he dared. The weight of him, slight as it was, reminded me that I could still die here in the sand if I did something reckless.

On my other side, Arwa hadn't so much as flinched at the prince's declaration, and I was inordinately proud of her. Tariq was breathing slowly, measured air going in and out, like he was spinning and wanted to match his breathing to the rhythm of his work. I took a deep breath and tried to do the same thing, but I felt it slip away from me immediately.

"Get them on their feet," the prince said.

"What about the girl?" said one of the guards.

Maram looked at Arwa for the first time, measuring her worth, as if one such as he could possibly fathom it.

"She has made her choice," he said. "She can live with it, for the time she has left."

He turned then and went back toward the encampment. They had not brought their horses with them, so we would all walk. The guards who stood with Zahrah led her behind their prince, while the rest of them turned their attention to us.

They did not bind us. There was no reason to. The desert had been a poor escape plan, as we had already learned, and there were many more of them than there were of us. Even if they needed to get a horse from their camp, they would still run us down soon enough if we made a break for it. Instead they searched us, taking knives and belts and going through our packs. None of these were returned, except for Arwa's. The guard who looked through her things was the same guard who had carried her out of the cave. He removed nearly everything from her pack, and then made a face like he had accidentally touched a hot cooking pot before returning the bag to her. One of his comrades leaned over to question him, and I did not hear the murmured reply, but clearly all the guards who did were in agreement.

I looked at Arwa, whose face was a determined mask. She looked at me for a brief second and her eyes flashed with something like satisfaction, though I couldn't guess the cause. Saoud looked relieved as well, and I wondered what in the world Arwa was carrying that she was so glad to keep while the men who had captured us were equally glad to let her. She pulled her veil over her face, as Zahrah had done, and I wished it was a bit windier so that the rest of us would have the excuse to do the same with our kafiyyahs. As it was, we were forced to march toward the camp with every defense taken from us.

The camp was a messy place, laid out with no regard for order or basic sanitation. We were taken to a small tent, and the four of us were shoved inside with little ceremony. I knew that there would be at least two guards posted outside, and that the thin walls of the tent would do nothing to cover the sound of our voices if we tried to speak to one another.

So we sat in silence and discomfort again, and waited for an end we did not know; though we knew it would be a while before we saw it. I thought of my mother, and wondered if she would ever learn what had become of me. She would have heard about Zahrah's kidnapping, of course. She might have seen the prince ride past on his way to her rescue. I didn't know if she would guess my part in it, if she would take the pieces—my leaving her, Zahrah's disappearance, the executions—and spin them into the thread of the true tale. I wanted her to die at peace, if she could. As I almost certainly would not.

But that was not my thread to spin.

THIRTY-TWO

THE GUARD CAME FOR ARWA as soon as the sun rose the next morning. We hadn't been given any blankets, so we had all slept in a pile together against the chill of the desert night. It had taken a long time to fall asleep, since we were spun so tight and stretching at the seams, and so we were groggy when the flap was opened. When we saw the guard's intent, Saoud did finally fight him. It was over before I could join in, with Saoud bleeding from the mouth and nose, and Arwa gone anyway with not so much as a glance from the guard who carried her. When I tried to open the tent flap to see where they were taking her, I was pushed back with a staff to the belly. It was the first time anyone had ever hit me outside of the practice ring, and it was several minutes before I could breathe properly.

By the time I had recovered, Saoud's nose had stopped bleeding. Tariq was sitting up, his face pale as he watched us, though he gave no other sign of distress. I was so proud of him, and of Arwa too, even though I wanted their freedom more than I wanted their strength.

"What can we do?" Tariq asked. It was the first time any of us had really spoken in hours, and it was a question I did not know the answer to.

"I think we must do our best to survive the trip back to the castle," I said. "We can't give the prince any reason to kill us between now and then."

"So we can die in Kharuf, before the king and queen themselves?" Saoud asked.

"I don't think Qasim and Rasima would allow it," I said. "They will listen to Zahrah. They might even recognize us, or at least the resemblance to our parents. I don't think they would really execute us."

"The prince would," Saoud pointed out. "What if he makes it a condition of his marriage? What if he calls Zahrah's reputation into question and says the only way for her to clear it is for her to give the order? What if it is a choice between us and Kharuf?"

He hadn't said anything I had not already thought of, but hearing it in words made it worse. He was right, of course. The Maker King's son was as cruel as the rumors suggested, and it was clear he wanted us to die—not just for some perception of justice, but because it would hurt Zahrah and show her that she was in his control.

"It is the only hope we have," Tariq said.

I was so tired of hope, but it had got us this far, and even though we were fools to trust it, Tariq was right. We fell silent again, aware that there were guards outside, and listened to the camp move around us. They must have been preparing to pack up and go back to Kharuf, but they were clearly no more orderly now than they had been when establishing camp in the first place. It was aggravating to be idle, even though there was nothing we could possibly do. My only consolation was that whatever they were doing to Arwa could not have been too painful, because we did not hear her scream.

After what felt like an eternity, Arwa was dumped through the tent flap. Saoud caught her around the waist and pulled her toward him, checking automatically for injuries to her head and hands.

"It's all right, I'm all right," she said, pushing him off. Still, she sat right next to him when he let her be.

"What happened?" he asked.

"You were right about the demon," Arwa said. "It's here, and it wants Zahrah very badly. Only, it was angry because she's not good enough at making things. They made me sew with her, and they're getting a loom for this afternoon. I told her that Yashaa was the only weaver, so they'd take him next."

I was a decent enough weaver, though I lacked practice. I could put up a show of it, though, and presumably if they needed us to teach Zahrah how to do it, there was no one of their number that was particularly skilled. Selfishly, I was glad that I would get out of the tent, not to mention see her again.

"How is she?" Tariq asked.

"She's fine," Arwa said. "We couldn't talk very much. The demon watched us while we worked. It was terrible, Yashaa. Its eyes were terrible, and it wouldn't stop looking. Zahrah kept working, though, like it didn't bother her at all. She's so brave, Yashaa. She's our princess."

It was cold comfort, but it was better than nothing. We had nothing to eat for breakfast, and no lunch was brought either. After our long days on trail rations, we were used to light meals, or missing them altogether, but they hadn't brought us any water, and that was going to be a more immediate problem. We had not drunk a lot yesterday while we were in hiding, and I knew that headaches and general malaise would only be the beginning if we didn't get water soon.

"I'm sorry we lost the salt boxes," Arwa said quietly. "Prince Maram threw them in a fire pit when the demon told him they were piskey-made."

317

"I think he hates everything that is beautiful just because it's not his," Tariq said. "It must be a lonely way to live."

"I don't pity him for it," Saoud said. "I pity everyone who has to live under his boot."

"Soon that will be all of Kharuf as well," I said.

"With luck," Saoud said darkly, "we will still be alive to see it."

He did not sound particularly hopeful, and we lapsed into silence again. I tried to think of how to tell them I was sorry for landing them all here, but every time I thought of words that might work, I remembered that Saoud had followed us of his own volition, and both Arwa and Tariq had offered as many suggestions as I had, back in the mountain pass. They had followed me here because they wanted to, not because I had made them, and if it was a bad end, then they would meet it on their own terms. The only thing I could really apologize for was raising the specter of hope again when it was all clearly lost, but even that sentiment rang hollow with me when I tried to give it voice.

Before I could think of anything, the tent flap opened again and a larger guard beckoned to me. I left the tent on my feet, my hands raised to protect my eyes from the light, and followed the guard through the haphazardly arranged tents until we stood before the tent that was clearly the best one. The cloth was dyed, to begin with, and there were clerestories in the uppermost areas of the peak, letting daylight in so that oil or candle smoke wouldn't make the air inside the tent stuffy. It was held in place by bronze pegs instead of iron. I shuddered when I recalled the reason for that detail.

We went into the tent, and I was immediately shoved forward onto my knees. Prince Maram sat on an ornately carved wooden chair, which I thought a foolish waste, as someone had to carry it while the prince rode on horseback. Beside him on a collection of pillows sat Zahrah. There was a frame in her lap with the warp already set, and a collection of cloth strips behind her. Judging by the colors, the strips had once been someone's uniform. At least they hadn't used our spare clothes.

"Spinner," said the prince, "I am told you can weave as well?"

"I can," I said. I was not his subject, and I would not grant him his title. The guard behind me pressed his staff into the back of my knee, pushing it into the ground, but I made no noise.

"I see," said the prince. He didn't sound impressed, either by my supposed talents at weaving or by my defiance. "It has come to my attention that my fiancée's lessons are incomplete. You will show her how to weave, as it is a skill all ladies ought to have."

The slight emphasis he put on "ladies" did not go unnoticed, but I said nothing further. I nodded and then moved to stand up so that I could go to where Zahrah was sitting. The guard pressed his staff down again, and I froze.

"You may crawl, Spinner," the prince said. "If you are lucky, I won't make you crawl all the way back to my beloved's castle."

I crawled. The guards laughed as I seated myself near Zahrah, and then the prince, seemingly bored of the game, dismissed most of them.

"Like this, my princess," I said, trying to sound formal, as I had done those days in the hidden valley.

I took the loom from her lap and selected a piece of cloth. We wouldn't be making anything in particular. The loom was too small for real work. Instead, she would learn the mechanics of how to weave the cloth as though it were a true lesson, and she would later move on to other projects. It wasn't real weaving, just the motions of it, as though they only needed to say she had woven something, and didn't care if she actually could.

I worked the first strip of cloth through the warp and then selected a piece of cloth for her. Our fingers brushed as I passed the loom back to her. Prince Maram, who had been watching dispassionately, nodded to the guard who stood beside me, and the guard cracked me across the knuckles with his sheathed dagger. It didn't break my fingers, but it hurt them. They would be swollen later, particularly if I kept weaving now, which I would obviously have to. Lessons, then, for Zahrah, in weaving, torture, and the prince's absolute control.

I risked a look at her, desperate to know if they had done the same to Arwa, even though Arwa had claimed she was fine. Zahrah gave the tiniest shake of her head and then raised a hand to her temple to cover the movement.

"My love, does your head ache?" asked Maram, his tone indicating that he already knew the answer to his question. "You must keep practicing. I have been told that will ease your suffering."

He meant her headache only, not the rest of her pain.

Zahrah began to weave. As always, she was beautiful at her work, even though the circumstances were abhorrent. She missed none of the cross strings in the warp, even on her first attempt, and was able to keep each line tightly aligned with the one above it with little effort. As she continued, a manic energy like I had never seen before lit her eyes, the only part of her I could see under her veil. I tried to think like Tariq, and wondered what was different now, and then I knew: the demon. Somehow it was driving her.

My hand was throbbing as I helped her begin the next row, careful not to touch her. There were so many magics upon her: the demon's to hurt, and the creatures' to inspire. She would feel all of those things at once. I was so proud of her for not fracturing under the pressure. But then, halfway through a line, she froze. She took a deep breath and looked up past my shoulder. I started to follow her gaze, and Prince Maram stood up out of his chair as the tent flap moved and a person who was not a person came into sight.

"Lady," Prince Maram said. "Have you come to see our progress?"

"I have," said the most terrible voice I had ever heard. Every part of me rebelled against her, but I couldn't flee. And even if I could have, I wouldn't have left Zahrah alone.

"Come, my little rose," said the demon queen. I hated it for using that name. That was our name, and she made it seem like Zahrah was a thing that could be cultivated and picked. "Let me see what you have made."

THIRTY-THREE

THE DEMON IGNORED ME, so I watched it as it circled the tent. It looked almost human except for its color, and the way that it held its head at strange angles. Instead of walking, it glided along the floor, moving first slowly and then much too fast. It made me sick to my stomach to look at it for long. When we'd fought the bear, the demon in it had been weaker, and we'd had iron. I sensed this demon was much stronger, and the iron I carried had already been taken from me.

It reached Zahrah and put a hand on her shoulder. Somehow Zahrah didn't shudder at the touch. She held up the loom, showing the work she'd done so far as though the demon were a favored aunt or teacher, like my mother. The demon laid a finger, or a fingerlike appendage, on the frame, and an odd light suffused both of them. Prince Maram didn't appear to notice anything, and neither did the demon, but when I looked at Zahrah's eyes, I knew that she could see the light, too, and that she didn't know what it meant either.

"Do you feel better now, my little rose?" the demon asked.

"Yes," said Zahrah, iron and thorns. "I do, thank you."

"It is so difficult to learn these tasks late in life," the demon said. "You ought to have learned them as a child. It would not have hurt so much then, and you wouldn't need my help to make the pain stop."

"I have dealt with pain all my life," said Zahrah. "It is a gift."

The demon recoiled at the last word, remembering its jailors, I hoped, and the misery and suffering it had felt in the mountains.

"You have so many gifts, my love," said Maram. "It gives me such pleasure to watch you use them."

The demon seemed to realize for the first time that I was in the room. It turned and looked at me, and I was glad I was still sitting or I might have fallen over. We had heard stories of the King-Who-Was-Good, who was *made* good, and how he had suffered before that. How the demons had come to the Storyteller Queen's family and burned them alive at her sister's wedding. It had not prepared me for the malice I felt directed toward me now. It didn't just want us to die; it wanted us to suffer. I knew it would not stop at Kharuf. It would have Qamih too, and the desert, and the world, if it could. Maram must be stupid if he didn't see this part of it. Or perhaps he knew and just didn't care. From what I had seen of him so far, I wouldn't think it too far a stretch for him.

"Maram, why is this spinner still alive?" the demon said.

"Because I haven't decided how he is going to die," the prince told it. "He and his cohorts kidnapped my beloved, and I must determine an appropriate punishment for them. Also, they have been useful. My men cannot teach her what you want her to know."

"But this one loves her," the demon said, and I flinched to hear the words from this terrible being. I hadn't said them yet myself, not out loud, and now Zahrah had heard the truth from this monster.

"How delightful," Maram replied, and he sounded truly joyous. I had their full attention now. "I'll make her light his pyre with her own hands. If he's very, very lucky, I'll make sure he's dead before I make her start the fire."

There is an odd sort of freedom that accompanies the pronouncement of your own death from a person who has the power to do it. I reached out and squeezed Zahrah's hand. It didn't matter if he broke all of my fingers. I needed her to know that it was all right. That I didn't blame her if she chose Kharuf over me. I had always known she might have to.

Maram smiled and called for a guard. He did not hit me again.

"Take these two back to the prison tent," the prince said. "My fiancée must learn another lesson, it seems."

"Yes, your highness," said the guard. His voice was oddly muffled.

"And make sure they're fed something," Maram said. "They have a long walk ahead of them."

The guard pulled Zahrah to her feet. While he had her, I would not resist. He took us back through the mess of a camp to the tent where the others were. There was a bucket of water on the ground by the flap, and Tariq was washing his hands in it.

"They let us out to use the privy, such as it is," he said.

The guard looked at Zahrah, who shook her head, and then to me. I nodded, and he took me to the foul and hastily dug pit that the prince's men were using for their privy. When we returned, he dismissed the guards for their dinner and shoved me into the tent. He didn't close the flap behind me, and we were grateful for the air. He sat down, a naked sword across his knees, so that he was half facing us, and half facing the camp. Then he unwrapped his kafiyyah, and I saw why he had disguised his voice.

"Father?" Saoud gasped, for here indeed sat the man who had taught us to fight with staves and survive in the forest. "What are you doing here?"

"I might ask the same of you, my son," he said. "I left you all in safety."

I thought of a thousand things at the same time. I had missed him so much when my mother sent him away, and I knew that my feelings paled beside Saoud's. I wished he had stayed with us at the crossroad camp. I wished we had met him before now, when we might have been saved. Now, though we could not all be saved, maybe some of us could be. Maybe Arwa and Tariq and Saoud.

"My mother sent us to the Maker King's court," I said. "But we didn't want to go, so we took our chances in Kharuf."

"I imagine it is quite a tale," he said, looking at Zahrah. "Except now it is quite a mess."

"Father," Saoud said. "We did our best."

"I know you did, Saoud," he said. "And there is something I must tell you. I ask you only to remember where you are—and that we will all be in great danger if you make a lot of noise."

We all nodded, and he turned to look at us. His eyes were different, I noticed. That was why I hadn't recognized him in the tent, when he'd obscured his voice. His face was the same, as was his speech now that he wasn't muffling it, but his eyes were strange.

"Saoud, I swear to you that I am your father still," he said. "But there is another that I share this body with, and he is the one who might be able to save us."

"I don't understand," Saoud said. "What do you mean?"

"When the desert king was made good, the Storyteller Queen broke the demon out of him," Saoud's father said. "The demon was sent to the iron mountains with all of its kin, but it was made good too, by the power of the Storyteller Queen's words."

"No," said Saoud. "I don't believe it."

"It's true," he said. "I met the demon in the mountains several years ago. It knew that there was mischief afoot between Kharuf and Qamih, that one of its own kin would bring us trouble, and it begged my help. It swore it would not risk me unnecessarily, and it swore it would do its best to protect you, and so I accepted its offer."

"That's when you started to teach us to fight," Tariq said. "It was the demon."

"Yes," he said. "I wanted you to be ready, though I never imagined you would need to be ready for this. And the demon kept its word. Look at my eyes and remember how I used to be. That is because the demon rested and let me be unremarkable for as long as it could. But now we need it, and so I have given it permission to take more of my mind for its own."

Saoud turned away and looked into the dark corner

of the tent. I couldn't imagine what he felt. The father he thought had left him behind had been in truth another creature altogether, and now he must have been second-guessing every conversation they'd had. I was past anger and confusion. Thanks to the demon I had faced today, I was numb to everything except the pain in my hand, and the cold determination to save Zahrah if I could . . . and the others if I could not.

"What can we do?" said Zahrah. She believed him, because she could see the truth with her gift. "Can you take me so that the other demon can't?"

"No," he said. "She has made you so that only she can have you. I am sorry. I would if I could."

"Then what?" I said. "What can we do?"

"I cannot face the demon queen alone," he said. "She has fed on the Maker Kings for years, and I have had only what was willingly given to me. She would crush me before my fighting her did any good."

I remembered the demon's stare and did not doubt him. I saw Arwa shudder and knew she had felt it too.

"But I can take care of the prince," he said.

"What happens to my father if you do?" Saoud asked. "Maram is rumored to be a good fighter, and I know that you are better than he is, but he has an army."

Saoud's father made no answer, and Saoud looked away.

"How does that help us?" Arwa said. "If the prince dies,

his men may fall into disarray, but there is still the demon, and we'll have to face it without you."

"The piskeys know we're here," Tariq said. "Or at least that we were headed in this direction. If they are watching, they might come to our aid."

"It's their task to do so," Saoud's father, or the demon in him, said. "And after I fight the Maker King's son, the demon will have to reveal itself openly to pursue you. That will certainly get their attention."

"So we run," I said. "And we hope."

I locked eyes with Saoud.

"It'll have to be fast," he said. "We'll have to go without recovering our gear."

He looked sideways at Arwa, who nodded. She still had her bag. Saoud looked at his father, who regarded him gravely.

"I made a promise to your father." This was the demon speaking. "I promised him that I would never make him do anything he didn't want to do. I can't, in truth. The Storyteller Queen made me good, and so I cannot force him to do this against his will. Do you believe me?"

"I have no choice," Saoud said. He looked at where his father sat, the demon flickering in his eyes.

"Yes you do, Saoud," I said. "You have trusted me, and you have trusted Zahrah, and you have trusted hope. We have made terrible plans, and you have done all you could to see them through. One more time, for me and for us. One more choice."

Saoud blinked, and I saw that there were tears in his eyes. He couldn't reach out to his father, in case someone happened by. We had already risked too much, talking this long. I felt my own eyes water, and missed my mother with a sudden flare of feeling. I wiped my eyes with my hand, and looked back at Saoud. This was his moment, and his grief. I would be ready for him when he needed me.

"I believe you," Saoud said. "I love you."

"I love you, too," said his father. "Tell your children about me and teach them what I taught you."

"I will," said Saoud.

"We all will," said Arwa.

"When the fight begins, you will know it," said the demon. "Be ready. And be strong."

We couldn't tell him that we heard him. We couldn't thank him. We couldn't say good-bye. Because as soon as he had said the words, another guard brought him his dinner and sent him to his tent, and we never saw him again.

THIRTY-FOUR

DESPITE OUR BEST ATTEMPTS, none of us slept very much that night. They brought us a poor supper of—what else— boiled vetch. Tariq took one look at it and began to laugh so hard I thought he might have trouble drawing breath. Indeed, soon enough he stopped making any sound at all, except for wheezing helplessly as he tried to calm down. Zahrah took his face in both her hands, forcing him to look at her, and then guided his breathing to match hers, even and deep, until he could be safely left to breathe on his own. It was difficult to choke down any food at all after that, but we knew we would need all the help we could get the next day, so we did our best.

Then, without talking, so that the guard outside would be unaware of what we were doing, Saoud did his best to make a map of Kharuf from what he remembered of the map that had been taken with his pack. It was a poor representation, which matched our poor plan, but escape was the priority. Saoud sketched out a straight line to where he thought the castle was. The ground we would cross was open and hilly, like most of Kharuf. If we were pursued by horsemen, we would be caught. We had to hope that they would be so put off by the death of the Maker King's son that it would take them time to reorganize. If their camp was any indication, we did not think too optimistically of them.

It was the demon that was the greatest threat, of course. We had no iron left, and it was unlikely that we would be able to get any on our way out of the camp, unless we stumbled upon it. Saoud's father had trained us with iron knives and still carried an iron sword, so we supposed that the demon's weakness to the metal was something we could not depend on. Without the creatures, we would be helpless.

"I think we'd be better to run for it," said Saoud, "and not waste time trying to find tools that might not help us very much."

"They helped us with the bear," Arwa pointed out.

"The bear was a physical animal, though," I reminded her. "You've seen the demon. Do you think we could cut it?"

She nodded and shuddered, and I realized she had not told us what the demon had said or done to her. Zahrah put an arm around her shoulders and shook her head at me. It wasn't something I could fix, I realized, and so we would deal with it later, in that time none of us were sure we were going to have.

It got darker and darker, and Saoud put his makeshift map away. We knew that we should sleep, but I felt like there was too much to think about. I thought I might fly apart. This was worse than when we had crossed Kharuf and were unable to spin. Instead of sleeping, I watched my friends get quieter and quieter, retreating into thoughts I couldn't share and couldn't heal. It was not a feeling I enjoyed. Zahrah slid her hand into mine, and it hurt, but I didn't let go.

At last Tariq sighed and cast himself on the bare floor of the tent. They hadn't put down a rug for us, so we were at the mercy of any insect that might come burrowing though the light material of the tent floor. Still, it was what we had, and tomorrow night we would have no tent at all. As we watched, Tariq curled in on himself, as though willing himself to sleep.

Arwa kissed my cheek, and Saoud's, as she had done when she was still a baby that we carried because it was too dangerous to set her down. Then she huddled beside Tariq, her arms wrapped around her pack so tightly that I didn't think anyone would be able to pry it from her. It was all we had left, and I didn't even know what was inside it. There had never been any good time to ask.

It got darker, and my thoughts were no more quieted than they had been before. We heard a chorus of wadi toads, though they were all but covered by the noise made by the soldiers who sat around their campfires and celebrated the end of their hunt. They were going home, or at least closer to it, and they had nothing to fear at the end of the journey.

I thought Saoud would sleep, or at least lie down and pretend to, but instead he sat up for a long time. This might be the only chance he had, I realized, to mourn the certain death of his father. We would have no opportunity tomorrow, and after that we could not say when we would have any respite at all. Saoud had promised to remember and to teach his own children about his father's bravery, but if Saoud died too, then there would be no one to carry the tale.

"If we fail," Zahrah said, "if we fail, and you die, and I have to wed the Maker King's son, I will tell the truth, for as long as I can. Before the demon takes me, I will tell anyone who listens that you all were my rescuers, not my captors, and that we tried to save Kharuf. I will tell them what we learned about the demons and the good creatures who live in the mountains. I will tell them about your father, about his sacrifices for us and for a kingdom that would have been proud to adopt him and his son."

Saoud said nothing, but we knew he heard. She could

promise him nothing more. The time for promises was done. We would make this last march together or not at all. So Saoud sat in vigil for his father, who was dead and not-yet-dead, and Zahrah and I sat with him, her hand in mine.

"I wondered why he was so eager to leave me," Saoud said, after he had been quiet for so long that I began to wonder if he had managed to fall asleep sitting up. "Why didn't he tell me?"

"Would you have let him?" Zahrah asked. Her voice was kind and sincere. She would have made such an excellent queen for Kharuf. "Would you have understood? Would anyone?"

I thought of the children we had been, bound and burdened by life at the crossroad camp. Directionless, and without any prospects beyond inheriting the meager work our parents did. No, we would not have understood. My mother would have driven Saoud's father out, and Saoud along with him, and I would have lost my brother before I truly loved him.

"No," said Saoud. "And even if I had, no one else would have."

"Your father loves you," she said. "And he helped make you strong. He wanted something better for you, and this was how he got it."

Saoud looked at her, and the tears that had been shining in his eyes began to fall. He leaned forward into her arms and wept. She held him, and I put my hands on his shoulders, and he mourned the father he had lost, and the father he would lose tomorrow. I had thought I would shed tears for him as well, but I found that I couldn't. Perhaps I had nothing left. At last, Saoud straightened. He bowed to Zahrah and pressed his forehead to mine, and then he crawled beside Arwa and collapsed into a fitful sleep.

Zahrah shifted and leaned against my shoulder. I put my arm around her, and she squeezed my hand. I hissed with pain.

"I'm sorry," she whispered. "I forgot."

"So did I," I admitted. "It seems like the least of my worries at the moment."

"Is it broken?" she asked. "I couldn't tell from how the guard hit you."

"No," I said. "Just swollen. The prince wanted pain, not infirmity."

"Everything I feared about him is true," she said. "He will ruin Kharuf just to watch it burn."

"And the demon will ruin Qamih," I told her. "But that is not a solution, to lose both countries. Our ancestress did not cross the desert for that."

"So we run," she said. "And hope we are caught by one of the Storyteller Queen's creatures before we are caught by the demon."

"It's a terrible plan," I said.

"Someday, Yashaa," she said, "you will have a good plan. I know it."

I kissed her, and the squalor and terror of Prince Maram's camp faded around us, discarded like burrs and clods of dirt pulled from new-washed wool. There was only her, and there was only me, and there was our foolish dream that everything was going to be all right.

"Does your head hurt?" I asked, when we stopped to breathe.

"It passes more quickly now," she said, not entirely answering the question.

"Does it feel safe?" As if safe were possible for us.

"Not as safe as this," she said and kissed me again, her hands making fists in the cloth of my tunic as if she never intended to let me go.

When she pulled away, still holding on to me, she was crying. I wiped her cheeks with my thumbs, which was not particularly effective, and she did her best to smile.

"I'm scared," she said. "And I'm sorry. If I had stayed in the tower, none of this would have happened."

"I spent most of the day trying to apologize to Arwa and Tariq for the same thing," I told her. "But there is nothing to apologize for. We made our choices, and we agreed on them when we did. We had to try, Zahrah, and we don't regret it."

"I know," she said. "But I still feel sorry for it. And angry that there is nothing I can do."

"I was angry for a long time," I told her. "And then I found something better."

"Flatterer," she said, but she laughed a little bit when she said it, and I knew that for however brief a time, I had made her feel better.

"Can you sleep?" I asked. My own mind whirled, a map of Kharuf spread across it with all the obstacles between us and Zahrah's castle starkly visible on it.

"I think so," she said. "And you are going to at least try."

I let her pull me down beside her, and she turned so that she was still in my arms. She was, I noticed, very careful not to put weight on my injured hand, though otherwise she was as close to me as she could be without physically crawling into my very skin. Her breathing became measured and even, but sleep eluded me. I looked across her to where the others were sleeping, or pretending to, and felt something sharp and hard in my stomach.

Saoud's father, and the demon he carried, had taught us the staff patterns and how to throw knives. He had taught us to survive in the forest. He had taught us how to find water. My mother had taught us the craft of our ancestors, and the stories they had carried with them from the desert. Those things had carried us this far. Tomorrow, none of that was going to do us any good. All we could do now was wait. And then, when the time came, we were going to run.

THIRTY-FIVE

THE DAY STRETCHED OUT, long and interminable, and we waited. They did not come for Zahrah, which was a blessing—we had not planned what to do if we were separated when the signal came—and a curse: idleness was worse than the wait. Arwa gathered loose threads from Zahrah's dress, and from her own clothing, and stored them in her bag. I couldn't even begin to imagine why, though I didn't say anything to her. She kept herself occupied, and it was a mercy. Zahrah's dress was ill-suited for travel, but the soldiers had taken our spares, and so we would have to make do. It was, I concluded, likely to be the least of our worries, and since there was nothing we could do about it, I didn't let myself linger in my thoughts for too long.

Instead, I thought of spinning, from the carding, which had been my earliest task in the spinning room, to the careful storage of the undyed wool as it waited on the distaff for use. I thought of my mother's fingers, cleverly pulling just the right amount of wool and feeding it into the dropping spindle, and then I saw my own hands learning the task. What began as lumpy and uneven became smooth with practice, until I had set the work aside to take up the staff and my knives.

But that was spinning too, or at least it was still a pattern. In the movements of the training circle, I had found the same peace my mother found in spinning. It was the peace she had hoped I would find in spinning someday. I had peace now, of a sort. Either we would succeed or we would die. I was reasonably sure that this was not what my mother had had in mind.

We stretched as best we could, to make sure that three days of sitting wouldn't slow us down too much, and we memorized the way each of us looked, in case there were fewer of us to remember it in the coming days.

When the sun turned to orange and began to light the desert in dark purples and blood-reds, we stilled and listened hard. The soldiers were cooking supper, from the smell, roasting a goat without herbs or any particular finesse to their technique, and those not on duty were seeing to the horses or waiting in their tents for the meal to be ready. There was only one guard outside our tent flap, the man who had carried Arwa, and he looked uncomfortable as he leaned on his staff. He had left the tent open after his shift began, which we appreciated for the air, except it made it difficult to act like we were meek captives.

"How are we going to deal with the guard, if he's still there when the noise starts?" I breathed in Saoud's ear. He looked at Arwa, or rather, at her bag.

"I will take care of it," he said, as quietly as I had. "You get Zahrah away."

I nodded, and the wait continued. The goat was finished, and a piece of it was brought to our guard. We had been given lunch and did not expect anything else. The guard ate his portion, turning away from us so we could not see him. I wondered if he had a daughter, and if that was why he was so ashamed.

Then there was a cry from the center of the camp, and a horde of running feet. We leapt up, all five of us together, and the guard spun to look at us, his staff clutched in both of his hands. Saoud had Arwa's bag and was moving to strike when the guard dropped his staff on the ground and held up his hands.

"Go," he said, and looked at me. "Can you use the staff so that I am wounded but not dead?"

It was not an easy task. His staff was heavier than the

342

one I was used to. I might kill him by accident. But I didn't hesitate.

"Yes," I said, and picked it up.

He kissed his hands and held them out to Arwa and to Zahrah, and then turned so that I could hit him. He dropped, and we stepped over him to run.

We tried for stealth at first, but soon enough we realized there was little cause for it and went for speed instead. The soldiers were entirely diverted, even the ones who had been feeding the horses their evening fodder, because Prince Maram's tent was in flames. The finely dyed cloth burned hot in the beginning of the desert night, and none of his men could get close enough to the conflagration to even try beating it out. As we circled the camp, we saw a figure emerge from the tent, screaming in agony as he burned.

He was too short to be Saoud's father.

We saw the soldiers tackle him, and frantically try to contain their prince before he could light the whole camp on fire with his own touch. Already the flames were spreading to other tents. The horses, smelling smoke, were beginning to panic and pull at their tethers. Saoud's father had bought us time, and we would be best set to use it.

We ran, giving heed only to our direction as we went. The stars were out and the moon was coming, and we ran beneath them, spurred on by desperate hope. When we crossed the border into Kharuf, we had to stop. Tariq and

343

Arwa both started coughing as soon as their feet passed the invisible line, and I felt my own lungs constrict. Zahrah and Saoud were untroubled, but when I waved them on, they did not go. Arwa passed her bag to Saoud, and Tariq straightened beside her. I took three deep breaths to prove I could, and then we were off again, though our pace was slower.

Zahrah had taken advantage of the short halt to tie up her dress, and she moved easier with it no longer wrapping around her legs. Arwa had lost her veil somewhere, and her long black hair streamed behind her like a banner. Tariq ran with a hand on his chest, as though each breath squeezed him, but his face was determined. Saoud carried the staff as well as Arwa's pack, and I fell to the rear of the group to watch for pursuers.

Time played with us as we ran. Our steps got heavier and heavier, our stops to rest more frequent; that should have made the night seem endless. Instead, the darkness passed all too quickly, and we could not run fast enough to make good use of it. Every moment felt squandered, but we could not go any faster.

It was not yet dawn, and we were weary with the night's long run when I saw the first sign that our escape had been noticed. It was too early for sunrise, and the east should have been pink, tinged with the promise of yellow day. Instead, it was silver, and edged with hate. I could barely gasp for breath at all, the run and the spinners' illness working against me, but I croaked a sound close enough to Saoud's name that he turned around and saw what I saw.

He stopped, his hands on his knees and his shoulders heaving. Behind him, Tariq fought to keep his feet, and Arwa swayed. Zahrah was resolute, even though she shook. The phoenix's gift was working. Her feet were bloody with cuts.

"My princess," said Saoud. "We have done what we can."

"You have my thanks," she said. "For now and always, no matter what becomes of me."

"No," I said, for I saw that she planned to sacrifice herself to the demon for our sake. "No."

"Yashaa, you must keep going," she said. "You must try. Run all the way to my father and warn him, and then warn Qamih."

"No," I repeated. I would not lose her, not again.

"Look!" said Tariq, who had not been watching the east, but the west instead. His eyes were lit with hope, shining in a moment of the truest belief I had ever seen on his face. He looked toward the mountains, and saw our salvation. It was how I was always going to remember him.

It was a swarm of purple and gold, the color of the Storyteller Queen, and the color of the creatures she had made. They had seen us. They had come.

They were too late.

The silver light grew brighter and then solidified before

345

us. Tariq gave a horrible cry as though something was pulling him to pieces, and then the ground beneath his feet opened, and he was gone.

Arwa screamed, and reached out for the space where Tariq had been. Saoud grabbed her hands and pulled her close to his chest, muffling the terrible sound. I could only stare at the spot, frozen. I didn't believe it. I couldn't. He was alive, somehow. He must be.

"Stop!" screamed my Little Rose, loud enough for the demon to hear her. "Stop and I will go with you."

"You have been mine since the day I first saw you, princess," the demon said. Its voice was even worse now. "I will have you, and I will do whatever I wish. But if you want, I will stop, so that it is you who murders your friends. They will see you do it, and I will make you watch."

Arwa's eyes were streaming tears now, and Saoud was shocked beyond horror, though his grip on her hadn't lessened. If the demon took one of them as it had taken Tariq, it would have to take them both, but there was nothing I could do. I was stuck in place, fixed by fear and by my grief.

"Choose, little rose," the demon said. "Choose the manner of their deaths."

The demon was so fixated on its prize and our pain, so overcome with joy at its perceived victory, that it did not see the piskeys until they were upon it, lifting it up into the sky above us, to battle on a plane we couldn't reach. The lights of them, warm and cold, strained against each other as we watched, and for a moment, we were locked in the awe of it. Then I shook myself free and fell to my knees, scrabbling at the ground with my bare hands over the place where Tariq had been standing when he disappeared. Surely he was not beyond retrieval. Surely, with magic, he might be brought back. My injured hand sent a wave of pain through me, and I screamed. Then hands locked on my shoulders and pulled me away.

"No," I said. Everything inside me focused on that single hope, that vain and foolish hope. "No."

"He's gone, Yashaa," Zahrah shouted at me, her voice full of tears and rage. "He's gone and we need you."

I howled, uncaring of everything in the whole world except that Tariq was dead and I couldn't save him. Zahrah shook me again, and I saw that the battle of lights still raged on, though the silver light had dimmed.

"They won't kill it, Yashaa," Zahrah said. "They can't. When the Storyteller Queen made them, she made them as jailors. They will only imprison it again. Yashaa, the curse will still be in place. Tariq will have died for nothing."

It was cruel, but it worked. I stopped up my grief, though I felt that it was boundless, and looked at her.

"What do you want me to do?" I asked, my voice cracking with the effort of speaking at all.

"I watched the demon while I was crafting, Yashaa," she said. Her voice was quiet—only for me—though Saoud and Arwa could hear her, and both of them were weeping enough to break my heart again. "It wants me so badly it is like a physical need. I'm nearly ready for it. If I tempt it, I don't think it will be able to resist."

"No," I said, at the same time Saoud looked up and said, "How?"

"I must spin," said my Little Rose. "Yashaa, you must show me how to spin."

"I can't," I said. "We have no spindles."

"Yes we do," said Arwa through her tears, and upended her bag.

Out fell the rags she and Zahrah had sewn in the mountains, the ones she had jokingly told us not to ask questions about, and that had been so distasteful to the guards that they hadn't confiscated them. Out of the dark of the bag, I could see that the rags were wrapped around four long objects that were heavier at one end then they were at the other. Arwa unwrapped them, her hands hovering over her own spindle, and then mine, and then finally closing around the spindle that Tariq had carried since he was old enough to do the work.

"Spin," said Arwa, and pressed the spindle into my hands.

My fingers ached, but I closed my grip on the spindle out of habit.

"Spin for him," Saoud said, and passed me the threads that Arwa had gathered so carefully from the fraying hem of my Little Rose's dress.

I laid the scraps out, already trying to tell which would make the best leader to guide the rest of them into a single thread. I attached the one I chose to the hooked end and reached for the next piece.

"Spin, Yashaa," said my Little Rose. "Please."

I knelt and dropped the whorl. It spun evenly in the light of the rising sun, and the thread grew beneath my hands.

"Take me home, Yashaa," said my Little Rose. "Find your mother. Tell her what we have done."

She learned quickly, of course. That was her gift. It was just as well, because I didn't have very much thread to work with. She watched me spin the whorl once, twice, three times, and then on the fourth, she caught it herself and continued to spin.

Saoud held her upright, and Arwa fed her thread. I could only watch as she fought. She fought to keep her hands moving as the silver light bore down upon her, unable to resist this offering even after the demon had been made weak by its fight. She fought to stay awake, as the piskey's gift came over her, and she swayed. Her eyes were locked with mine, her work forgotten even as her hands continued to move. She blinked, and I saw instead of my Little Rose the exultation of the demon queen, who had at last the body it wanted more than it had sense to see the trap. She blinked again, and I saw my Little Rose, still fighting. For me. For us. For Kharuf. She reached for the spindle again, and grasped it this time at the tip.

The spindle dropped one last time, and no one caught it. A drop of blood fell to the ground, and for a moment, I thought the entire world shifted underneath my feet. Then the thread unspooled, the curse shattered, the prison bars closed in around the demon's head, and Zahrah, my Little Rose, fell asleep.

1.

They built the tomb of iron, though neither of we who sleep here are dead. To guard against rust and decay, the dragons and the phoenix smelted the ore in their own fire, before turning the molten metal over to human smiths. As long as their power holds, the tomb will stand, apart from the castle but close to its heart. The bier is iron, and the walls are iron, and the roof is iron. But Yashaa dug a moat and filled it with roses, and their thorns grew sharp and long.

A monster slept there, and so most folk avoided it. But there were some few who came to sit by me, and they reminded me of why I chose this, when it seemed I had no choice at all.

My parents did not come. They gave Yashaa whatever he

asked for to build the tomb, and watched the procession that carried me there, but they could not come themselves. I understood their pain, and I felt it in turn. They had done too much damage for it to be repaired without talking, and those who sleep cannot talk.

There was almost always at least one piskey hovering around my head, shedding fine gold dust that glimmered in the torchlight. It made the iron seem less cold. I thought perhaps they wept for me, or for the tangle of magic one of their kind had made of my life. They were a comfort to me, though. Like the iron, they weakened the demon that shared my sleep, and gave me room enough in my own mind to fight it.

Others came too, once or twice each, to pay their respects. They were the ones who had gone out from Kharuf when the curse was laid, and who could return now that I had broken it. They kissed my hand—kept warm and unmarred by time, thanks to the piskey's gift—and sometimes I felt their tears, too. Though I had not known most of them, or at least I did not remember knowing them in life, in sleep I could feel their work in their hands, and knew that they loved me for my sacrifice.

And then there were the ones whom I loved.

The guardsman would bring his whetstone and his knives and sit at the foot of the bier. He talked about the rebuilding of Kharuf, and later, of his wife and his children. He told me that the tower I had lived in was a shrine now, where girls lit candles and boys made rash promises in the name of love. I felt them:

the flames and the power of the words said there. I felt the words the guardsman said to me, too, as much as I heard them. They gave me strength to continue my battle with the one who slept with me, and every new flame, every whispered prayer, made me stronger in the fight.

The mountain goat came, too. She did not settle as easily as the other did. Her dreams were haunted by fire and dirt, suffocating her one minute and burning her the next. But in time, she too found peace and joy again. She would bring all manner of craft with her when she came to see me: weaving and fine embroidery, bread dough for kneading, fine copper wires that could be threaded through bright glass beads. I felt her work as much as I saw it, and it strengthened me as much as the guardsman's tales of candles and promises.

The spinner came whenever he could, and his visits were always long. He would sit in silence, or else he would tell me the smallest details of his day. He told me when his mother returned, and how she was teaching him the ways of their craft again, now that it was safe. He told me when she died: too young, but happy to have seen the curse lifted from her fellow spinners. He did not ever touch my hand. I missed his touch, though I understood why he could not give it, and I used his freely given words as fuel in my struggle.

When he could not visit, he always told me why he was gone. He went often out into the world, looking for the magic that would set me free of my demon and free of my sleep. He remembered the stories he had learned, and spoke words for the boy who could not, and he believed for all of us. He told our story to everyone he met, and the words moved across the world. They changed, as stories do, and the truth warped like strings on a broken loom, but it was enough to learn what he needed to know.

It was years before he found the answers he sought, far away in the desert kingdom where our ancestors had once lived. My father was dead, and my mother was old, and my kingdom had no one else to take the throne. Yashaa was old too, which was enough to break my heart, except I needed a whole one to finally quell the demon. To fuel my fight, I used the thirty years of lit candles and spoken promises, the days that my friends had spent beside me, the attention of the piskeys and the sprites, and the memory of the boy who had died in the desert but who always knew the right story. I brought to bear the full force of my will, made strong beyond human measure by myself and those who loved me. The demon, though it had plagued me for almost as long as I could remember, was gone between one breath and the next, so pitiful it was when faced with me, the focus of the will for everyone who had ever lit a candle at my shrine.

I felt the piskey alight on my chest, felt it look inside me and see that I had been victorious. The curse was broken, and now I could safely wake from the piskey's gift, if what Yashaa had learned was true. I felt the surge of happiness tinged with melancholy from my friends, who had watched me for this long, and who I would soon see with my waking eyes. I felt their children and grandchildren, eager to meet me and see if I was as interesting as their parents had said.

And I felt my Yashaa, bearded and wrinkled, when he pressed his lips to mine.

Acknowledgments

AND ANOTHER ONE!

Josh Adams, agent extraordinaire, thank you so much for not believing me every time I told you this book was going "fine," and then talking me back into facing it anyway.

Emily Meehan, Hannah Allaman, and the whole Hyperion team did such a wonderful job with *A Thousand Nights*, and I was so pleased to work with them again on *Kingdom of Sleep*. Thank you for another beautiful book.

And thank you, as ever, to my crit readers: Emma, Colleen, Faith, Laura, and RJ, and to Katie and Erin, who read the third draft while I had a panic/processed my *Star Wars* emotions.

Kingdom of Sleep began on a dining room table in Waterloo, took a major detour through another novel altogether, and was finally written while sitting in a chair (it's a big deal, trust me), at the southern intersection of Westmount and Fisher-Hallman.

About the Author

EMILY KATE JOHNSTON is a forensic archaeologist. She has lived on four continents, including summers spent in Jordan experiencing the desert first hand. Her inspirations come from her work, travels and her university studies in biblical Hebrew and Arabic. She loves telling stories, and has been doing so across different mediums for over ten years.

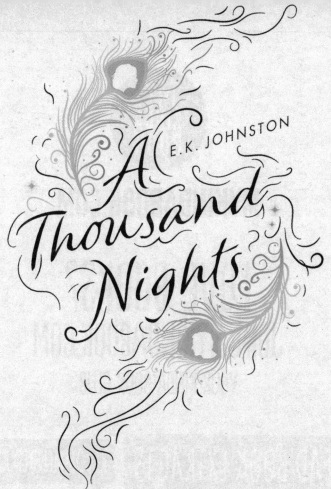

E.K. JOHNSTON

A Thousand Nights

He killed three hundred girls
before he came to my village looking for a wife.

When a powerful and dangerous king arrives in the desert to take
one of the village girls as his next wife, one girl will stop at nothing
to save the life of her sister – even if it means sacrificing herself.

At his palace she is sure death awaits. But the king's fascination with
her keeps her alive night after night, as the tales she weaves for him
create a strange magic between them and her words come to life
before her eyes. As her stories become more intricate and beautiful,
her magic becomes more powerful, but will it be enough to save her?